ATLANTIS

Atlantis

THREE TALES

Samuel R. Delany

To José —
All good thoughts
for all good things
— from
Sam R. Delany
NYC '98

Wesleyan University Press

PUBLISHED BY UNIVERSITY PRESS OF NEW ENGLAND

HANOVER & LONDON

Wesleyan University Press
Published by University Press of New England, Hanover, NH 03755

A limited first edition of *Atlantis* was published by Incunabula in April 1995.

In slightly different form, section *b* of *Atlantis: Model 1924* first appeared in *The Kenyon Review*, Fall 1993, Volume xv, Number 4; section *d* and part of section *c* first appeared in *The Kenyon Review*, Fall 1994, Volume xvi, Number 4. Copyright © 1993, 1994 by Kenyon College.

In slightly different form, sections of "Eric, Gwen, and D. H. Lawrence's Esthetic of Unrectified Feeling" first appeared in *Callaloo*, Spring 1991, Volume 14, Number 2. Copyright © 1991 by Charles H. Rowell.

In slightly different form, sections II and v of "Citre et Trans" first appeared in *Fiction International*, 1991, Number 22. Copyright © 1992 by San Diego State University Press. In slightly different form, sections I, III, IV, v, and vI appeared in *Pacific Review*, Spring 1991. Copyright © 1991 by *Pacific Review*.

The author extends his warmest thanks to editors Ron Drummond, Marilyn Hacker, Charles H. Rowell, Harold Jaffe & Larry McCaffery, and Suzanne M. Sato & Sinda Gregory; and to John D. Berry for his fine sense of book design — and great patience. As well, thanks go to Edward Brunner for Crane and train lore. And for generously sharing their expertise on '20s pulp magazines and record players, happy thanks go to Frank Robinson and Bill Blackbeard.

Cover art: *The Voice of the City of New York Interpreted, 1920–22: The White Way I*, by Joseph Stella, Collection of The Newark Museum, Purchase 1937, Felix Fuld Bequest Fund.

Edited, designed, and produced by
Incunabula, Post Office Box 30146, Seattle, WA 98103-0146

Printed in the United States of America

5 4 3 2

CIP data appear at the end of the book

For
Iva Hacker–Delany,
John R. Keene, Jr.,
and
Dennis Rickett

All the little household gods
    Have started crying, but say
Good-bye now, and put to sea.
    Farewell, dear friend, farewell...

—W. H. AUDEN, "Atlantis"

The long shadow thrown from this single
    obstruction to its own light!
Thought flies out from the old scars of the sea
    as if to land. Flocks that are longings
come in to shake over the deep water.

It's prodigies held in time's amber
old destructions
and the theme of revival the heart asks for.
        The past and future are
full of disasters, splendors
shaken to earth, seas rising to overshadow
    shores and roaring in.

—ROBERT DUNCAN, "Atlantis"

CONTENTS

ATLANTIS: MODEL 1924

Distinctly praise the years...

> —HART CRANE, "For the Marriage of
> Faustus and Helen"

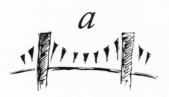

a

It is for the other world that the madman sets sail in his fools' boat; it is from the other world that he comes when he disembarks.

— MICHEL FOUCAULT, *Madness and Civilization*

Voyage through death
                     to life upon these shores.

— ROBERT HAYDEN, "Middle Passage"

I. Skyscrapers — that's what he was most eager to see. But before entering the city the train dropped between earthen walls tangled with winter trees, sometimes becoming out the window, for a hundred feet or more, concrete.

II. The tallest building in the world was in New York — the Woolworth Building. Most people knew that; but *he* knew, counting basements and sub-basements, the Woolworth had exactly sixty stories — and not many people knew that.

III. Bring such information out at the right time, and people said: "What a smart boy!" which made up a little for the guilt he felt over his school grades: they'd been bad enough to silence Papa —

IV. recently elected bishop—and make Mama cry. Finally they'd decided to let him leave (clearly school was doing him no good) and come north to stay with his brother. Sam's toes felt sticky in his socks.

V. Last night, he'd decided not to take his shoes off, afraid his feet might smell. This morning, however, though he'd already gone into the little bathroom with its metal walls to wash his face and hands,

VI. nothing about him felt fresh. Stretching, he arched his back, pulled his fists against his chest; the noblet of flesh on the left side —one male, milkless teat—caught a thread or fold in his shirt,

pulling till it cut.

He sat forward quickly, trying to look disinterested, waiting for the soreness to fall from his chest. A minute on, when he sat back, cambric brushed him: the sensitivity had become, surprisingly, pleasant. Again, he felt himself shift within his wool trousers. Insistently alert to his body, sensual and stale under cloth, he glanced around the car—especially at the women in their seats, black and white, beginning to arrange themselves.

Five times now he'd noticed, first with distress, then with curiosity, and finally with indifference, that if he sat on the rumbling plush, relaxed, and let his knees fall wide, through loose wool the train's joggling gave him an erection.

Pulling his knees together, he sat back again and arched his fingers on the cushion, so that blue nap slipped under his nails. (Amidst the wheels' cacophony, Sam could hear a "...tut-tut-tut-tut-tut..." just like the song.) The first joints of his fingers (and his toes—but people didn't see those) had grown too much: tall as he was, the initial joints had clubbed into those of someone even bigger. *Digitus clavigerae*, or something like it, his oldest brother, Lemuel, had said it was called. Not that that made him feel any better about it. Youngest child, lightest child (hair once cornsilk pale before puberty had turned it rough and red—

and adolescence darkened it further), a surprise child, Mama had called him. Mama's pet, the others said, which, while sometimes it held their ire, now had become a term of fondness—for most of them, most of the time. But he was the one among the ten who hadn't finished high school. Well, when he'd worked awhile in New York and grown more serious, the older ones could settle him into night school and help him toward a diploma. That's what Papa said; and since she always listened to Papa, Mama said he could go. And see the skyscrapers.

On either bank—Sam slid from one seat, moved across the aisle, and into another, to peer by purple tassels — against November gray, fili-greed branches separated wooden houses, one and two drab stories.

Watching the dawnscape, still iceless, flip along, he contemplated for the thousandth time the astonishing process by which the seamless and inexorable progression of the present slipped away to pack the past with memories, like numbered stanzas in a song, like cells in a comb, like cakes in a carton, to be called back (though, he'd already ascertained, most he'd never recall) in whatever surprising, associative order.

There'd been, he remembered now, that poor-white family with the six children the white conductor had brought into the Jim Crow car last night and, after looking around, settled — with their twine-tied boxes and traveling baskets—in the three rows of seats at the car's head. "If you all want to sit together, this is about the best we can do." One of the girls and two of the boys had been barefoot, just as if it were summer. "In a couple of hours you all could come in here anyway." The father's coat had been out at both elbows and his hair stuck straight down from under his straw hat in blond blades. Holding the shoulder of his moth-er's sweater, with a fall of silver silk over each ear and eyes like circles cut from gingham, above the seat back the littlest stared at all the car's dark faces, to fix finally — pink lips lax in a thoughtless 'o' — on Sam, four seats behind and across the aisle, as if Sam, and not they, were the anomaly here. Sam had slid his fingers under his thighs.

But why did that make him remember, how many days before, Lewy, arguing with — well, discussing with — Mama, in an extraordinarily grown-up manner, how going north would be good for him — while

Sam sat, silent, impressed, across the kitchen table, listening to them go on earnestly for fifteen minutes, as though he weren't there.

For moments Sam thought again about the memory he didn't have—because he'd dozed through it: that moment, on leaving Washington, when the Jim Crow car in which he'd started out had become a car like any other, along with all the white cars on the train; and he and anyone in it could sit anywhere they wanted. Immediately on waking, with half a dozen others already up and collecting things, though it was after one o'clock in the morning, he'd gotten his two cases and moved. Sprawled against each other, the white man and the barefoot children slept on. Beside the bigger boy, who wore shoes like his parents, the white woman gazed at the black window. At her shoulder, the blue-eyed child stared up, as Sam pushed, sideways, by.

Then there'd been the porter, whom, while he'd been exploring the train last night, Sam had caught smoking in the vestibule between cars; the two of them had stood in the chill chamber and had cigarettes together. The porter—whose name was John Brown, like his friend John at home—had *not* said: *Ain't you too young to smoke, boy?* He'd said: "I'm usually on the Chicago–Calgary run—but I got deflected. I got to get me home to Chicago; eventually, somehow. That's where my girlfriend live." He'd chuckled as the night's iced air whipped and snapped smoke back from the dark shelves of his lips. Sam told him about his friends, John and Lewy, and how John's name was the same as his. "My daddy," the porter said, "he was just John Brown crazy. Back when Dr. DuBois' book come out, he made me read the whole thing out loud to him." Sam laughed, and told him how his father had read it out loud to *his* whole family too—though he'd not been five years old; and often in bed. But he remembered lying awake, listening. Then the porter told Sam he'd just read another book about Brown by someone named Oswald Garrison Villard, who was the editor of a magazine. Sam didn't remember the magazine's name, but he remembered Oswald Garrison Villard because it sounded so eccentric he'd laughed.

How could a memory of laughter make you smile now? But, turning away from the window, Sam smiled.

ATLANTIS: MODEL 1924

Four seats ahead was the middle-aged white woman who'd started three different conversations with him—the first on the train platform yesterday at noon, then twice more since Washington—the third even after he'd told her, during the second, that he was Negro. Now, she was fixing her wide, ivory hat to salted auburn, with one, then another, then a third (taking them from between her teeth) pearl-tipped hatpin. She'd said she was Scottish and lived in Flatbush—in the heart of Brooklyn. He'd said that, just the morning he'd left, his older sister, Jules, had decided the vat of soap out back of the house had bleached enough to slice loose some half dozen cakes, wrap them in waxed paper, and send them in Sam's wicker trunk to his brothers and sisters in New York. (Holding a fold of her apron, there'd been Jules, in the yard, looking at the soap tray, eyes narrowed, lips pursed; she was comparing it with Mama's or Elsie's, he knew. What she really wanted was to get to her piano lessons with the little girls who'd start coming in at one—almost an hour after he'd be on the train. When would he hear Jules in the parlor, guiding scales again?) The white woman had said *she'd* made her own soap for a while, but it wasn't worth it—there in Brooklyn. At Borough Hall she could get either subway or trolley into Manhattan, and a general store not three streets away from where she lived sold bars of store soap any time she wanted it.

Ivory, like it said in the advertisements, was the best. He'd looked down at the flounce on her skirt, to see if he could glimpse an ankle— another memory.

Sam thought about going to inquire of her now. (Ankles of ivory. Ankles like moons…) But finally (for now was gone) he went back to ask John Brown, who, in his blue-black uniform, was just coming down through the car: "Sir, we in New York State yet?"

Seemingly constructed of blue-black coal, Brown's face turned in mild surprise: "Well, we just gone by Hell Gate." And with that damnable dawn news, John Brown stepped around him, to move on between plush seat backs, bending here, leaning there, asking the older passengers if they would need help with any of their bags—the older white passengers, anyway, Sam noted: a stately Negro woman, with black hat

7

and veil, blue coat frayed at the shoulders, and doubtless going to a funeral—well, the porter, like a dog avoiding another dog's tree, had walked *right* around her!

Sam breathed.

If Mama had been with him, she'd have muttered, "…no-account!" then told Sam to go immediately to that woman and offer a hand: and would probably say something cutting to the porter. Mama could get quite self-righteous over the behavior of other Negroes she didn't approve of—as if she carried responsibility for the whole race on her issue-free shoulders. Sam started to go to her—then remembered his own, two large cases, one leather, one wicker. Well, when he got them off and Hubert was there, he'd go *back* and help.

Out the window a snarl of underpasses and stuttering sunlight became a tunnel, through which they roared a long time: the light from the white glass shades every two seats took on the yellowish cast they'd had at night.

Genitals, buttocks, nipples, tongue all seemed so insistently present inside Sam's mouth and twenty-four-hour-worn suit. Once, well back before dawn, when the train windows were still black and the other passengers slept, he had stared at one white round glass, thinking of the moon, when, at once, he'd stood, to bring his mouth closer and closer, as if to kiss this night light at the aisle's end, pulling back only when the heat about burned his lips. He'd seen the Scotswoman from Brooklyn — she *would* be the one awake — turn away too, smiling. (Why do something like that? And, if you did, why remember it?) No, he didn't want to speak to her.

"Here," Lewy said, under the moon-mottled magnolia, "it's my journal. It's got everything I don't want Sam and you to know about. Go on, look."

But when John opened the cover, Sam peering over his shoulder, it was in code — two columns, one barely comprehensible, the other *complete* nonsense. "You don't want none of them jewboys to get hold of this," John said. "They could figure it out on you."

8

The tunnel went on at alarming length.

Then the white conductor ambled through, calling, "Grand Central Terminal coming up! Change trains for *aaaaall* connections! Grand Central Terminal...!" and people stood to haul their bags down from the overhead rack; men squatted in the aisle to lift them from under the seats. It wasn't yet eight in the morning.

And the train itself, he thought, will be only memory in moments: "...tut-tut-tut-tut..." Then he was lugging his cases down onto the rectangular stool the porter had kicked out the train's door, its squared wooden corners clucking cement.

As Sam stood on the platform among debarking passengers, swaying with the train's remembered sway, Hubert, in his tan-wool overcoat, pushed up in front of him. A grin started out on Sam's face. Then, as suddenly, confusion tore it away—because Hubert was focused all behind him, even before either of them could say hello.

"Here, ma'am! I'll get that for you!" Hubert said to someone beyond Sam's shoulder—which, as Sam turned, he realized was the ponderous woman in mourning.

"Just a minute now, ma'am," which was John Brown, who, at Hubert's intervention, had become as solicitous of her as if she'd been queen of the car's whole hive, handing the heavy creature firmly down to the stool, passing her three bags one after another to Hubert, who swung them, over its metal rail, up on the broad cart with the other baggage that the porter from the sleeping car was loading for the redcaps clustered up at the platform's head.

Hubert was asking her if everything were all right. She was saying, in subdued tones, in an accent that put her well to the west of Raleigh: "Why, thank ya — thank ya, young gen'l'man. Ah'm Mrs. Callista Arkady and Ah'm goin' to the funeral of mah son. It's so kind of y'all to help a bereaved mother. Thank ya — God'll thank y'all. Thank y'all so much!"

Before turning off, the porter leaned over to Sam, to explain softly, sullenly, snappishly: "She didn't tip me none! When she first got on the

JC, yesterday, I took as much time with her as with anybody else—I did!" John Brown's accent was considerably to the north. "But she didn't tip me. You don't got enough to pay your tips, you don't ride the train! Even niggers got to know that!"

"Yes, but she's still a—" he was about to say "lady," while he wondered should he give John Brown a nickel. (That's what John D. Rockefeller tipped *his* train porter; it had said so in a northern magazine.) Of course the porter hadn't touched Sam's bags at all—and, as well, he'd swung back up into the car by now to help the other, white, and—certainly—better heeled passengers.

The woman plowed—mournfully—up the platform through the packs of porters and debarkees, when Hubert turned back to him:

"Well, now—Sam! And how are *you* there—" to clap him on both shoulders, then, with his blue bow tie and buttoned-up double breasted showing between tan coat flaps, to give Sam a bear-like, brotherly hug. "So you got here after all!" In almost the same gesture, Hubert hefted up the wicker trunk, leaving Sam with the leather case. "How's everybody down at the school?"

Sam followed Hubert up the platform, behind the uniformed Negro pushing the baggage cart—far enough ahead so that it would be difficult to catch up and get their bags on. "Mama's fine, Papa's fine. Papa says you should write him another letter like the last long one, tellin' him about the boys in your class. He read that one out to all of us, at Thanksgiving dinner. It made Mama laugh so!"

Hubert chuckled, as Mrs. Arkady vanished around passengers descending, like billows, from the train's several doors. As he pushed after Hubert through the crowd, Sam looked aside two or three times, expecting to see a blue-eyed child staring at him over its mother's knitted gray shoulder. But apparently the family for whom there'd been no room in the white cars had gotten off at some prior local stop, so that, Sam realized, with the myriad details that were his train trip north, they too had sunk into yesterday's consuming sea.

Now and again, Sam glanced at the black ceiling, crossed by pipes, girders, cables, and hung with incandescent bulbs in conical shades, insides enameled white. Train stations, Sam thought, even ones this central and this grand, should sit out under sky, with, yes, an indoor waiting room to one side. But as many times as he'd heard Grand Central Terminal mentioned, it had never occurred to him it would be a structure that wholly closed over…well (he looked through a dozen dark columns above how many trains), a dozen tracks at least! "Hubert," Sam asked, "*where* is the sky…?" thinking his brother, two steps ahead, would not even hear the—after all—ridiculous question.

But at the ramp's end, as, with the crowd, they pushed through a low entrance with a wrought metal transome above, sound around them became hollow and reverberant. They'd stepped into a vast space. With his free hand, Hubert pointed straight up. "They put that there—for folks like you."

Sam looked.

The hall's arched ceiling was watery blue — tile blue. Set here and there in it were lights. The whole was filigreed over with gold: a crab, the head and forelegs of a winged horse, a scorpion, a shaggy-haired warrior holding up a club in one hand and, on his other arm, hefting a shaggy pelt. A gilded line, the zodiacal circle, curved to cross another, the ecliptic. Sam stopped, set down his case. People with small bags jostled him. A flat of baggage rumbled by. Directly above was pictured a gilded bee, a pair of carpenter's triangles beneath her. Awed, Sam pulled his cap from his pocket and, still gazing up, positioned it on his head.

Beyond a central booth bearing above it its own multi-faced spherical time keeper, far bigger across than two tall men laid out foot to foot, a great clock hung between columns.

Curlicued arrows at their tips, oar-long hands lay a diametric certainty across its face, a horizon ruled on the rising moon, on the setting sun. Short hand lower at the left and long hand higher at the right told Sam it was within seconds, one way or the other, of eleven past eight — a slant horizon forward of the dark prow of his trip, lifting and listing from spurious waters, if not the pointer on some turn and bank

John borrowed a mule from the older boys down at the agi-barn and rode it up to the house, big indicator of the sort Sperry had been putting into aeroplanes since the war's close, an artificial horizon unknown to him a year ago, when he'd watched John, shirtless in the field, with his rusty hair and freckled skin the hue of a tobacco leaf, play at being a bomber, dancing like a deranged Indian over red earth, feet—blam! blam!—on the earth's red flesh, running into waves of hip-high grass, holding one hand aloft, thumb and little finger spread from the others, swooping left, turning right, blood remembering some aeronautic invasion, crying Vrummmmmmmmmmmmmm, while Sam and Lewy stood at the field's edge, laughing, clapping, celebrating fantastic catastrophes.

The hands' exact slant was repeated on the smaller, spherical clock's four faces.

Sam and Hubert made their way

boots flapping at its slate-colored flanks.

Mama ran out to shake her apron at them. "Get him out of here! Get him out! Boy, what do you think you're doing? He gets in my Swiss chard and I'll skin you alive, so help me!"

(Sam had heard her swear like that maybe twice in his life. That's probably why he remembered it.)

The mule jerked to the side—and John slipped right to the ground. Then Mama started laughing. Splayed on the grass, John was laughing too.

"Get up... from there, John—" Mama called, between hysteric eruptions. "And get him... out of here!" while the mule wandered over to the porch steps and ate a hollyhock.

through waves of men and women. Again, Sam the Navigator gazed up at sky-tiles like an overturned sea.

For a moment, not the distant lights of the Pegasus in their gilded starbursts—across from the balcony at the halls' right side, across from Orion above squared pilasters practically without capitals—but the gold lines with which Pegasus was drawn, suggested a caricature of Callista Arkady's broad, veiled face, but with an ecstatic smile, gazing down.

With some gentleness, as people plunged in echo by, Hubert said: "Come on, Sam," to bring his eyes down. "We have to get the train."

The train — *this* train — was a subway. They didn't even step outside to get to it. Going down the stairs, Hubert asked him: "You got a nickel?"

At the steps' bottom, again Sam put his suitcase down, pushed into his pants pocket—feeling scrape his wrist the ten dollar bill Lucius had told Mama should be safety-pinned there, because Sam was going to New York, where things could happen—to pull out his coins. On his palm, Sam forefingered aside the fifty-cent piece, two dimes, two nickels, and five, six, seven, eight pennies: change from the Coca-Cola he'd bought on the train platform yesterday, which, there, had cost two cents more than at the colored grocery—

"Come on," Hubert said. "I'll pay for you. I got two—come *on*, Sam! This is New York; you can't dawdle here!"

"I'm *not* dawdling; I'm looking after my money." Only he glanced up to see people cascading down the steps, breaking to left and right of him, like water at a rock. Jamming coins back in his pocket, Sam snatched up his suitcase to follow Hubert, who pushed one nickel into the slot ahead, then another into the one beside that. As they hefted the cases over, they were practically pounded through shadowless stiles by the wooden paddles swinging round behind them. "What does it do?" Sam looked back, frowning. "Whack you in the butt every time you go in?"

"That's just to make sure people like you go and get on with it." Hubert hurried ahead. "This way!" he called over his shoulder. "Let's get the first car!"

Hubert was twenty-three. Last year Hubert had gone to Europe and traveled there four months. When he'd got back, he'd worked in the tobacco fields in Connecticut. This eagerness for the first car—something he'd imagine from John or Lewy—was not what you expected from a big brother about to start his second year in law school—all of which Hubert could claim. But with a sister in between, Hubert was his brother nearest Sam in age; perhaps that enthusiasm was what had kept them so close, in spite of it all.

They didn't make the first car, because the subway was already pulling in when they got down to it.

They made the second:

"...tut-tut-tut..." Sam was surprised he could still hear it.

Inside, posts went from the floor to the curved ceiling—green-paint-ed metal up to about stomach height, then white enamel for the rest. In metal fittings, leather loops hung from a pipe just above head-height, in a row down each side of the car. Up by the ceiling, eight-inch-high cardboard strips told of Sloan's Liniment and Ivory Soap ("ninety-nine and forty-four one hundredths percent pure") and Pine Tar Honey—one (in color: red with yellow letters, a round face grinning beside them, in a bottle cap hat) was for Coca-Cola.

It had never occurred to Sam they'd have Coca-Cola in New York.

The subway seats were the same woven wicker as the trunk Hubert carried. Looking down at them, Sam saw their interstices were black—and realized it was dirt!

"Come on," Hubert repeated, as the train started more smoothly than Sam expected: had a day and a night on the locomotive from Raleigh gotten him his rail legs?

Hefting up his bag, Sam followed Hubert to the car's front. A door-way made a vestibule there—half the size of the one on the railway car in which he'd smoked with John Brown. Inside, a wheel hung against the wall; and pipes; and cables. To one side was a flat, green door.

Over racketing wheels, Hubert said: "The engineer sits in there."

"This is the *engine*?"—for through the window in the door ahead he could see into the forward car, as it swung, intriguingly out of sync with theirs.

Hubert laughed and opened the doors between, to lob the wicker through, then turned to explain over the noise (louder between the cars) how, on the subway, any car could be the engine. All you had to do was put it first.

They went through the next car into the little booth at its head—*this* was the first car. Hubert told him to look out the front window; Sam stood, hands up beside his face to shade the light. Beyond the glass, with its inch-sized, hexagonal wire reinforcements between layered panes, darkness rushed him, cut by girders, punctured by lights—blue, red, green—a matutinal career through seas of shadow, past nocturnal carnivals.

"Now when you ride on the subway by yourself—"

Sam pulled back from the window. In the booth's yellowish light, Hubert's dark eyes were serious above his short mustache.

"—in the morning," Hubert went on, "when people are going to work, or in the evening, when they're coming home—rush hour—you don't come in here by yourself, now."

"Why not?" Sam turned to Hubert.

"'Cause things can happen to you in here."

"What things?"

"People can do things to you—like you can get your pocket picked, for one."

Sam was going to say, just to be silly, *You been deflected, Hubert?* But Hubert swung—suddenly—the back of his hand against Sam's pants lap, which made him flinch:

"Hey—!"

"You got to watch out for yourself, that's all." The train was coming into the station. "That's all I'm saying. Now come on." Carrying both trunk and case now, Hubert strode into the car, grinning again over his shoulder.

Parting black rubber rims, dark double doors rolled open, and Sam followed his brother onto still another wholly enclosed platform. "*What* sort of things, Hubert?"

Hubert put the suitcase down for Sam to take. "You just have to re-member," Hubert repeated, "that this is New York," and the gravity with which he spoke seemed—apparently to Hubert—to cover the situation.

The subway station they were in, Times Square and Forty-second Street, was even bigger—and more crowded—than the one at Grand Central. They had to go up stairs and down. With their gilt signs, the plate glass windows indicated clothing stores, barber shops, bakeries. One store even sold magic tricks: through its window, when, with his case, Sam went over to look, a small man with a sharp beard turned to smile out at him—thick glasses made his eyes huge marbles—over red and blue boxes, through chains of metal rings, past cardboards with small figures attached to them, by black top hats, colored scarfs, oriental bird cages, and black wands with white tips. (Sam vowed he'd come back to that one.) The store windows were right in the ivory tiled wall, as if this were some outside street, so that he kept glancing up, expecting to see the sky above this buried city.

Saturday morning not that many people were traveling. Still, most of the ones who were stood across the tracks, off between the girders on the other platform. Drones at work in sweet, rich New York.

Following Hubert through resonant tunnels, considering his trajectory, like a bullet's through a beehive, Sam wondered which of the enclosed images he'd recall in a day, in a decade. Then an idea came to rupture his contemplation of — even in the quick of excitement — the evanescence of time, that made him near break out laughing. Imagine writing a letter to Lewy and John (they *were* his best friends), with a page even for Mama and Papa, telling the wonders of his trip so far: he'd fold it, pack it into his cap so that the pages were fixed beneath the band. Then, by its visor, he'd sail the gray and brown tweed into the air, so that, as if become helmet, it shattered all these artificial ceilings, crashed out and up from under the flagpoles on the skyscrapers above, into liquid air, to go soaring south to Raleigh — really, about as

John said, "They could figure it out on you."

But, chuckling, Lewy wandered away, barefoot over fallen blossoms, as if codes and journals and secrets and cyphers had ceased to interest him as he searched the spring night.

sensible as putting a message into a jeweled box and floating it off on the water, in hopes somehow it would wend home. Still, the image stayed. What might John or Lewy say if they saw a cap falling at them, a dark disk, an eclipsed moon—that turned out stuffed with his adventures?

"Is it *all* underground...?" Sam asked, wonderingly—having just realized that the "sub" in the "subways" Hubert and Lucius and Lemuel and Corey and Hap and Elsie had all, in their turn, been talking about, whenever, over these last years, they'd come home for one vacation or another, was short for "subterranean"!

"Some of them — on Third Avenue," Hubert said, with mock seriousness, "or Sixth Avenue, or Ninth, run up above the streets, through the sky...!"

Cities underground...? Cities in the air...? With subterranean and superterranean ways between? And all were among New York's honied algebra of miracles? Hurrying after Hubert, a-grin at the marvel and mystery of it, Sam tried to fathom it and keep from laughing. All this — *and* skyscrapers?

(Where were they...?)

They took another two trains — or was it three?

"Where do we get out?"

"A Hundred-twenty-fifth Street," Hubert said. "This is us."

A Hundred-twenty-fifth Street sounded awfully far from Grand Central or Forty-second.

They carried the cases upstairs — into another covered concourse.

How long would it be, Sam wondered, before they got outside?

He noticed now, with curiosity and relief: all the people in this station were black—heavyset ladies in dark or light stockings, men in straw hats with brown or red bands, sometimes even a bit of pheasant feather.

Sam and Hubert pushed out the gates beside the row of stiles (where people were — *ka-chunk, ka-chunk* — hurrying in), turned left, and started up the steps between the off-white tiles. A winter wedge of blue widened above them. Then, diagonally across it, slid a sculpted cornice.

At the steps' head, Sam put his case on the sidewalk and looked down from the cloudless sky. (That empty air he'd recall for years.) The building—though it ran the length of the block—was two stories tall. Shops filled the ground floor. On the second, with tan Venetian blinds lowered to their several heights behind the glass, black or gold letters spoke of accountants, law firms, a billiards parlor — and the next was unreadable behind the sun's reflected silver. Still, none of the names were very different from those in gold letters across the second story windows in the downtown building, back home, in which their older brother Lucius had his law practice.

"Shoot...!" Sam said. "It ain't as big as what we got in Raleigh! The biggest building there is *six* stories and got an elevator!" He looked at Hubert, the first presentiment of pain the city had ceded him nudging his features toward bewilderment.

Hubert shook his head—to drawl in a voice that suddenly and surprisingly brought back sixteen-year-old Hubert from Carolina, making Sam electrically aware how different that was from the twenty-three-year-old law student he was to live with now: "Boy," Hubert said, "you a *real* country nigger, ain't you!"—the words carrying no interrogation at all, only their hugely playful, hopelessly damning, inescapable sibling judgment.

The leadership and conduct of the war were on the one side in the hands of our city, on the other in the hands of the kings of Atlantis. At the time, as we said, Atlantis was an island larger than Libya and Asia put together, though it was subsequently overwhelmed by earthquakes and is the source of the impenetrable mud which prevents free passage of those who sail out of the straights into the open sea.

— PLATO, *Critias*

I sometimes had pleasant nightmares in which I fancied that New York was being destroyed by an earthquake: its towers snapped like pine trees in a storm, a tidal wave poured through its streets…

— MALCOLM COWLEY, *Exile's Return*

On the top (third) floor, Hubert's was around the corner from Mount Morris Park.

"I got to wash up." Sam put the suitcase on the rug's foot-faded red, looking around the first of the two small rooms.

"Sure." With his shoe, Hubert pushed the wicker trunk under what would be Sam's bed. "Unless you want to wait till later when we get over to Elsie and Corey's. They got hot water."

"That's all right. I want to do it now. And change my clothes."

"All right." Hubert took the wash basin out from under the corner sink. "Here you go. But you got to hurry up, before Clarice gets here."

Using Hubert's yellow bar of kitchen soap, lathering his arms, his buttocks, his knees, hopping now on one foot, hopping now on the other, Sam washed in cold water. Sometimes he glanced at Hubert, who sat in the wing chair: Hubert's forehead furrowed above his glasses, as, in the corner, he paged through a book. *Views of…* something.

Hubert was one of three colored teachers recently hired to teach first grade in the colored all-boys public school, only six blocks from here, Hubert had explained to Sam. That tall body had cut tobacco in Connecticut; that strong body sat so straight when he studied. And there'd been "…Miss Hutchinson told me about a trick she used when she taught those rough boys in the colored schools outside Cincinnati. She said if it would work for a woman, it would certainly work for me. Just as she told me to do, before classes began I procured an old, cracked baseball bat, and on the first school day I brought it with me before any of the scholars arrived. Before going in, I hit it on the curb outside school till it cracked more. I then took it into my classroom and leaned it in the corner by my desk. When the boys came in—they were loud and lively and full of high spirits—within five minutes, while some of them were still taking their coats off and playing tag around the room, one of them asked me, 'What's that for?' Sitting at my desk, I looked over my folded hands and said, in a firm and resonant voice: 'I had some trouble with one of the boys in my last class—and I'm afraid I broke my bat on his backside. And by the way, you must learn to call me "Sir."' They all turned around, eyes about to bulge out of their brown, round faces. And when I called them to order and they rushed to sit, you could see them squirming on their benches, each attached to the desk behind. Their eyes kept going to the bat in the corner, their little behinds stinging in anticipation. You knew they were wondering how it felt." About the bony wreckage of the Thanksgiving carcass, everyone was laughing too loudly for Papa to go on—as, here, he put down the letter a moment to touch his clerical collar. Mama took her wire-framed glasses off and dabbed her eyes with her napkin.

Sam hopped, and shook quickly from his mind another memory ("...an *animal*...!" The crate's slats smithereened across Hubert's shoulder, and dragging the chain across the gravel where the grass had worn from around the pump, Hubert cowered back: *"Papa! No...!"* He remembered his father's grunts, precise and ugly), hopped again and scrubbed at his groin — finally to squat among the splatters over the dark floorboards and maul the balled rag first over, then under, his out-sized toes. "Hubert, did you really do that thing with the baseball bat?"

"Hmm?" Hubert asked, over his book. "What—oh, sure. Only I don't think I really had to. Miss Hutchinson, when *she* did it, she was teaching big, rough, country boys—field hands right in from pickin' cotton. They were all field niggers — wasn't a house nigger among them, she told me. A lot of them were too old for high school anyway—she said some of them were older than she was. And there were a few who just didn't want to take no guff off a woman. But my boys are just children— and city children, too." He dropped his eyes to the book, raised it a bit from his lap: *Views of Italy.*

Sam wiped the splatters up and, still squatting naked, turned to pull the wicker from under the daybed. "You mind if I smoke me a cigarette?"

"Go ahead if you want. But like I say—finish up before Clarice gets here. She don't approve of smoking."

Only on opening it and pushing aside shirts and underwear (which he didn't really wear, unless Mama insisted) did Sam see the folded paper bag with Jules' soap. "Hubert, don't let me forget this when we go over to Elsie and Corey's." Taking a bar from the bag to leave Hubert, Sam put bag and bar up on the pink quilting. Translucent as isinglass, the bar's paper immediately unfolded, like a thing volitional.

With a notable amount of white moneys—but a treasured portion of black — by his astonishing energy (that, even now he was over sixty, awed Sam), Papa and several of his friends had helped develop the small Negro college. Papa was now Vice-Chancellor. Mama was Dean of Women. That same energy had already pushed Sam's slave-born father to learn Aramaic, Arabic, Hebrew, Greek, and Latin. Two years ago it had gotten him elected Bishop of the Archdiocese of North and South Carolina — this prodigy of black learning, this learned black prodigy, this prodigious black learner. Black and white ministers both had elected him. Papa was a voyager on the ocean of theology and ancient languages. Sharp-tongued Corey had seemed, for a while, the one likely to follow Papa into that sea. Then she had turned from its waters—sharply—with the realization there was little enough a black man could do with Greek and Aramaic. (Though Mama always insisted it was more than well-deserved, the suffrage bishopric was after all an anomaly.) Still less, a black woman. She had followed her younger brother, Hap, first to New York, then into dental school.

Cigarette still fuming between his teeth, Sam was just buttoning his shirt when, outside in the hall, someone twisted the doorbell key.

Clarice came in.

Hubert's girlfriend was — like last time — another pale-complected creature, who looked, really, whiter than Hubert. (This one's name was Clarice!) "This is your little brother? He's not so little at all! How come all you boys in this family are so good looking?" Within moments Sam learned, now from Clarice, now from enthusiastic Hubert—when Clarice suddenly remembered to be modest — that she wrote poems that got published in newspapers and sometimes in small magazines (Hubert brought some out to show him) with titles like *Broom* and *Spark*. Their ragged-edged pages were thick as fabric as you turned them. Passionate about the Negro Question (as was Hubert), she read *The Messenger* and *Opportunity* and knew writers and artists, black and white— Wally and Richard and Bruce and Jean and Angelina and Waldo and talked about them at length and a woman named Lola at whose house on Ninth Street she had met a number of them—from Washington to New York, from Harlem to Gay Street, the block-long colored enclave in Greenwich Village, she explained. Greenwich Village was where Hubert went, in the evenings, to his law classes at New York University Law School.

And they were all expected at Elsie and Corey's at four o'clock for Saturday dinner—Elsie and Corey were his and Hubert's oldest sisters;

and Saturday dinner, Hubert said now, was easier for them than Sunday, because of Elsie's studying for School on Monday—not to mention Hubert's.

The surprise, that evening, was that Hap — another brother — and his wife came too.

"Sam, how's everybody down at the college?" Dr. Corey wanted to know. Calling her "Doctor Corey" was something of a joke, because she was a woman. (They didn't call Hap "Doctor Hap" — or Lemuel, his oldest brother who was a real doctor, not just a dentist, "Doctor Lem.") But Corey had decided it was her due. She'd tell you in a moment, if you asked: "Filling teeth and getting paid for it is a lot better than teaching Greek to a bunch of hands, straight out the field, who couldn't care less about the difference between a first and a second aorist!"

Mama's fine, Papa's fine, they all laughed over that long Thanksgiving letter Hubert wrote—Sam repeated.

"Oh, yes," Elsie said. "Hubert came and read it to us before he sent it. I thought that would tickle Mama."

Corey sent him to the bathroom to wash his hands.

As Sam stood, caressive water falling warm over his fingers from the verdigrised faucet, in the alley outside someone called, again and again, sounding now like, *"Dandelion...!"* now like, *"Handle-iron...!"* The voice was shrill—the shrillness of a man who was going to call for a long time and wanted folks to hear. Sam tried to imagine the body with that voice: brown face under a squashed-down hat, hard hands, bony hips in loose pants, sharp shoulders in an old vest...

More because he was tired than because he had to go, Sam dropped his pants and sat on the commode's wood ring. (At Hubert's the commode was behind a door out in the hall.) Newspapers lay on the two-tiered stool beside him. Lifting up the first few, he saw a green-covered magazine and slipped it out, certain it was one with Clarice's poems. He read the title: *Mnemosyne.* Flipping through a few pages, however, he realized a good deal of it was in Latin. Turning back to the cover, he caught the date—1918: no, it was one of Corey's journals from the time of her language pursuits. Again he opened it, to page through—132, 133,

134—where a passage Corey had marked caught him. The article explained the lines were from a Chorus closing the second act of Seneca's *Medea*.

> *Venient annis, saecula seris,*
> *Quibus Oceanus vincula rerum*
> *Laxet et ingens pateat tellus*
> *Tethysque novos detegat orbes*
> *Nec sit terris ultima Thule.*

In careful pencil, at a gray slant, Corey had inscribed her marginal translation (five days ago? in distant 1918? sometime in between?):

> An age will come, in distant times,
> When Ocean will release the chains 'round things
> And the whole broad earth—as well
> as Tethys's new world's end, Thule,
> Not as the limit of lands—will be revealed.

The article explained how Christopher Columbus's son and biographer, Fernando, had marked just this passage in his own copy of Seneca, jotting down in the margin:

> *Haec propheteia expleta est per patrem meum*
> *Christopher Colon almirantem ano 1492.*

Corey's marginal gloss:

> This prophecy was fulfilled by my father
> Christopher Colon _____ in the year 1492.

Beside that, she had written: "*almirantem?* Ask Papa. C.C.'s place of birth? Elmira? But it's not capitalized."

When Corey and Elsie had first visited New York, almost ten years

ago now, with Mama as chaperone, they'd taken the boat up from Nor-
folk. But Sam had been mad to take the train—nearly as eager over that
as he'd been about the skyscrapers. All that water…? He closed *Mnemosyne*, put it down on the newspapers—then, in afterthought, pulled up
two or three papers and put them back on top.

Outside, the shrill cry was blotted up by silence.

He'd often thought he'd have liked to follow Papa and Corey in their
linguistic explorations. But (said Papa) he was too mercurial for such
diligence. Sam stood, reached up and pulled the wooden handle on the
flush chain. As the water roared from the wooden tank above, he bent,
pulled his pants up, buttoned them, and buckled his belt.

After washing his hands once more, he opened the bathroom door—
to be startled by the mirror in the hall right between the glass-chim-
neyed gas lamps, where his surprised double surprised him, pausing, bewildered in the frame, Sam the Stranger, unknowingly about to walk in
on him.

In the living room, where the table had been moved in from the
kitchen, he gave out Jules' soap; and Hap, who was the *first* dentist in
the family (and had got his nickname—Hap—because he was so happy), said: "Well, I'll get my teeth *real* clean with this!"

"Now you don't use that on your teeth," Elsie said, "more than but
once a week!"

"For the rest of the time, you just use tooth powder, like everybody
else," Dr. Corey said. "Why you have to tell a dentist what to brush his
teeth with, I'll never know!" Since her graduation from Dental College
at Columbia, she'd shared an office with Hap.

They all laughed. "Tell us about Thanksgiving," which had been only
last week. "How was it this year?"

So he did—about the turkey and the dancing to the records, which
Papa had allowed because it wasn't Sunday, even though they made two
trips to chapel, once in the morning and once at sunset. Right after his
election, Papa had decided not to get a Victrola but a more expensive
Edison Player. The medallion beside the flocked turntable said: "Dia-
mond Disc Official Laboratory Model." The song Sam and Lewy and

John all liked and had played over and over to the point of exhaustive hilarity was the quarter-inch-thick record of Billy Rose and Ernest Hare singing Harry Von Tilzer's "In Old King Tutankhamen's Day," with its infectious refrain: "Old King Tut-tut-tut-tut-tut-tut-tut…" though Jules and Laura preferred the other side: "Barney Google." The other record Sam and Papa loved to play was the late Enrico Caruso and Mario Ancona singing the duet from Bizet's *The Pearl Fishers*. In his study, Papa slipped the crank back into its metal clip on the dark wood and asked: "Do you want to ask Batouta the Moor to come in with us and listen?" (This month Batouta the Moor was Papa's nickname for Lewy.) "But then, he's probably out somewhere exploring." (He was.) So they sat by themselves and listened to the cascading male voices, each rippling down over the other; and Sam would imagine weedy waters and flickering tidelights over submarine grottoes — not that that had much to do with Thanksgiving nor, really, was there much to say about it.

So he told them instead about Lewy and the poetry book with the gold star in it for excellence Lewy'd won in Mrs. Fitzgarn's and what Reverend Fitzgarn had said about Papa's sermon and about how John had brought the mule into Mama's yard and had fallen off it and how it ate Mama's flowers and she'd just about skinned him alive and—again —about the laughter at Hubert's letter, when, after Thanksgiving dinner, Papa had read it out.

Once, when he paused, Elsie smiled: "I think we can let him stop now."

Hap's wife said: "It's so good to hear how things are going. And it's so good to have you up here, Sam."

Then they talked about other things and laughed lots more and all said how much he'd grown.

Sam was, in fact (it had taken most of the day to register), as tall as Hubert now.

On the way back to Hubert's rooms Sam *saw* his first skyscrapers—late that evening, when it was already dark. They'd stopped to stroll in

Mount Morris. (Hubert had already given Sam the key and was going to walk Clarice home to her aunt and uncle's at a Hundred-twentieth Street and Seventh Avenue.) In the November's-end dark, the three of them climbed the stone steps to the high rocks. Then Hubert and Sam left Clarice, to climb up the rocks themselves. "Those lights over there, like pearls — that you can just see? — " Hubert explained — "*those* are skyscrapers... mostly."

Far away, specular and portentous, they glimmered behind haze-hung night. (It felt as if it might rain any moment.) Sam seemed to be looking across some black and insubstantial river to another city altogether — a city come apart from New York, drifting in fog, in air, in darkness, and wholly ephemeral: the idea of a city—with no more substance than his memory of his memories on the train.

When they climbed down, Clarice was leaning against a low boulder. The park lamp behind her threw her into silhouette. "Now doesn't she look older than the rocks among which she sits?" Hubert asked.

"What's *that* supposed to mean?" Clarice asked, her hands in her coat pockets, legs crossed under her skirt.

"My rag, my bone, my hank of hair; and *she* doesn't care—"

"*Hu*-bert—!" Clarice objected.

"I'm teasing you," he said.

She stood. "Now what Sam — *Eshu!*" Clarice pulled her coat around her — "Sam should do, if he wants to see skyscrapers, is take a walk across the Brooklyn Bridge. That's the way really to see New York." (Sam had already realized Clarice was a person who said "really to see" and "truly to think." She had declared, loudly and insistently at dinner, that she thought it particularly important Negroes speak with proper grammar. "After all, we've been here longer than most of these crackers!" It was practically an echo of Mama, down on the campus. "And that's why you will not hear me split my infinitives!" "Or hear her say, even jokingly," Hubert added, "'a girl like I.'" That made Clarice laugh too. Still, those unified verbs sounded even stranger than her clipped, northern accent.) In the damp night, Clarice said, "That's the city at its best — *Eshu!*" A second time she sneezed.

27

Hubert moved toward her. "We better get you home."

Distant in the night-haze, the lights burned with soft, pearl-like fires —so different from what burned in Sam.

On their way down, wrapped 'round in shadow, Sam tried to remember Clarice's body beneath the dress, beneath the coat she pulled even more tightly to her throat. That body had all sorts of lines, gentle, pleasant, that became clear under the fall of her skirt or sleeve when she'd leaned to pass this, sat back with an embarrassed smile, turned in her seat to hear what Hubert said. (Did Hubert ever kiss her? he wondered.) Under a park lamp, he saw her raise a lace-edged handkerchief, pulled over one knuckle, to her nose. Over Hubert's arm around her shoulder, her breath added its own lace to the fog already wreathing her dark hair. Completing the thought begun minutes ago, she added: "Over the bridge—*Eshu!* That's what I'd want to do."

Sam's first job in the city was washing walls for three guys who knew Hubert and were painters. He was fired loudly and ignominiously after a week. He just wasn't fast enough. Perez—the loud, bony one—said, consolingly afterwards, that Sam was a smart boy and shouldn't be doing stuff like that anyway. And Louis, the fat fellow (who spelled his name completely differently from Lewy down home), said Sam damned well ought to *learn* how to do stuff like that; smart or not, it didn't hurt nobody to know how to wash a damned wall! The third one, the one he really liked—whose name was Prince, followed by something Caribbean, Marquez? Cinquez? — had said nothing to him at all, but had smiled at him a few times while they'd worked and had looked on seriously while Louis and Perez bawled him out.

There really wasn't enough work anyway, Hubert explained that evening back at home—trying to make it easier for sulky Sam. People wanted their houses painted in spring and summer, when they could keep the place open and air it out. Not in winter. That's why the fellows had been so touchy, because they weren't making any money themselves.

Three days later Sam got another job as stockboy in Mr. Harris's men's haberdashery over on a Hundred-seventeenth Street — mostly packing things down in, and getting things up from, the cellar. The wreath on the door and the tinsel strung in front of the counter surprised him. And the heavy black girl who worked there and who looked like Milly Potts down home — though she had none of Milly's sense of humor—wore a Christmas pin on her blouse. But then, Christmas was less than two weeks away.

When Sam came in, Clarice was sitting in the wing chair, in her purple blouse, reading aloud:

"'Evidently the author's implication is that there must be a welding into one personality of Kabnis and Lewis: the great emotionalism of the race guided and directed by a great purpose and a super-intelligence.'"

Chin still prickling from the cold, Sam could hear, in the other room, Hubert thumping books on his desk. Clarice looked up, smiled, then went back to her peroration:

"'...In the south we have a "powerful underground" race with a marvelous emotional power which like Niagara before it was harnessed is wasting itself. Release it into proper channels, direct its course intelligently, and you have possibilities for future achievement that challenge the imagination. The hope of the race is in the great blind forces of the masses properly utilized by capable leaders.'" She looked up again, frowning.

Indeed, Sam was astonished at how little of Christmas stayed with him that year: he and Hubert celebrated it, of course. He gave Hubert an embossed leather notebook, which cost two dollars. Hubert gave him three sets of long johns, which was supposed to be kind of funny, but Sam started wearing them that morning: they were a pretty good idea. And Corey and Elsie had a tree hung with both glass and colored-paper ornaments, strung with cranberries and yarns of popcorn and cotton wool all around its base, just like at home; but (and it was the first time Sam had ever experienced this, so that for a few days it really bothered him) it just didn't *feel* like Christmas.

When it was over, the only thing that remained with any vividness was a pre-Christmas Saturday morning trip to the post office for

29

"Lord, Montgomery *does* go on about him, doesn't he...?" Clearly she spoke to Hubert, behind the wall against which Sam's bed stood — still unmade from this morning.

"What's that?" Sam began to shrug off his coat.

Clarice smiled again. "It's about my friend I said looked like you...?" She held up *Opportunity*. "Jean...?"

From inside, Hubert said: "Sam, if that's you, would you *please* clean up in there a little!"

"I was *going* to spread your bed up," Clarice said softly from the chair, "only he wouldn't let—"

But, coat back on his shoulders and ears hot with embarrassment, Sam was already across the room, tugging up the sheet, swinging over the quilt.

Elsie and Corey, to mail the three shopping bags full of gifts back to Raleigh. (One bag was Hubert's and his.) The building like a fort—

The lines of people—

Within, pine bows were draped all around the upper molding on the marble walls—

Bells of shiny red and silver paper hung, soundless, in each corner. Black rubber mats were splayed over the floor, slopping with the slush people tracked about in rundown shoes and open galoshes with jingling clasps. Wreaths with red berries and red ribbon were wired to the doors. But even inside, the marble room was chill and damp enough for your breath to drift away in clouds.

Were all these black and yellow and tan and brown faces, in all these lines in front of all the brass-barred windows, sending presents back to some ever-shifting, generalized, and hopelessly unlocatable place (but never baffling the postal readers of the carefully printed or clumsily scrawled addresses on brown paper under twine) called home? Certainly, to look at the bags and parcels they carried, it seemed so.

The clerks behind the bars, Sam had noticed, were all white.

Postal clerks were white at home too, but there were only three windows in the post office he went to in Raleigh. Here, between marble columns—and it wasn't even the central post office—ten windows lined the wall, so he'd just expected, well...maybe *some* dark faces behind the squared brass bars.

With broad, brown cheekbones, brown eyes large and crossed, and wearing an old black coat, a girl settled herself next to him, to stare up. From within her blunt, strabismic gaze, a glint of blue surfaced in Sam's mind—from the staring boy back on the train. Then it sank into the estuary of her curiosity, to swirl away. Looking down at her and in a voice more friendly than he felt, Sam asked her age-absent stare (was she eleven? was she fifteen?): "Now who are you?"

She held up her hand to him, or rather her wrist—with her fingers bent down. The hand was deformed—or at least...its deformity surprised, even shocked, him: the forefinger was thumb-thick and longer than the middle, which was, in turn, longer than the ring finger, which was longer than the little—all of them, indeed, fatter than fingers were supposed to be. The nails were dirty, spiky. Her teeth were set apart in bluish gum—some of the lower ones, Sam realized, missing. "What's your name?" he asked again, of this unappealing child.

The woman behind him said, "She's showing you her wrist beads." Then—small, brownskinned, with nicely done hair and a green cloth coat (the child's hair stuck out in tufts, from under a gray kerchief tied not under her chin but off center by her cheek, the cloth ends frazzled like something someone had sucked on)—the woman took the girl's wrist and held it up. Black-gloved fingers moved a band of white beads from under the threadbare cuff. "Baby beads—just like when you're born. In the hospital." (Sam had been born at home, and had had the details of Doctor Haley's three-in-the-morning visit, when they'd thought there might be complications—but there weren't—recounted to him many times.) Each bead had a black letter on it.

"See," the woman said. "E-L-L-A A-B-L-I-R...this is Ella Ablir." Each lettered bead had two holes in it. Running through were, Sam saw, not threads but wires, twisted together below the pudgy wrist. The woman smiled. "She's looking at you because you're white."

"No." Sam smiled. "I'm afraid I'm not. I'm colored, too, just like everybody else here."

"Oh, I'm *sorry*...!" The woman was suddenly and greatly distressed—while again Sam glanced at the white clerk behind the bars and at the woman at his window in red coat and red hat, with thick-heeled shoes buttoning inches up stockings white as some nurse's: she seemed to be buying many small stamps for a penny or two pennies, but wasn't sure how many she wanted; now she asked for two more, no three more — well, maybe another two; and one more please? Thank you. Now, if I could just have two more of this kind — please?

"Sometimes," Sam said, "when people first meet me, they think I am. But I'm not."

"Yes. Of course," the woman said. "If I had just been paying attention, I would've seen it."

Sam looked down at the girl, who still stared up: "Hello, Ella," he said, becoming aware that, behind the woman, five or six other children shuffled — girls, most of them. No, all of them. Ragged, unkempt, each had something distinctly wrong with her.

"Where're y'all from?" Sam asked.

"We're from the Manhattan Hospital," the woman said, indicating a rectangle of cardboard pinned to her lapel, with something printed on it, "for the Insane." The girl had the same cardboard pinned lopsidedly to her coat. So did the girls behind. The eyes of a tall and stoop-shouldered girl did not look in the same direction. "Over on the island. But they ain't really insane at all." She smiled. "Not even a little bit of it. They're just some very nice little girls — who all been very, specially good. And I been out with them since eight o'clock this morning, taking them around on a Christmas pass."

The woman in red finished at the window. So Sam said:

"You go on ahead there. I'm not in that big a rush." He hefted the three shopping bags, two in his

Their young women goe not shadowed (clothed) amongst their own companie, until they be nigh eleven or twelve returns of the leafe old, nor are they much ashamed thereof, and therefore would the before remembered … sometymes resorting to our fort … but being over twelve years, they put on a kind of semecinctum lethern apron before their bellies, and are very shamefaced to be seen bare.

— wantons before marriage

right hand, so that the handle cords moved half an inch across his stinging palms.

"That's awful nice of you. They do get restless sometimes, when they have to stand still so long. I appreciate it a lot." She turned and announced to the shuffling gaggle: "Now you all stay with this nice colored gentleman right here. I'm going to the window there to get you your penny postcards." She smiled at Sam in turning and stepped toward the bars.

The girls moved up around him. One, though in another torn coat and with the same kind of rag over her hair—and her expression just as vacant—, was actually pretty, as she looked off to the side. Her face was the darkest. The bones in it were fine. Her figure, beneath her poor coat, seemed fit. For a moment Sam imagined her some displaced tribal princess, stepped from an ancient African sect to be dazzled by the modern day—till she turned: the far part of her face was a scarred cascade from a burn.

There was not even an eye in it.

Tides of black and brown made a torrent down her skull. So as not to stare, Sam dropped his eyes—and saw, beneath her torn hem, her ankles and the legs above them were as badly burned as her face. She wore only some sort of slippers, which her heels had slid over the edge of, onto the mat slewed with snot-colored slush. Sam turned a little, lifted his eyes again—and caught a whiff of unwashed sourness. Could that be one of them?

Really, he thought, the things that could be wreaked on the body!

Sam's bags were weighty with Hubert's and Elsie's and Corey's—and his own—gifts. But the floor was too wet to set them down.

Just then the Ablir girl ran forward to the window beside theirs, shouldering aside the generous-breasted, humus-skinned woman who had just handed in a package as the bars had been, for a moment, unlocked and swung aside.

The bars clicked closed; the woman said, "Hey, you—!"

and household drudges after, it is extremely questionable whether they had any conception of it.

With all her brachydactylic fingers, Ella pointed through.

Inside, the white clerk brought forward a toy horse, that Ella must have seen. He stuck one plush hoof through the bars and waved it at her. Ella took a breath, grabbed it, and tried to tug it out—but, still smiling, the clerk pulled it from her grip and raised it higher between the bars, beyond her reach, to wave the leg once more.

Silent, determined, Ella jumped, missed, jumped again. She didn't jump very high; and the little lift she managed suggested her physical coordination was deeply impaired.

The woman who'd just handed her package through looked down now, frowned, then began to smile.

From behind the bars, the clerk said with a notable brogue: "All right, little girl. Now you have to let the other people mail their letters."

Biting her broad underlip, Ella Ablir backed from the cage, gazing within.

A bunch of penny postcards in one hand, not yet put into her pocket book, the woman in the green coat stepped away from the next window over to receive the child's shoulders with guiding gloves. At the contact, the woman's worried look relaxed. "All right," she said. "Let's all behave. Come on, now—let's go. I got your penny postcards for you. We're going to take them back home and draw pictures of what we want for Christmas and send them to Santa Claus at the North Pole. That's what we're going to do now." As she stepped by Sam, she smiled her gratitude for his brief vigil—and explained: "They won't never get nothing. And they can't write. But they like to draw the pictures and send them to Santa." She turned to the girls. "Now all of us. Let's go!"

Their cardboard tags at their several levels on threadbare cloth (the tall one's coat was ludicrously too small), they shuffled before the woman, like wounded angels or emissaries from another world, up between the lines of Christmas mailers loaded with letters and packages to be sent by sea and rail and air to where and wherever.

Postage on all Sam's three shopping-bags full came to two dollars and seventeen cents.

Turning from the window, the bags at his side empty and all in one hand now, flapping like wind-abandoned sails, Sam saw the big clock on the wall above the door. It was circled in eight concentric rings of metal, each one set back from the next (for the eight planets, perhaps?), the face a ninth and central wafer, whiter than ice, arrow-tipped hands upthrust, long one right and short one left, telling him it was five past eleven.

That noon was the first time Sam tried to find the underground magic shop at Forty-second Street. For most of his exploration, he kept making the same turns and going along the same underground alleys, even as he tried to get somewhere new, finally to give up: he didn't want to be late for dinner at Corey and Elsie's. When he was unsure of what train he was actually supposed to take to get back to Harlem, he asked an elderly Negro in a suit with baggy knees and the jacket and vest grayed with powdered plaster, who was carrying a chest of tools on the platform—and came home.

New Year's Day was practically balmy. For a while Sam retained a memory of strolling down Lenox Avenue, just a sweater under his suit jacket. Hands in his pants pockets, he whistled jets of music and condensed breath, ambling by the pine trees discarded that morning at the curb over soiled snow clutching the sidewalk's rim. Wooden stands were still nailed to the trunks: crossed planks, a board square, or some more complicated contrivance with braces. The needle-bare branches transformed the trees into long-slain carcasses.

The next day the temperature dropped to a previously unknown and, till then unbelievable, paralytic cold. What had been snow and slush became a rind of ice over the city. That night, ears stinging and face a mask of pain from the wind, Sam hurried toward Mount Morris past a mound of trees, delicately afire in the corner lot, one still with ornaments on its charring branches, black before crackling flame.

Late in February's icy circuit, when Sam answered the door, Clarice came in, waving a newspaper, cheeks blotched red with cold. "You've got to see this. This is too much. This is, I tell you, the living end!"

35

Hubert got up from the wing chair. "What is it?"

"What *is* it?" The room was chill; and though Clarice's coat was open, she didn't shrug it off. "Here—now did you believe you were ever going to live to see something like this in a paper—even a New York City paper?"

The picture took up a quarter of the second page.

White actress Mary Blair knelt on the ground beside a seated, twenty-six year old Negro actor, Paul Robeson, kissing his hand! The play was Eugene O'Neill's *All God's Chillun Got Wings*, scheduled to open at the Provincetown Players in Greenwich Village sometime that spring. Robeson played a young, Negro law student—

"See. He was a lawyer, Hubert—like you."

"He *plays* a lawyer," Hubert corrected. "In the play."

Sam read over Clarice's shoulder.

"No, he really *was* a lawyer," Clarice said. "Before. But he gave it up for the theater!"

"He wasn't a lawyer; he was a football player!" Sam said. "See." Football was Sam's own sport—he had played center in high school, till Papa—when John's brother broke his leg in the game, the sharp bone coming through his brown, bloody shin—decided it was too rough and had forbidden him: everyone at home had encouraged him to go out for basketball, for which Sam had no particular love. "It says he was All-American Halfback in 1917 and 1918."

"First he was a football player—when he was at Rutgers," Clarice explained. "*Then* he was a lawyer. Then he became an actor."

"Well," Hubert said, "I can't imagine his being a very good lawyer, then. Where'd he go to law school?"

"Columbia."

"People are going to try and stop that play from going on," Hubert said. "You just watch."

"There's a statement in here by the actress," Clarice said. "She thinks it's an *honor* to be in the play."

The picture was…well, uncomfortable making. But maybe that was because you just didn't *see* pictures like that.

"Is that man dreamy—or is he dreamy?" Clarice asked. "Oh, Hubert—!" she added. Because Hubert was frowning. "I'm *teasing* you!"

Still, in March Clarice dragged them off to see Robeson in Nan Stevens' *Roseanne*, over at the Lafayette Theater. "We've *got* to go!" she insisted. "It's only playing for a *week!*" On Saturday afternoon they met before the yellow, horizontally striated walls with the other Negroes at a Hundred-thirty-second Street and Seventh Avenue. In their gloves, scarves, hats, a lot of people must have read the articles that had been appearing. There'd been a slew of them since the first one—and the picture had been reprinted by now in half a dozen papers. Clarice said: "This is surely a lot more people than usually come to this sort of thing." She took a hand from her fox muff to rub one knuckle on her nose.

The tickets were thirty-five cents. The matinee was supposed to start at two-thirty, but it was almost quarter to three before they let people in. And a tall, West Indian looking — and sounding — man called out something, very loudly, about "a C.P.T. matinee," which made some people laugh.

"Oh, that's *terrible!*" Clarice whispered. "Come on, let's go inside. I'm freezing!"

Before the curtain went up, a stolid, brownskinned man, Mr. Gilpin, head of the Lafayette Players, came out and made a speech saying the Lafayette was the only Negro dramatic company in the country; and if the audience liked what they were doing for the colored community, they could make extra donations in the lobby. Clarice leaned toward Hubert. Sam heard her whisper: "You read that article in *The Messenger* I showed you...? Where Lewis got on them so for only doing white plays with black actors...?" In the light from the stage, Hubert nodded.

Then Gilpin went back in through the curtain. A moment later red drapery pulled aside from the stage.

Robeson played a Negro preacher—it was hard to see him, at least at the beginning, and not think of Papa—whose actions became more and more sinful. And he was certainly wonderful. When he got excited, his voice filled the theater. He seemed half again as big as most of the other actors, and he moved around, towering, handsome, like some half-wild, wondrous animal barely caged by the set. Canvas walls and mâché trees shook as he strode by. Indeed, the glee, the wild joy with which he embraced his sins—drinking, crap shooting, shirking his Sunday sermons, and finally falling into the arms of a no-account Negro woman and getting her with child—made those weaknesses seem almost like some socially rebellious strength. Finally, though, his congregation turned on him. He was only saved in the end by a brave black woman—Roseanne —who'd been in love with him all along and who made an impassioned speech to the black people, who'd gathered to lynch him, about his humanity and his weaknesses and how *his* weaknesses were really *their* weaknesses. (Robeson spent a lot of time on his knees in the play, though not the actress.) But in comparison to Robeson's performance, the long-suffering Roseanne's words to the angry townsfolk seemed preachier than any of Papa's sermons.

Clapping wildly, Sam stood up with everybody else when Robeson came to the front of the stage to bow.

But as they were walking down to a Hundred-sixteenth Street, Hubert said, "Another weak-willed nigger and another strong-headed woman. And niggers lynching *niggers?* Where, I wonder, did they get that one from? Now you *know* the woman who wrote that play had to be white!"

Clarice was thoughtful—walking with rapid, thoughtful steps, once in a while coughing into her muff. Possibly it had made her uncomfortable too.

A blizzard rose in the last days of March; and, with only an hour out here and an hour out there, the chill effluvia still fell on April Fool's Day.

each Friday at Mr. Harris's he went to the bank at lunchtime thirty-five or forty dollars in pennies nickels dimes quarters and fifty-cent pieces in two thick canvas sacks metal fastenings at the top through the brass bars he exchanged them for an envelope of paper money out of which back at the store Mr. Harris carefully counted Sam's nine dollars for the week the sales girl gum-chewing Missely's twelve and put the envelope with the rest in his inner suit coat pocket the only profit it looked like Mr. Harris allowed himself from the business Missely was Milly Pott's weight and Milly Pott's color but with not half Milly's sense of humor two Fridays on Mr. Harris came in and unwrapped his scarf "Feels like snow again don't it" and after hanging up the length of maroon wool on the coat rack's brass hook said "Before you go downstairs Sam run over two buildings and hunt up Poonkin he'll probably be in the cellar see if he got those boards he told me about and if he do you bring as many back here as you can carry I want to put me up some shelving downstairs in the back all right" and Sam said "A Mr. Poonkin" and Mr. Harris said "I don't think there's any 'mister' in with it just Poonkin" and he grinned gold tooth bright between the white ones in a face as deep a brown as Papa's "Poonkin was in the Civil War you know ask him to tell you about it sometime but not on my time now get going" and in only his shirtsleeves Sam went out in the gelid noon through steely cold he hurried two buildings up the wooden planks of the cellar doors gaped between snow banks he ducked down they rose like green board wings beside him as he dropped one foot then the other to a lower step in deepening shadow "Mr. Poonkin…" because he was a well-bred boy and his father said you call a man mister now you hear me white or colored but especially a colored man a lot of people won't call a colored man mister it shows you have breeding Sam stepped further down the ceiling of the cellar was crossed by tarred eight-by-ten beams bowed now and gray pipes the joints shiny with new solder low enough so that there'd be no standing easily here "…Mr. Poonkin" as he trod on the cement floor that two feet on be-

As my eyes grew accustomed to the light, details of the room within emerged from the mist, strange animals, statues, and gold — everywhere the glint of gold. For the moment—an eternity it must have seemed to the others standing by—I was struck

came earth a voice cracked like the ground beneath his shoes "What you want…?" and the blades of light that came in at the ceiling's edge from some cracks up to the street were much brighter it seemed than the aluminum light outside "Mr. Harris in the clothing store he dumb with amazement, and when Lord Carnarvon, unable to stand the suspense any longer, inquired anxiously, "Can you see anything?" it was all I could do to get out the words, "Yes, wonderful things…"

sent me over here I work for Mr. Harris? and he told me to come over about some wood? you had for him? he wants to make some shelves — in his cellar?" the voice answered "Oh. Yeah…" and stepped forward the face wizened as a prune and what of it visible a moment passing through a beam not much bigger shoulders sagging beneath layered sweaters and two jackets the hands in knitted gloves with the fingers out the nails yellow passing through the light as they felt through cold air toward him talon-long on the floor the foot in its black shoe grated through scuffed light Sam tried to imagine that body holding together such an impoverished galaxy of details and lost all bodiliness until the voice fixed that darkly and shabbily invested corporeality "Come on back with me, and help me carry 'em" Sam wondered how old you had to be to have been in the Civil War anyway because Papa who was over sixty-five now had been a slave till he was seven years old in Georgia and that meant you had to be seventy-five eighty could this bent black man be that old on the second trip three boards was all Poonkin could carry at a time the light fell through the window high in the wall to light half a cardboard carton on the ground bottles standing beside it and as Sam took the boards from those wide withered hands webbed in gray knitting he glanced down to see what was in the box and resolved he would come back for a third load despite Mr. Harris and when he was back for three more boards they'd taken nine over so far he stood by the carton and said "Mr. Harris said you were in the Civil War" and Poonkin now he'd met him Sam could think of the man as Poonkin a title rather than a name Poonkin let cackled syllables fall like pebbles to hit the floor and skitter into the dark at no predictable rhythm "Yessir, I was in the war in 'Sippi. I weren't but fifteen. But I had me a rifle and I hid in a' ol' barn behind some spruce trees, and anybody what come up to it I shot" and Sam laughed "Did you shoot rebels or Union men" the cackle failed was replaced by crackling words "I shot anybody who come up. Some of 'em was blue. Some of 'em was gray. But the ones who come up too near was the ones I shot. It weren't like this last war. This last war, it look like about everybody got killed. But I'm still alive — and I believe pretty much most of the ones I shot is dead. But you more interested in that box than in the war, ain't you, boy. What's in there you want?" which was true because back in '22 when the news had filled the papers of the discovery of Tutankhamen's tomb Sam and John and Lewy had begun to find in the candy stores and the newsstands in downtown Raleigh the most amazing magazines with flat spines and colored covers and titles like *Adventure* and *Mystery Magazine* and *All Story Magazine* and they had bought them for a quarter each and had read "Khufu's Real Tomb" by Talbot Mundy and Adam Hull Shirk's "Osiris" ("Have you been reading about King Tut? If so, you'll be interested in 'Osiris'!") and *Weird Tales* and *Popular Magazine* and John had found a copy of Sax Rohmer's *Tales of Secret Egypt* and they had traded them and they had sat in the glider together out on the back porch reading or off alone on the benches beside St. Agnes which after it had been closed down as a hospital years before had been re-opened as the first building on campus or crosslegged on the attic floor reading and reading and rereading of gray-eyed suntanned Englishmen and intrepid American reporters and rich well-spoken young women who rebelled against their fathers by helping the young man anyway evil Arabs and dangerous African tribes diamonds that had been in the family for generations and rubies fixed to the jade idol's forehead since time first dawned over the sands moonlit chases with gunshots echoing among the pyramids bullets biting into the sandstone of the sphinx's paw as they had not since Napoleon's time temples in the jungle the small plane's engine growling as it settled among the monuments in the Valley of the Kings the sound of the twentieth century infiltrating the silence of a past so deep its bottom was source and fundament of time and of mankind itself and Poonkin's voice acute to his own century said "You want those — you can have 'em. Somebody livin' upstairs left 'em. Last white man in the building to go, too. Moved out four months ago. I used to read me my Bible," Poonkin explained "First thing I did when the war was over was learn me to read some. Only one in my family, too; but I wouldn't read stuff like that. Can't see good enough to read no more nohow" and when Sam came back after working an anxious two more hours in Mr. Harris's basement warmer by a corner paraffin heater and better lit by two kerosene lamps the magazines were in a shopping bag on a dry sheaf of newspapers beside the cellar doors closed now the bag leaning up by the brick wall when he lifted it on the paper beneath was a picture of KKK men in bedsheets holding high a torch menacing the darkness of the black newsprint from within the photo's right framing the shopping bag just sitting there Sam thought where anyone could have taken it

Anyone at all.

That evening Sam worked late at Mr. Harris's. When he left the store, the sky above the second story cornice was blue-black.

Carrying the shopping bag filled with a dozen and a half of Poonkin's magazines between the snow mounded against the stoops and the slush by the cars along the curb, it struck him: it was the powerless who produced most of the myths of power, as it was the poor who articulated the most staggering fantasies of wealth—in the same way it was probably the Philistines and illiterates who perpetrated the soaring images of art and poetry which, once they came loose from the Edgar Guests, from the Courier-and-Ives, the rest of the world was seduced by; and real poets and artists doubtless exhausted their lives trying to make them happen. And so desire fueled the engines of the world. But because he was neither a poet nor an artist himself, Sam did not even try to hold onto the insight. And by the time he was climbing the tall stoop around the corner from the park, he had forgotten it.

Inside, Sam took off his coat, took off his shoes, pants, shirt, socks, till he was just in the long johns Hubert had given him—and put on his suit jacket. Hubert was in class tonight—and would go over to eat with Clarice in her aunt and uncle's kitchen afterward. Sam sat in Hubert's wing chair, took a magazine from the shopping bag, slid one bare foot atop the other...and began to page through for the stories about the blinding sand, the brittle mummies, the cursed scarabs, and the lean, light-eyed men whose years away from civilization had burnt them black as Arabs or mixed-blooded Negroes, dangerous men, wise in the ways of the jungle, the East, the desert, quick with their fists and fine shots to a man, who knew what to do, what to say....

On the wall across from his bed, the back window had a curtain over it—and a drape. But, on finishing his fourth story in his second magazine and turning to the fifth, Sam glanced up to see the light at the drape's edge. Frowning, he closed the pages, put the magazine down, and stood. Was there some sort of light shining up from the alley?

Sam walked across the rug and pulled away drape and curtain.

Through the window, the yard below was blinding: by the black walls, snow had ceased falling, and some high breeze had swept clouds away from—his eyes ascended to the ascent of the moon—the full orb. It blazed on the platinum alley-scape—crossed and recrossed by catenaries of clotheslines piled with white. The only things not silver, gray, or black were three windows in the wall across from him, behind the ropes and fire escapes... One had the yellowish hue of incandescent light. Two had the dimmer yellow from hidden kerosene lamps, flaming quietly and darkly. In one of these, the light came through cloth no thicker than a bedsheet, hanging in folds behind the glass. Even as Sam noticed, a shadow moved on it.

Yes, on the rippled textile was the shadow of a body—a woman's body. A woman with hair, and breasts—he started—and, he was certain, wearing nothing! The slim darkness of an arm raised on ivory cloth; on the hanging folds, her silhouette turned. The sill was at her thigh, and as she strained to do something behind, he could see the apex of light between her legs as one went back. The line of a hip—her breast again. Body of shadow, body of light, held a moment—and the illumination that articulated her dimmed...then puffed out!

Within gray stone, the window's rectangle was black.

The surprise of her vanishing made him gasp. With thudding chest, slowly he went down on the knees of his union suit before the painted wainscot beneath his own sill. The drape fell against his jacket shoulder, slid behind him.

Her window remained dark.

Cold air leaked under the edge of his own.

After a moment, down on his knees, Sam lifted his elbows out and up, grasped the metal handles on the lower sash, and raised it. Over the tiny chill real cold fell in under his thumbs, wrapped its feathery tickle around his chin and neck, pried inside his long-john top. Beyond the wooden trough—a black, splintered canyon in water-rotted wood—out on the dry stone a snow pillow curved away, glittering. He raised the sash another inch, then a foot—then six more inches; raised himself to look again toward that black window. His breathing had become so shallow that, now, he gasped a chest full of icy air. On his knees, it made him reel. Rising again, he leaned forward, thrust his face under the sash —brought his mouth slowly to the snow.

And kissed it.

Crystals melted before his lips — he closed his eyes — and a water bead ran along the crevice between. He opened his mouth just a little— and a cold drop rolled within, warming. Mouthing snow, he took in only the tiniest bit of air through lattices of white fire.

Two days later on his third trip underground to Times Square and Forty-second Street specifically to find it, almost by accident Sam turned to see the window full of false noses, exploding cigars, and sneezing powder—more jokes in the window, actually, than the magic tricks that had first caught his attention. The shop's exotic name was Cathay. It also had lots of Chinese boxes for sale, and ivory carvings with black wood bases, Japanese fans and Oriental scarves that were not particularly magic at all. Maybe he had passed it before and, for all the other things there, hadn't recognized it. But there was the top hat, the wand... Inside, the bearded man with the bottle-bottom glasses was a Mr. Horstein, who, soon as they got to talking, explained how he'd been a magician back in the 'nineties—oh, yes, the magic was the first reason for Cathay's existence. The rest was all because sailors on leave and sometimes tourists liked to buy them. Clearly Mr. Horstein loved to talk to his customers. He talked about the great Harry Houdini, who, no, never came to Cathay. But Mr. Horstein had met him in Chicago and then again in Syracuse. Apparently they were acquaintances. "Not friends. But we say 'Hello,' as men who share the same profession." Last year when Houdini had played the Jackson Theater, Sam and Lewy had not been allowed to go—because neither Papa nor Lewy's stepfather would allow their children to go to a segregated theater. John's mother didn't mind though; and Lewy and Sam might well have snuck in with him. (Going with someone whose parents said it was all right made it not quite so much like sneaking.) But that week John was sick and had his throat tied up with a scarf full of asafœtida.

Mr. Horstein (Sam had been in the store for almost three hours) had introduced Sam to several of his customers by now: "This is Sam—isn't this a good-looking, intelligent colored boy? He's a real credit, and I like to have this kind of young fellow here."

Riding home on the subway, Sam read an article in a red pamphlet with lots of fancy symbols on the cover about astrology Mr. Horstein had sold him for a nickel: it talked about the Transit of Mercury, that happened this year, and might even—this part Sam wasn't clear on— fall on Sam's birthday, though such transits were more common in November than in May.

When he got home, Hubert—or Clarice—had left *Views of Italy* open under the reading lamp. He picked it up, turned the lamp on, and held it down under the light to look at a photograph of a hill—northwest of Sienna, the caption said. The hilltop was ringed by a wall, set at equal distances with blocky towers: seven towers, Sam counted — though the caption said there'd once been fourteen.

Insistent through sleep, voices like water met him, within some dream, listening. The long sounds of morning, the tired sounds, indistinct— metal hit metal somewhere and reverberated. Someone shouted. As far away as the train tracks a siren complained of its windy wound. All muffled in sleep, signs tangled in the sheets around him, vanishing. (*Who is this woman with us...?*) A truck lumbered east. Another one braked—and a motor started. Someone shouted—again. Something hit something else, dully. Outside, in half light, beyond the window, April snow *still* fell — and sounds rose; morning sounds carrying away his drowsiness. He turned under the quilt (to face the draped window), wondering if they might return it. Soft sounds slid around him, slipped over him like a sleeve, waiting in the winter-dimmed city. Outside, the black stones of Mount Morris would be a pillow of white. (*A black woman clothed in white moving through the white city...a white woman on a cloth of light.*) He could see, through the edge of the glass beside the drape, smoke spill from a roof vent into smoke, to wander up the sky, wash off in winter wisps.

Under the covers, Sam thought: *And beside me...*

He moved his hand with their thickened fingertips out from the depression his body had warmed to the cold place where no one lay. (*A white woman in the heart of...a black woman in a city of light.*) Somewhere a siren sounded, weaving together for him the possibilities of his vacant day.

Saturday at Corey and Elsie's there was a short, sharp argument between Sam and Hubert: Sam was happy to do his tricks for Hubert— and even Clarice—back at Hubert's, but Hubert suggested after dinner that Sam perform one of Cathay's wonders for his sisters: a vanishing coin. Sam had brought the trick over, after all, in his inner jacket pocket, precisely *for* that. But Hubert's request got only Sam's refusal, first a quiet one, then an insistent one, then—with red-cheeked embarrassment—a loud one, when Hubert wouldn't stop.

But, at least partly, it was because Mr. Carter, a Columbia Teacher's College friend of Elsie's, was there that afternoon for dinner — a mahogany-complected, articulate young man from Philadelphia, who cut all his food with his fork. But Mr. Carter displayed a smiling, inquisitive awe before Elsie and her siblings that Sam recognized: it was the air other ministers, especially white ones, displayed when they visited Papa socially at home. And nothing made a social situation more uncomfortable for Sam. It turned everything you did into a performance, and always left him somewhere between tongue-tied and belligerent.

"*I'd* like to see you do a magic trick," Mr. Carter had prompted across the remains of dinner, in what clearly he thought was an encouraging way.

"Go *on*, Sam!" Hubert said. "That's what you brought it over here for—to *show* people!"

"*No!*" Sam said. "Come on, now—I said *No!* Didn't you *hear* me?" His voice was too loud, his hand was actually shaking, and the silence after it was much too long.

Corey rescued him: "Now Sam is still learning these things. And you've got to practice them before you do them for other people. He just needs to practice and will show us all his trick in his own time, now."

Hubert dragged his forearm from the table, sucked his teeth — his turn to sulk.

But nothing dented Mr. Carter's simple, irrepressible good will. "Can I ask you something seriously, though?" His dark fingers moved on the handle of his unused knife.

"I don't know." Corey smiled. "Can you?"

"Would you please tell me—because I have heard this story about you two ladies so many times before, but just in snatches and fragments, so that you never know what you're really supposed to believe and what you're not—just so I can tell other people when I get back to Philadelphia—what *really* happened at that movie, there—was it six or seven years ago?"

"What movie?" Elsie asked.

"That movie," Mr. Carter said, "where you two got into all that trouble?"

"Six years ago?" Elsie said. "What movie does he—"

"Oh, I know what he means," Dr. Corey said. "Arnold—" which was Mr. Carter's name to Corey and Elsie, but not to Hubert, Clarice, and Sam—"that wasn't six years ago. That was seven, eight—" she frowned. "That was *nine* years ago now!"

"But...what happened?"

"Might as well go ahead," Hubert said. "After all this time, everybody ought to know."

"What movie?" Sam said. Though he knew the outlines of the tale, the fragmentariness was as much there for him as for Arnold Carter—since, nine years ago, when Corey and Elsie had first gone up to the city, where they'd stayed for two years before coming home, Sam had been...well, nine.

"That great big movie they made, about the south—and the Ku Klux Klan and all," Hubert said. "About the wonderful white south and the black devils who were raping all those white women—"

"Oh!" Elsie said. "That awful movie—that made everybody go out and start lynching all those people!"

"It didn't *start* them lynching," Corey said. "But it certainly made them go out and lynch more."

"What did you have to do with it?" Sam asked.

"We were picketing—a peaceful picket line. With a lot of other Negroes."

"With a lot of other *angry* Negroes, I bet," Hubert said. "That's what I heard."

"We *were* angry," Dr. Corey said. "Who wouldn't be angry, at a movie like that?"

"How did a movie make people lynch people?" Sam wanted to know.

"It was a movie about those damned Ku Klux Klansmen—" Corey didn't use language like that and it startled Sam to hear her cuss like Louis—"and told how wonderful they were and how they were protecting southern white womanhood."

What came back to Sam was a memory of his cousin, or a woman whom his mother had called their cousin: yes, he'd been nine, eight, maybe younger, when her and her husband's mutilated bodies, under gray canvas, had been brought, in the creaking wagon, back through the evening trees, to the campus—

"We were picketing," Corey said. "That's all. With the others, across the street from the theater."

"Well, that wasn't *quite* all," Elsie said.

"Then what else *did* we do?" Dr. Corey asked, indignantly.

But Elsie had some devilment in her eye.

And there was a grin back of Dr. Corey's indignation. "We certainly didn't do very *much* else—that anyone with a grain of sense wouldn't have done. There's no forgiving a movie like that—stirring people up to violence against their fellow man!"

"What did she do, Miss Elsie?" Mr. Carter asked.

"Well, we were picketing, there across the street. The policemen were keeping us back. And you could see that it wasn't doing anything to keep people from going into the movie—"

"The thing we wanted to do," Corey said, "was to stop them from going to see it, you see. That's what we were trying to do."

"So finally," Elsie said, "Corey says to me, 'Come on.' Well, I didn't know where she was going."

"You did too!" Corey said. "I *told* you—"

"After we got in line," Elsie said, "you told me. We left the pickets, went down to the end of the block, crossed over, came back, and got on the ticket line to the movie. That's when I asked you, what we were going to do. And you told me, 'We're going to go inside and see that movie!' Well, I was afraid to leave her, because I knew she was probably going to do something foolish—and I didn't want her to get in trouble."

"You went *into* the movie?" Clarice asked. From her tone, Sam realized this was new to her as well.

Corey nodded.

"We went into the movie," Elsie said, "took our seats, and waited for the lights to go down and the man at the organ to start his playing—and I asked: 'Corey, what are we going to do now?' And she whispered, 'Hush!' and just to sit there and to do what she did. Well, I thought, dear Lord, give me strength! What has this crazy girl, my own little sister, got it into her head to do?"

"Then what happened?" Sam asked.

"The lights went off, the man started to play the organ, and the movie began—and Corey jumps up, scoots out into the aisle, with those long dresses we used to wear back then, catching on everybody's knees, saying real loud, 'Excuse me—excuse me, please!' and I'm coming right after her. I think people thought she was sick—and had to use the facilities. So they were making room.

"But then, when she got into the aisle, she ran right down toward the front of the theater — and I'm running to keep up. And she climbed onto the stage—"

"I *jumped* onto the stage," Corey said. "I got hold of the edge, and I went up like a boy over a fence—though I don't know whether I could do it today—"

"And she grabbed hold of the edge of the screen, with the light from the projector all over us, and people starting to stand up and call out to ask if something was wrong, and she *ripped* it—"

Corey laughed. "I certainly did. I remember, you stood there, on the stage, in front of all those people, and you said, 'Oh, Corey—!'"

"Then *I* grabbed hold," Elsie said, "and started ripping too!"

"Once we began, *she* ripped more than I did," Corey said. "I really think Elsie was having fun."

"I was scared to death," Elsie said. "But, by then, I figured it didn't make much difference. I knew we were going to end up in jail, no matter —so I decided it'd be better at least to do what we'd come for. Yes, I got hold of it—and I ripped it too. In about a New York minute, the two of us tore the whole screen down!"

Clarice hooted, hands over her mouth.

"But *then* what happened?" Sam said, between his own guffaws.

"I mean," Clarice said, "how did you two get *out* of there?"

"Very quickly," Corey said. "We were lucky. Someone in the audience by that time had started fighting. There were other people on the stage now—you remember that man who asked us, so politely, while we were ripping, if something was wrong? But the fist fight in the audience, that was taking up all the ushers' attention. So even while they were putting the lights on, we rushed backstage and down some steps and around through a door that opened right into the alley — and got out!"

"This is so funny," Clarice said, recovering herself. "A couple of months ago, I was reading in *Opportunity* about the 'riot' they had at the premier of *Birth of a Nation*. And you mean you two *were* the riot?"

"I guess we were pretty much *most* of the riot. It was in the newspapers," Elsie said, "the next day. But I wouldn't think they'd still be talking about it now. It was nine—almost ten years ago; and it was just a movie, after all. Who'd want to remember something like that?"

"A low down, dirty, rotten movie," Dr. Corey said, "that made people go out and *kill* each other!"

"Mama and Papa never talked about that," Sam said. "I don't think they'd like something like that, you all being in the newspapers for gettin' in some kind of trouble!"

"We didn't want to worry Mama and Papa," Elsie said. "So we didn't tell them. But I guess other people told them just this bit and that bit—and it all gets out of hand."

"But we didn't do anything to be ashamed of," Dr. Corey said. "I thought it was right then. And I'd do it again today, if I had to. The lynchings went up all over the country in nineteen fifteen—because of that movie. That's probably why they're up now. Not a man or woman, black or white, Christian or Jew, with free-thinking ideas and care for his fellows was safe anywhere in the country while that movie was on."

"Jews?" Sam said. "They don't lynch Jews." Back home, John and his brother had told Sam that, because Jews had all the money, everybody was afraid to cross them and that's why they were taking control of just everything. "They got too much money."

"Don't lynch *Jews?*" Dr. Corey declared. "And just what makes you think they don't, boy? That poor Jew, Mr. Frank, he was lynched down in Georgia, right near where Papa was born, the very summer that movie was showing. Don't lynch Jews? Where have you been, boy? Back when the Jim Crow laws came in, *everybody* was getting lynched. That was the crime of it, see? That's what taking the law into your own hands is all about. Anybody they didn't like, got lynched—for any reason. You think they didn't lynch Jews? They lynched white people, they lynched black people—they lynched women, children, *and* Jews. Don't let me hear you talkin' nonsense like that anymore, Sam. Sometimes I think you don't know anything!"

"Now they did lynch *more* colored than anybody else," Elsie said. "You know that, Corey."

Corey just *humphed*.

"You remember that sign they put up in the park in downtown Raleigh, when the Jim Crow laws came in? 'No Jews or Dogs Allowed'?" Elsie laughed. "They didn't even think enough of niggers to put up a sign to keep us out."

Sam had heard about the sign; but by the time he'd got to go downtown, there were just the usual signs for where coloreds were supposed to go and the water fountains you were supposed to drink from and where whites were supposed to go and drink. There'd been a mysterious time, Sam knew, that had ended just around his birth, when everyone went to the theater together; when people even went to school together. His older brothers and sisters—Lemuel and Elsie and Corey and Lucius —often spoke of it, when everyone in Raleigh had gone to the Jackson Theater and sat wherever they'd wanted to and watched plays by Shakespeare and dastardly melodramas and uproarious comic skits, in which people sang and danced and minstrels Tommed in black-face, and men in top hats did magic tricks. (Mr. Horstein had said that, personally, he'd never played the Jackson in Raleigh—but magicians had come to Cathay who had.) But now all the theaters in Raleigh were segregated, and Papa wouldn't let him go at all. A few times he'd snuck in with Lewy and John. (John's mother taught Mathematics and Women's Deportment at the college—his father had died three years ago—and didn't care.) In the balcony, John's brother's crutches leaning over the seat back, the boys sat with the other colored children—nigger heaven, everybody called it—to watch Mary Pickford and William S. Hart and Douglas Fairbanks… Though Corey probably had her point, John was pretty smart, and Sam was not yet ready to dismiss completely John's judgment of the Jews…

"That's true," Corey said, uncharacteristically pensive, "that's true…."

And for a moment Sam wasn't sure if memory had made him miss something important in the present.

That night, after Hubert came back from taking Clarice home and went into his own room to study, then to sleep, Sam got up, moved the drape and curtain back, to hang them in a great down-descending arch over the wing of the chair. Then he got back in bed and lay awake, covers over his mouth and ears, blinking at the moonlight out the window.

At work a few days later, Sam asked: "Mr. Harris, you seen Mr. Poonkin?"

"*Awww...*" Mr. Harris said, like someone with something real sad he'd forgotten to tell you: "Last week, Poonkin—he got the pee-neumo-nia. I guess it was on the Tuesday you didn't come in. They took him over to Manhattan Hospital on Ward's Island—"

"—for the *Insane?*"

Mr. Harris frowned. "Well, they got a lot more people out there than just the looneys now, you know. I guess they got pretty much everybody over there who can't pay for hisself. But Poonkin got the pee-neumonia —the old people's friend."

Sam looked puzzled.

"That's what they call it." Glare slid left to right across Mr. Harris's gold tooth. Denting green silk, Mr. Harris's tiepin was gold. "At least it's the friend of old people like Poonkin who ain't got nobody to care for 'em. It takes 'em quick and, as dying goes, goes pretty easy. I wouldn't be surprised if old Poonkin's dead by now—though nobody's told me that, yet. Though why they'd come and tell me, I don't know. I'm no kin of his. Poonkin been around here long before I got here. Now he's gone."

While he worked in the cellar, sometimes looking over at the boards against the cement wall, Sam thought about going to visit old Poonkin on Ward's Island. He tried to picture himself in a great public hospital, endless dividing sheets rippling white between the beds, talking to the old man, propped on his pillow: "Mr. Poonkin, tell me about what you did in the War—about the rifle and the barn—behind the spruce, before you could read—what of it you can remember...?" But he didn't really know if Poonkin were first name or last. (Those idiosyncratic memories of the War, what it was to be a fifteen-year-old black boy with a rifle in a barn, not to mention everything that had brought that child to the cellar two doors away, an aged, half-blind, brief and taloned guardian to those magazines—suddenly winking out. Memories—like spume from a broken wave...) In the hospital, weakly he calls to me. I start to leave, he calls again, but before I turn...there was Hubert, chained to the water pump, and Papa gasping, drawing back the orange crate in his brown hands, his collar loose and no shirt under his black vest, the arms of a man in his fifties, yes, but deeply dark in the evening blue. "You are not a man—you are a little *animal!*" Papa shouted. "And if you will live like an animal, I will *treat* you like an animal! I will *beat* you like a *beast* till you *beg* to be a *man* again...!" Crate slats splintered against Hubert's shoulder; he remembered the precise sound of his father's grunts. *"Ah...!"* The slats splintered again. *"Keh...!"* On the next blow they smithereened. *"Dah...!"* Hubert fell, pulled himself backward, shouting: "Papa! *No, Papa...? No — !"* Papa hit him with the stump of what hung from his hands, then hurled the bottom, missing Hubert, gouging grass. *No...*

No. (Sam walked slowly through the cold street.) For suppose he went over there and Mr. Harris was right: Poonkin was already dead.

"You shouldn't *do* that!" Clarice said one day. "You don't do it at Elsie and Corey's. I'm sure you didn't do it in front of your Mama and your Papa at home." Which was true.

"If he's going to do it," Hubert said from the wing chair where he'd begun to read, "I'd just as soon he did it in front of me. You don't want the boy sneaking off to do it behind my back, now."

Sam was surprised at Clarice's upset. He'd thought her unconcerned about the matter till now.

"Hubert, you should speak to him—you *said* you were going to speak to him. Oh, I'm sorry—it isn't any of my business! And I shouldn't have said anything." Then, with her coat still unbuttoned, she went to the door and out.

Pulling it to after her, it stuck—with a noise like *Pra*, then, when she opened it an inch and pulled it to again, with a *Ja*. Outside, she yanked it to, and it closed on two beats: *Pa-Ti*. The tensions of her leaving turned the sound into a kind of thunder that left the room whispering its silence. Sam thought about saying: *Hubert, you said you didn't mind if I—*

But Hubert cut the thought off: "You know, I used to work in the tobacco fields—and by and large, it's a pretty ordinary sort of Negro you find there."

"That's right. In Connecticut. What do you mean?" Sam asked; because Hubert was speaking in his serious, older-brother voice. Another sort of thunder.

"Well, you got hardworking Negroes. You got lazy Negroes. Then you got no-accounts—but that shouldn't be any news to you…"

Sam nodded.

"But you got another kind you're going to run into up here — only thing to call 'em is animals. Maybe there're white people like that too— I guess there must be, someplace. But, now, there were some good men working with me in the Connecticut fields. And there were some lazy ones. Lots of them were no-accounts—but even more of them were just animals." Hubert pointed his finger. "And *that's* why I don't smoke no cigarettes."

"I don't understand…?"

"When they pick tobacco," Hubert said, "they cure it before they make those. But they don't wash it."

"I still don't—"

"Where does an animal make water or do his business?"

"Right where's he's standing."

"Well, *that's* what I mean," Hubert said. "And I don't mean once or twice; I mean all day every day—right in the row where they're hooking tobacco. They don't even go to the side. And at least ten times or more I come across some feller doing a lot worse than making water or his

55

business—grinning and telling you he's gotta do it now 'cause there ain't much more to life but that and getting drunk and he's just *got* to do it! Right on top of what you're putting in your mouth and sucking into your body! They know white people going to be smoking them things— they think it's funny."

"What's a lot worse?" Sam took the delicate white paper from his lip, feeling its faint adhesion unstick, to look at the tube of fire and flavor in his clubbed fingers.

"If you can't figure it for yourself," Hubert said, "it's not my place to tell you. It's not my place to preach to you, neither. And I'm not going to talk about it to you anymore." With a theatrical finality Sam found much more maddening than any preaching (that, at least, with Hubert, meant you could turn it back into an argument), Hubert got up from the wing chair and walked, slowly and with the deliberation of a silent, primal force, into the other room — and did *not* close the door. Sam watched him pull out the chair, move two heavy law books over, sit down, settle one forearm on the desk, and begin studying.

Within the silence, which was almost a rumble, like a train's thundering off somewhere, Sam tried to detect the instructions that would release him from his own paralysis. He really *didn't* know what Hubert meant by "a lot worse." But the veiled suggestions went immediately with the things that could happen to you in the vestibules of subway cars. It wasn't scarifying so much as it defined an area wholly constituted of his ignorance. Sam hated that and felt stupid before it.

It didn't stop him from smoking. But it stopped him from smoking in the house when he was around Clarice—or Hubert.

C

He sees an image of the bridge springing from a remote past
and propelled upward, spiraling, arching the sky, casting its
shadow down upon us and vanishing in space.

    —HORACE GREGORY, "Far Beyond Our Consciousness"

Lost three this morning leaped with crazy laughter
to the waiting sharks, sang as they went under.

    —ROBERT HAYDEN, "Middle Passage"

The intricate interpenetration of the senses, woven into that proto-
historic textile—the tapestry of day—sleep and forgetfulness unravel, as
effectively as any Penelope, largely before the next day's panel is begun.
(Forget a city in which you've once lived, and it might as well have fallen
into the sea.) But it would be as naive to think that all forgettings are
random as it would be to think thus of all dreams: the first things to go
are, systematically, the incidents confirming our own weaknesses which,
because we are lucky enough not to *have* to talk about, there's no particular reason to recall. The incidents we will, likewise, retain are among
those that tell of a certain strength. We may talk about them or not. In
between are all the positive and negative lessons of life that life itself will
not let us lose. But even among these, on imagination's intricate loom,
one can be reworked into the other with astonishing rapidity, strength
into weakness, weakness into strength.

It was astonishing how quickly Sam forgot Poonkin. Guilt he'd felt for not trying to see him on Ward's Island was replaced by guilt at not wrapping up some of the magazines, trudging to the post office — stripped now of its green and red and silver —, and mailing them to Lewy, who, with his small dark hands, with his chocolate chest, with his crisp-haired enthusiasm, would pass them on to tobacco-colored John: a much smaller guilt, since they'd all already traded so many. Back home, they'd received dozens from Sam; Sam had received dozens from them. Probably they'd seen most of these anyway. (Five among the eighteen Sam had actually read before.) But when the last bedsheet-sized pulp was closed and returned to the pile under the daybed beside the wicker, both guilts extinguished each other. He never thought of Poonkin again.

Or anything Poonkin might have remembered.

Over the next few years, half-a-dozen-odd encounters with Paul Robeson, now in a concert, now in another play — along with the tremendous presence Robeson acquired in the black community — soon muddled for Sam the exact memory of the first time he'd seen Robeson on stage. *Had* he seen *All God's Chillun*? No. But then, what was the name of the play he'd seen at the Lafayette? Had he seen Robeson in *The Emperor Jones*, that alternated with *Chillun* at the Provincetown through that spring and summer? No—but some years later he saw the movie. And there was so much talk about, and so many articles on, Robeson, that, on occasions one or two decades by, Sam *said* he'd seen *Chillun* because he knew he'd seen *something* with Robeson in it from around that time. And when, in 1944, Sam and his second wife attended —with Hubert and *his* second wife—the Robeson production of *Othello* at the Metropolitan Opera House, with José Ferrer as Iago, Uta Hagen as Desdemona, Margaret Webster as Emilia, and Phillip Drury as Cassio, they all went very much as Negroes who'd frequently seen Robeson perform.

Sam had seen him just not *quite* so frequently.

He remembered the little girls at the post office a good while. Taking care of them for even those moments had allowed him to retain their ruined visages with a kind of pleasure.

But the other thing Sam remembered was the first time he walked across Brooklyn Bridge.

Two weeks after the full moon, Clarice told him: "If you're going down there, honey, you've got to dress warmer than that. May up here just isn't like May where you and Hubert come from."

Thoughtfully, Sam stood at the secondhand bureau Hubert had gotten him just for his things. (He had on Hubert's long johns.) With what little was left over from his pay, after he'd contributed his two dollars a month to Corey and Elsie for food and three-dollars-fifty-cents a week for his half of the rent, Sam had still saved enough to buy first one, another, then a third magic trick from underground Cathay.

Sam fingered the objects on the dresser.

Just that afternoon, down on the table in the hall, he'd found a brown paper package, wrapped in twine, the mailman had brought — from Lewy! Ripping off the paper, he'd found May's *Weird Tales*, featuring the first installment of a novel by...Harry Houdini!

Imprisoned With the Pharaohs.

Folded up and slipped around the first pages, Lewy's letter said: "High Priest Manetho here to Imhotep off spying in the Upper Kingdom," which made Sam smile at their mutual joke from the afternoon before he'd left that he'd forgotten till now: that Sam was supposed to be a spy in the north and report back to Lewy and John what was going on. "Hi, y'all! You have got a birthday coming up, as I recall. And I got this yesterday—just finished it last night. (I wonder if it's *really* by Houdini?) Consider it your present. And write back quickly and tell me what you think. Though I don't expect a letter from you too soon, as I'm sure you're awash in beautiful women and bathtub gin (while freckled Rust-Top and I do content us with simple moonshine) and the general sins of the northern fleshpots—and you simply haven't the time. But I know you: you'll wait (or try to wait) for the next two installments and read the whole thing at a swoop! But if, in another two months, I haven't heard from you, then I shall do me magic and ju-ju spells on the assumption that thou hast forgotten thy brothers in the southlands."

Sam slid the oversized magazine into the top drawer, wondering whether he'd really have the patience to wait for the next two installments before reading it in a night.

The first of Mr. Horstein's tricks he'd bought was the magic coin that disappeared. Actually, the trick was just a length of black elastic with a clip on one end you could fasten up your sleeve and a bit of gum on the other that you could stick to any quarter or nickel. But now, as he kneaded the stickum, he realized it was losing its adhesion. More and more times it pulled loose from the coin, letting it fall to the rug as often as it snapped the metal glittering from sight.

The most effective trick—and the most expensive (eighty-five cents) —was a little guillotine in which you could cut a cigarette in half; but if you put your finger through the same hole, you could make the blade slip aside so that it appeared—magically—to pass through your finger, leaving it unhurt and whole.

The third one—though it had cost only a dime—didn't work at all: a hollow, metal cup in the form of a thumb's first joint. Smoking a cigarette, without letting anyone see, you secreted the false thumb in your fist. Then you took the cigarette and poked it into your fingers, putting it out on the bottom of the metal cup the false thumb made. You kept packing the cigarette in, until it was inside your fist completely. Finally you used your other thumb to tamp it down further—only you slid your thumb into the false metal one, got it seated good—then opened both your hands.

The cigarette had disappeared. And nobody was supposed to be able to see the thumb cap (with the cigarette inside) over your real one.

The cap was large enough so that, when Hubert tried it on, it just fell off. And Hubert's hands weren't small. Still, Sam's own thumb was too big to wedge into it. Also, the thumbnail on the cap didn't look like the broad, oversized nails curving down over Sam's fingers. And it was painted a luminous pink, that, when Clarice examined it, she said didn't look like anyone's skin color she knew—black, white, gray, or grizzly!

Hubert had suggested Sam ask Mr. Horstein for his dime back. But then, though he liked Mr. Horstein, he was still a little afraid of him (he *was* a Jew, after all), and a dime wasn't a lot.

Sam pushed all three tricks off the dresser, into the drawer on top of *Weird Tales*, and closed it.

And, for Clarice, he put on his suit jacket. And his cap.

"Remember — " That was Hubert, reading the paper in the wing chair; he had folded it back to an advertisement for a new kind of suit-case, made from something called... Naugahyde? "Elsie wants us all over there by four." Hubert looked across the dark room from under the tasseled lamp. "Since your birthday's this coming Tuesday, she and Corey are probably going to do something a little special today. So don't you be late, now."

When he asked the man behind the bars how to get to the Brooklyn Bridge from the station, Sam was told he should have gotten off at City Hall—which was closer. This was the old stop (Brooklyn Bridge) for workers who repaired the bridge—not for people who wanted to walk across it. But if he went two blocks to the east and turned left, he'd come to the walkway.

Beyond the Oriental ornateness of the Pulitzer Building, he saw the structure between—and above—the swoop and curve of trolley tracks, the girders of the El.

It really *was* immense!

He turned left onto Rose Street, which took him down under one of the bridge's stone archways. The arches left and right were walled and windowed, with padlocked doors.

Did people live there, in the base of the bridge? Sam turned into the stone underpass.

Hung from the middle of the overhead stone, its rim painted fresh green, a wooden sign read:

BRIDGE WALKWAY

Beside it was an opening in the stone. The stairway's walls were close set. As he stood there, two colored girls with gingham showing from under their yellow cloth coats ran down. He glimpsed their shiny shoes, their white socks over their little-girl ankles, bare little-girl legs above— and smiled, as they descended toward him, out of the shadow, laughing —while an older sister in a straw hat with a grownup-looking bluejay feather came down behind, more sedately. She was almost as old as Clarice — and, from the way she turned her shoulders and nodded so faintly without a smile, clearly considered herself to look smart.

And (he turned to look after her) she did.

Then all three were gone.

He was left only his own smile and their brief memory. Shrugging his suit jacket together, putting his big, country-boy hand against one stone wall, he started up.

And came out onto the concrete ramp rolling toward the first stanchion. Beyond green rails, cars passed left and right of him—along with a trolley. As its troller crossed beneath sustaining guys, its antenna jangling under the overhead wire, sparks spit down. Rocking away toward Brooklyn, a cart lagged behind, its gun-gray horse and its colored driver, in his gray slouch brim, impassive beside the electrical crackling, the blue-green shower of light.

Hart Crane was born on July 21, 1899 in Garrettsville, Ohio. He was the only child of Clarence Arthur and Grace Hart Crane.

Between him and the traffic, a cable thick as an oil drum lifted slant and vertical cords toward the double vault of stone. Sam started forward, walking toward where the cement flooring gave way to wood. And as hundreds on hundreds of thousands of pedestrians had thought so many times before, Sam thought: Lord, this is marvelous!

In July of 1923, Edna St.-Vincent Millay married Dutch coffee importer Eugen Jan Boissevain. The couple lived at 75½ Bedford Street, at nine feet wide the narrowest house in New York City.

At first it seemed the walkway stopped when it hit the bridge's stanchion. But when he got closer, some white boys, one copper-haired and none more than fourteen, ran round the central stone column, down—those were metal *steps* up to the higher level, not a ribbed green metal wall—the stairs. Check these off.

Braithwaite died in 1962. Angelina Grimké in 1958. Fenton Johnson in 1958 also…. Effie Lee Newsome was doing poorly this past summer, I was told by a lady from Wilberforce, but she was still alive. Her address has been Box 291, Wilberforce, Ohio.

Nanina Alba's address is 303 Fonville Street, Tuskegee, Alabama. Shall I write her for bionotes, or would you like to?… There is a Charles E. Wheeler, Jr. listed in the Chicago telephone directory, but I can't get an answer there — yet. Will try again. I am not sure (in fact, I doubt) this is the poet…. Jean Toomer is still in a nursing home in Doylestown, Pa. His wife Marjorie Toomer can be reached at their home, "The Barn", R.D. 2, Doylestown. *She will answer letters promptly.* I have visited her twice. She is active for civil rights. Jean's literary disappointments after *Cane* were shattering. He tried desperately to repeat that artistic achievement (but not as a Negro) and failed…. I persuaded her and him to give his papers and literary effects to Fisk. A large collection. There is now a chance that

Once Lewy had made a clock from a ten-gallon kerosene can, a hole punched in the bottom to dribble water ("No, no—!" Mama said. "Don't bring that in here. Set it out by the pump!") and a board float in the top, fixed to a cord, that, as the float lowered, turned a spool on another board that rotated an elaborately scrolled hand, from an old clock Lewy'd found, about a cardboard dial. The first dial Lewy had drawn was marked with minutes in five-minute groupings. It kept time for practically three-quarters of an hour. But that evening Lewy came over and closeted himself with Papa in the study, and the next day he'd replaced the dial with one far more elaborate, drawn on a piece of parchment, inked in reds and blacks and greens and suggesting some medieval illuminated compass, now marked with a time scale of three fourteen-minute intervals, each divided in two, then further divided into three, with the major divisions indicated by signs from the zodiac and the smaller ones notated in Hebrew letters, representing a special,

Cane may be reprinted along with some of Jean's unpublished writings.... The sonnet by Allen Tate is perfect for *The Poetry of the Negro.* His background as a Fugitive and redhot I'LL TAKE MY STANDer adds to its effectiveness. As Countee said about himself, Allen's "conversion came high-priced," no doubt.... and there are letters from him in the Toomer Collection. Hart Crane was trying to arrange for the two (Toomer and Tate) to meet. In any case, we can now see that the early anti-Negro expressions of the Fugitives probably reflected guilt feelings, as this "Sonnet at Christmas" makes clear in Tate's case.... By the way, I also sponsored Frank Lima for his Opportunity. We should let him pass for colored, if he wishes. I thought he was Puerto Rican at the time. Nobody would object to a Mexican identifying as a Negro. Not even a black muslim or a black panther. And I will not object to a couple or so poems by Mason Jordan Mason so long as we make it plain in the biographical note that at least we are not sure. He certainly writes in Negro, as Karl Shapiro says of Tolson. And he's good.

I don't expect us to find any-

ancient, mystic time scale, out of Africa from before the dawn of the West — which Lewy had just made up. Lewy had explained, laughing, to Sam and John: "Now white boys do not do things like this. Your daddy told me that when he was helping me with the letters last night," and John said, "You should've used Arab letters on it! Or Egyptian!" And Lewy, who knew what John was getting at, said, "I like the Jewish letters. They're easier to remember. And the Bishop doesn't speak Egyptian — yet." Helping Lewy fill the clock, or sitting, the three of them, out by the pump, watching the hand's imperceptible progress across the mystic signs, at such moments Sam could forget the occasional throbs of desire to be the same clear and earth-dark hue as Lewy and his own father. Well, nobody had trouble telling John was colored, for all his rusty hair. Strange though, Sam thought; such an instant as that was what let him look with sympathy at such a group of city white children — who, he was sure, from their ragged socks, worn shoes, and the rope tied around one's waist in place of a belt, were *just* the boys thing from the Allen Ginsberg cabal that meets our criteria. So why don't we close the door now.

who didn't do things like that. They broke around him, running—and were gone.

Beside the steps stood a wooden booth with a glassed-in window, before which were the same brass bars he'd become familiar with in front of tellers at the bank and clerks in the subway's change booths and post offices. Below the wooden shelf with its worn depression for the change to slide into, was another sign—

Toll:
Pedestrians 1¢

—faded and flaking. But perhaps the toll was not in effect today—or, indeed, had not been in effect for some time: the booth was closed; no one sat behind the bars to collect.

Sam climbed the stairs and walked around the great stone column—on the near side of which a black-bronze plaque explained that the bridge had first been opened to traffic in 1883—forty-one years ago!

He strolled out on the walkway, looking down over the green rail, at the tracks between him and the trolley wires.

Dead in the afternoon — hasn't the sky? —, gas lamps at intervals stood along the walkway's sides. A sailor in early whites came toward him, hurled balled waxed paper from a late lunch over the rail, to follow it with a delicately flipped toothpick from his lips' corner. He was carrying some kind of Japanese fan. Over its folds, pastel waves were painted in blues and blacks. The sailor hawked across the bar, returned from moving the other authority recently dropped, and gave Sam a grin: Sam imagined sputum sparkling down between girders to the water. The fellow sauntered away around the stone. (The fan. Where was it from? Where would it go?...Cathay.) Benches with wrought iron backs sat along the walkway, wrested as much of that severe sunshine as you need now. Now turning, Sam saw the lower city's skyline, towers above the water — yes, and there, on the way you go, were his skyscrapers!

Cowley and Crane at Sweets. Fitzgerald and Agee at the Chrysler. Agee's first poems

And there in the other direction was the green woman with the up-raised torch — Liberty! Tug and sail and barge traffic moved lazily about the sound. bore a title from Crane's exhor-tation to Emil Opffer: Permit me voyage, love, into your hands.

But what Sam hadn't been prepared for was the bridge itself. The reason why it happened only since you woke up — he walked along the planks, head high — is letting the steam disappear from those clouds. Imagine a giant harp, when the landscape all around is hilly sites. No, imagine *four* giant harps, side by side. Then rotate the alternate ones — just a little, so that some cables were vertical and some slanted across them. Now put two of these double harps at each side of the walkway, that will have to be reckoned into the total, and let the wind play silent music through and against crisp blue.

For there to be more air —

He dropped his head, still walking, to look for a moment at his shoes — and had the disorienting experience of being suspended more than a hundred feet in mid-air above glass-green water!

He stopped.

The boards were again under his leather shoe soles.

Heart pounding, he swayed a bit. Then, still looking down, he started to walk again: between each foot-worn three-inch plank and the next was a quarter-inch gap. What had happened, he realized, was that to move over them with any speed was to let the light from the river glitter up through the spaces, creat-ing the illusion that the walkway had vanished — or at least had gone largely transparent! Green as trolley sparks, the water — thousands of

Precisely as we move, we move through time. Time is a function of motion — but of the micro-miniature motions of the atoms in their crystal lattices and the cosmic motions of stars and the collection of stars we inhabit.

millions of drops of it — flowed below.

How many epochs could those waters clock, passing under the bridge?

Sam strolled a dozen steps more, looking down, relishing the feel of this miraculous suspension above the brilliant river—till a dinghy, with chipped gunwales of flat gray-green, slid into sight. In a wide straw hat, a—shirtless?—man tugged and leaned on the oars.

The boat looked smaller than some wooden bath toy, small as a match box—Sam sensed all over again how high he was.

Again Sam stopped—man and boat vanished. He could just glimpse the boat's rim moving under a single crack. Again Sam walked.

Rower and river reappeared. Yes, the man was shirtless. Was it warmer down on the water than it was up here in the sky? The rower's bare feet were wedged against one of the boat's cross-braces. His pants were brown, and—small as he was — you could see one knee was frayed; a simple rip crossed the other, so that that knee—like a bone from Negro flesh—stuck out. The boat moved at an acute diagonal to the sunside of a shadow on the water—the shadow, Sam realized, of the bridge.

Archie also mentioned Hart Crane, whom he had once persuaded *Fortune* to take on for a trial. Hart had been completely unable to do it. It did not cross my mind that this had any relevance to me.

Sam was about to stop and start again, to make the man disappear and reappear—but now the rower pulled in his oars, took off the straw hat—his hair was black and his shoulders were sun-darkened enough that, for a moment, still walking to hold the sight, Sam wondered if the fellow *was* colored. The man tossed the hat to the dinghy's back seat, then stood.

The fellow's hands went to his waist; then his pants dropped—first to his knees, then to his feet! With the awkward step you use in a rocking boat, he got one foot free of them, then the other. Nor was he wearing underwear.

The minuscule figure grasped his genitals—

—and winked out to become only water. What had happened, Sam realized, was that the visible area was only the fraction of an arc directly below; and when he'd walked more than sixteen feet or so, the area he could see moved over: his arc of visibility no longer included the boat!

Without even looking up, Sam swung around and began to stride back. Yes, there the fellow was, doing what Sam had assumed he'd been about to do: urinating. Ripples spread in translucent rings, through sunlight, from where, some feet from the boat's side, the fellow's waters conjoined the river's.

Man as water clock…?

Striding, Sam watched, wondering why any man, to do what all men do, had to strip himself naked in the midst of the water—

When he collided, that is, banging his jaw on someone's head, confused, with…yes, a man, who grasped him by the shoulders, steadied him, more fitness, pushed him out to arm's length: "Hey, there, young fellow—!"

"Oh…!" Sam said, read into the undeduced result. "Oh…! I'm… Are you…?"

It was a white man, dark complected but not swarthy, maybe Hubert's age, though at least a head shorter, with wire framed glasses like Mama's. His jaw was broad, his mustache brown.

"I'm sorry…Oh!" Sam repeated. "Are you all right?" His own jaw throbbed, though he did not want to touch it.

"I'm fine. What about you? Heads up on the bridge now, young fellow!" Then, with a warm grin, the man walked on.

After that, Sam thought about looking down again at the crazy

I must at once acknowledge an even greater indebtedness to Mr. Willis Clarke for his generosity toward me. In 1903 Mr. Clarke began to collect copies of letters and facts for a life…but was so baffled by conflicting statements that he dropped the work. His shorthand report of an interview with Crane at Brede is quoted in Chapters 1, 3, and 4 and 7 of this book.

rower pissing from his boat. He rubbed his jaw. But even though no one was nearer than land, it wasn't something you wanted to be *caught* looking at. So after that, he raised his eyes again to the cables; and walked… more slowly.

Well, the bridge *was* magnificent.

Besides the man he'd collided with hurrying off, only half a dozen people strolled along the boardwalk. This means never — two cyclists pedaled across: a young man, followed by a young woman in blowing skirts, both in yellow hats with black ribbons. (Certainly they'd be in love...) Getting any closer to—a seagull swooped in rings between the cables, circled again to perch unsteadily on one slant cord, bobbed its tail, and, for all its unsteadiness, let fall its liquid waste, a white gleam along gray cable, before it splatted, in a lime-like star, over the planks fifteen feet ahead. The whole world, it seemed, was expectorating, urinating, defecating. Was that the basic principal operating behind spring in New York?

A day of natural functions?

He thought about it and continued walking. The time to look at skyscrapers, he decided (still entranced with the bridge itself)—rather than to the distracted entity of a mirage—, would be on the way back.

Ten minutes later, Sam reached the second stanchion's platform, to gaze over at the Brooklyn shore. No skyscrapers there. Right, low buildings hugged the water. Other than that, there was not too much of anything, really—save scattered wooden houses. As Sam came down the steps and started forward on the bridge's landward leg, ahead and to the left was... an early cornfield!

In February of 1929, Edna St.-Vincent Millay had not yet heard of Hart Crane—according to Mary Blair's soon to be divorced husband, Bunny Wilson.

He began to slow his pace, found himself frowning, the half-meant, half-perceived motions. Really, this was, in its way, more disconcerting than the visual revelation of his height above the water at bridge center.

Already Sam had learned to see the city, with its numbered streets and avenues, even with those exceptions like Hamilton Terrace — or Gay Street or Rose—, as a grid in which everything had its place, in which nothing could be lost. Even after a few months, the country had become in memory a kind of field, verdant and vasty, of fronds out of idle depths, pleasant to the eye, but in which nothing much could be found, especially if it wasn't your own bit of it that you'd spent your whole life learning as best you could, but only a stretch—like this—like it: which are summer. The city behind him, in whose concrete crevices he'd been learning to find his way, the city he'd been learning to work in, to make himself comfortable in, even more, to have some bit of fun in…well, though it was still supposed to be New York, *here* was no city at all!

Ahead, the bridge spilled out onto macadam that ribboned through the land—land not terribly different from what he'd left in Carolina. He could see a couple of churches.

There was a cluster of white frame houses you might even call a township; and two, four, or twelve miles further along the road (he knew) there'd be another. But the bridge here, he realized, connected the city to the country. And country was what Sam thought he'd left behind.

For the first time in months, he remembered the white woman on

Hart Crane and Vachel Lindsay took their lives that spring. Great gifts always set their possessors apart, but not necessarily apart from any chance to exercise them; this gift at that time pretty well did, what is meant is that this distant image of you, the way you really are,

the train — Scottish — who'd been so eager to talk…who *lived* in the heart of all that. Brooklyn? Her gregariousness had made him uncomfortable. This sudden view of the place she lived—gregarious in its own way, with all he realized now he knew of it—made him as uneasy as she had.

Turning, and expansion into little draughts, he started back for the stanchion steps.

Then, across the railing, beyond the trolley wires, down on the water he saw the boat — the green dinghy. The reply wakens easily, darting from untruth to willed moment. This much closer to shore, the bridge had imperceptibly lowered, till it

what did you see as you fell, what did you hear / as you sank?

was only a third as high above the greeny river as it had been in the center. That was why it took him an eye's blink, a heart's beat, to recognize it. It seemed much larger—the tiny thing—turning slowly, moving out from the rail's edge. But, yes, there was the yellow hat, still on the back seat. Something dark trailed from the side into the water—a leg of the doffed trousers?

Now, maybe twenty feet away, an oar floated out, making the same turns as the boat, moments back, following the same current. Sam frowned, then walked to the rail, to gaze across the traffic lanes a dozen feet below.

No, the boat was empty.

He could see the braces across its bottom. He strained to see the pants, the hat—one oar docked inside, the other loose and floating. He watched a long time. It took the boat almost two minutes to do a complete, lazy, long rotation. And he watched it do two, then three, while he scanned the water, first near it, then further away, for the sunburned arms and shoulders cutting through (swimming strongly), black hair thrown back, glistening, breaking the ripples...

is the test of how you see yourself, and regardless of whether or not you hesitate, Sentimentality and Inhibition are the Scylla and Charybdis of the criticism of this decade, it may be assumed that you have won, that this wooden and external representation

He saw nothing.

I *should* have looked again, Sam thought, returns the full echo of what you meant. In the middle of the bridge, after I ran into that fellow, I should have—though, he pondered a moment later, what good might

In the lunar year, the sun's death month—and the death month of the young god—is the thirteenth month.

I have done him even if I *had* seen him from up here dive, fall, or, heaven forbid, jump? Whom could I have called? It would take me half an hour to get to the shore, even from here—to find someone about

with a boat, much less get out in the water to help him.

71

No, there were no ripples from the vanished rower, no fugitive swimmer to be seen. Sam looked about. Had anyone else seen it—or seen more of it?

Had it been a young man? Or an old? *Was* it a white man? Or a black? (He remembered the sailor hawking over the bridge rail.) Was it some blue-eyed Larry just out of Kansas, younger than Hubert if older than he, voyage balked on his first brush with the ocean—but how could you tell? (It had all been so far away!) Had it been some cement-handed old salt, with a shark's tooth round his neck, an aged, fierce old man, a battered, wrecked enigma, mind and language shattered by a lifetime's collision with the sea?

Was it the disillusion of age or youth the river had just drunk up?

The past, Sam thought. The past, the past. The past—

The boat turned, looking now as though it would miss the rocks along the farmland's edge—by a hundred feet! And he could no longer see into it.

Frowning, Sam put his hands into his trousers pockets and started back, scarcely called into being. At the top of the steps, when he'd left the stanchion to walk toward the bridge's center, once he looked down again, to see green water flash its coherent, sunny surface through the gaps at his feet—and the bridge's shadow cut away light, with nothing left over. (Had it moved, even in ten or fifteen minutes? From that circumference now alight with ex-possibilities?) Yes, he passed two women and, yes, one of them pushed a stroller, with a fringed parasol built out to cover it—so that certainly it contained some minuscule creature, mittened and bunted against cool May, to make its mother proud. Become present fact, and you must wear them like clothing. But in the anxiety he walked with now, they just didn't compensate.

Above hung the stone and steel harp, moving in the shadow of your single and twin existence.

A third of the way back, waking in intact appreciation of it, Sam stopped to sit on one of the benches and gaze off at the clouds over Brooklyn. Sputum, urine, feces: while morning is still, Hart Crane committed suicide on

72

before it swells, the way a waterfall drums at different levels, at least he should find a policeman and tell him what had happened. He even got up, thinking to start again for the nearer, Brooklyn shore. But as he stood, he realized the one thing

April 27, 1932, by jumping into the sea from the deck of a steamer bearing him from Mexico to the United States, and before the body is changed by the faces of evening

he would never find — among those fields and farmhouses — was a policeman.

Policemen were in cities.

Sam sat again. Certainly boat, hat, and the man's odd unconcern about his nakedness seemed connected, in Sam's mind, with the more rural—

I, / *Catullus redivivus*

"Excuse me," someone said behind him. "But you're Negro, aren't you?"

d

The One remains, the many change and pass;
Heaven's light forever shines, Earth's shadows fly;
Life, like a dome of many-coloured glass,
Stains the white radiance of Eternity.

—PERCY BYSSHE SHELLEY, *Adonaïs*

...plough through thrashing glister toward
fata morgana's lucent melting shore,
weave toward New World littorals that are
mirage and myth and actual shore.

—ROBERT HAYDEN, "Middle Passage"

Sam turned on the bench, to see, standing behind him, the man he'd
bumped when he'd been staring through the planks.

"Yes," Sam said. "That's right. I am."

"I know it's none of my business," the man said. "But I'd bet a lot of
people meet you and think you're white."

Well, a lot of people up here did. "Some of them."

"The reason I suspected, I suppose, is that I have a colored friend—
a writer. A marvelous writer. He writes stories, but they're much more
like poems. You read them, and you can just *see* the sunlight on the

75

fields and hear the sound of the Negro girls' laughter. His name is Jean—"

"—Toomer?" Sam supplied.

"Now don't tell me you're related to him...?" The man laughed. "Though you look somewhat like him. You know, Jean just ran off with the wife of my very good friend, Waldo—so I don't think I'm really *supposed* to like him right through here—it's the kind of thing you don't write your mother about. But I do—like him, that is. He's handsome, brilliant, talented. How could one help it? Maybe that's why I took a chance and spoke to you—because you do look something like him. New York is the biggest of cities, but the smallest of worlds. Everybody always turns out to know everyone else—"

"No," Sam said. "No. I'm not his relative. But he's a friend of my..." How did you explain about your brother's strange girlfriend—who was the one who *knew* everybody. "A friend of my brother's. Well, a friend of a girl my brother knows." Though Clarice had said he looked like Toomer, she hadn't mentioned the absconsion. "She was the one who told me about him." He couldn't imagine Clarice approving of such carryings on.

"Oh, well, there—you see. You know, that man you were watching, in the boat—do you mind if I sit down?"

"No. Sure...!"

The young man stepped around the bench's end, flopped to the seat, and flung both arms along the back: "Lord, he was hung! Like a stallion! Pissed like a racehorse, too!" He looked over, grinning behind his glasses. "To see it from up here at all, someone's got to throw a stream as thick as a fire hose. It was something, 'ey?"

Sam was surprised—and found himself grinning at the ridiculousness of it. People didn't strip down to stand up and make water before all New York—but if someone did, even less did you talk about it. That both had happened within the hour seemed to overthrow the anxiety of the last minutes, and struck him as exorbitantly comic.

"But did you see what he did?" Sam asked. "Did you see?"

"I saw as much as you, I bet—maybe more, the way you ran off."

The fellow hit him playfully on the shoulder with the back of his hand.

"I mean, he must have jumped in...for a swim. Or maybe—"

"No," the man said. "I don't think he'd have done that." He seemed suddenly pensive. "It's much too cold. The water's still on the nippy side, this early in spring."

"But he *must* have," Sam said. He'd stopped laughing. "I saw the boat, later on—over there." He pointed toward Brooklyn. "There was no one in it. I know it was the same boat. Because of the hat, and... because of his hat."

"No one in it?" The man seemed surprised.

"It was floating empty. He must have fallen overboard—or jumped in. Then he couldn't get back up. The boat was just drifting, turning in circles. Really—there was no one in it at all!"

The man narrowed his eyes, then looked pensively out at the sky while a train's open-air trundle filled the space beneath them. Through the green v's of the beams supporting the rail, over the walkway's edge, Sam could see the car tops moving toward the city. Finally the man said: "No, I don't think that's what happened. He was probably one of the Italian fishermen living over there. I live over there, too—not too far from them. A clutch of Genovesi." He too waved toward Brooklyn. "God, those guineas are magnificent animals! Swim like porpoises—at least the boys do. You can watch them, frisking about in the water just down from where I live. Fell in? *Naw...!*" He burlesqued the word, speaking it in an exaggerated tone of someone who didn't use it naturally. "It's a bold swimmer who jumps into the midst of his own pee. You think he went under in his own maelstrom, while your white aeroplane of Help soared overhead? Oh, no. The East River's not really a river, you know. It's a saltwater estuary—complete with tides. So even that whole herd of pissers from the Naval Shipyard, splattering off the concrete's edge every day, doesn't significantly change the taste. Jump? I'll tell you what's more likely. After he spilled his manly quarts, he lay down in the bottom and let his boat float, with the sunlight filling it up around him as if it were a tub and the light was a froth of suds. And when, finally, he drifts into the dago docks, he'll jump up, grab hold of

it, and shake that long-skinned guinea pizzle for the little Genoese lass-
ies out this afternoon to squeal over, go running to their mothers, and
snigger at. No, suicidal or otherwise, his kind doesn't go in for drown-
ing."

Sam started to repeat that the boat had been empty. But—well, *was*
there a chance he'd missed the form stretched on the bottom? Sam said:
"You live in Brooklyn?" because that was all he could think to say. (No.
He remembered the oar. The boat had been empty, he was sure of it—
almost.)

The man inclined his head: "Sebastian Melmouth, at your service.
One-ten Columbia Heights, Apartment c 33." The man took his glasses
off, held them up to the sky, examining them for dust, then put them
back on.

Sam said: "I think he fell over. Maybe he was drunk or crazy
or...drunk. Maybe that's why he took his clothes off—?"

"— to piss in the river?" The man cocked his head, quizzical. "It's
possible. Those guineas drink more than I do. A couple of quarts of
dago red'll certainly make your spigot spout." He looked over at Sam,
suddenly sober-faced. "My name isn't really Sebastian Melmouth. Do
you know who Sebastian Melmouth was?"

Sam shook his head.

"That was the name Wilde used, after he got out of Reading and was
staying incognito in France. Oscar Wilde — you know, *The Ballad of
Reading Gaol*—'each man kills the thing he loves'?"

"*The Importance of Being Earnest*," Sam answered.

"The importance of being earnest to be *sure!*" The man nodded deeply.

"They did that down on the school campus — the play — where I
grew up."

"School?" The man raised an eyebrow.

"The college — it's a Negro college, in North Carolina. My father
works there. My mama's Dean of Women. The students put it on, three
years ago, I guess. We all went to see it."

The man threw back his head and barked a single syllable of laughter.
"I'm sorry—but the idea of *The Importance of Being Earnest* in blackface

—well, not blackface. But as a minstrel—" The man's laughter fractured his own sentence. "…Really!" He bent forward, rocked back, recovering. "That's just awful of me. But maybe—" he turned, sincere questioning among his features nudging through the laugh's detritus—"they only used the lighter-skinned students for the—?"

"No," Sam said, suppressing the indignation from his voice. "No, they had students of *all* colors, playing whichever part they did best. They just had to be able to speak the lines."

"Really?" the man asked, incredulously.

Sam put his hands on his thighs, ready to stand and excuse himself. There seemed no need at all to continue this.

"You know," the man said, sitting back again, again looking at the sky. "I would have *loved* to have seen that production! Actually, it sounds quite exciting. More than exciting—it might even have been important. In fact, I wouldn't be surprised if it's the sort of thing that *all* white people should be made to see—Shakespeare and Wilde and Ibsen, with Negro actors of all colors, taking whichever parts. It would probably do us some good!"

Surprised once more, Sam took his hands from his thighs. His sister Jules, who had played Gwendolen Fairfax (and was as light as his mother), had said much the same thing after it was over—though the part of Cecily Cardew had been taken by pudgy little black-brown Milly Potts ("Memory, my dear Cecily, is the diary we all carry about with us…"), who'd jazzed up the lines unmercifully, strutting and flaunting every phrase as much as it could bear and then some, rolling her eyes, shooting her hands in the air, and making the whole audience, including Papa, rock in their seats, clutch their stomachs and howl (the women's cackles cutting over and continuing after the men's bellowings)—to the point where the other actors couldn't say their own lines, trying to hold their laughter. Later, a more serious Papa had said that though it was *supposed* to be funny, it *wasn't* supposed to be funny in the way Milly had made it so. But now it was hard to think of the play any other way.

The man said: "I don't live in Apartment c 33, actually. You know what that was? That was the cell number Wilde had at Reading. 'The brave man does it with a sword, the coward with a—'"

"What?" Sam asked.

"Kills the thing he loves," the man intoned. "I was going to put c 33 on my door, once. But then I thought better. It's a nice room, though. It's right in front of Roebling's old room."

"Roebling…?"

"Washington Roebling. He's the man who made this bridge." The man raised his head, to take in caging cables. "Who hung these lines here? *He* took over the job from his father, John Augustus Roebling. The Bridge killed his father, John, you know. He'd already completed the plans and was at the waterfront, surveying to start the work—when a runaway cart sliced open his foot. It became infected until, three weeks later, tetanus did him in—with spasms that near broke his bones, with crying out for water. So the son, Washington, took it up. The problem, you see, was to dig the foundations out for those great stone towers." The man gestured left, then right. "How to excavate them, there in the water, the both of them, with those gigantic dredging machines. They had to dig out, beneath the river, two areas a hundred-seventy-two feet by a hundred-two—for each about a third the size of a football field! You know how they did it? They built two immense, upside-down iron and wooden boxes. The bottoms—or, better, the roofs—were made of five layers of foot-square pine timbers, bolted together. They caulked them within an inch of their lives, covered them over with sheet tin, then covered over the whole with wood again. Then they dropped those upside-down caissons into the drink, with the air still in them. They let the workers down through shafts that were pressurized to keep the air in and the water out. Working on the bottom, the poor bohunks and square-heads they had in there dredged out muck and mud till they hit bedrock—seventy-eight feet six inches below the high-tide line on the Manhattan side and forty-four feet six inches below on the Brooklyn side. The workers had a nine-foot high space to dig in, all propped up with six-by-six beams. The pressure was immense—and they used what they called clamshell buckets to haul out the dredgings. Right at the very beginning, young Roebling was down in the caissons inspecting—

came up too fast and got the bends. He was a cripple for the rest of his life. So he stayed in the room at the back of where I live now, surveying the work through the window with a telescope and directing it through his wife—the bridge—who went down to the docks every day to bring his orders and take back her report: spying through his glass at the stanchions he'd raised—twin gnomons swinging their shadows around the face of the sound, insistently marking out his days, till new navigators remap those voyages to and beyond love's peripheries, till another alphabet, another hunt can reconfigure the word. There're twenty corpses down under those towers. When it was all done, they poured concrete through the air shafts into the work space, filled it up, sealed it down to the bedrock. Twenty corpses, at least—"

"They buried the men in the caissons?" Sam asked, surprised.

"I'm speaking figuratively. Some twenty workers died in the bridge's construction—and do you know, no one is really sure of their names? I like to think of those towers as their tombstones. This one falling from the top of some steam-powered boom derrick, that one hit in the head by a swinging beam. I see them, buried, all twenty, in those hypogea at the river bottom, while the stanchions' shadows sweep away the years between their deaths and the sea's mergence with the sun, while the noon signal sirens all the dead swimmers through the everyday..." For a moment he was pensive. (Uncomfortable Sam thought again of the...Italian fisherman?) "Everybody always talks about John Augustus —a kraut, you see," the man went on. "There's nothing dumber than a dumb kraut, but there's nothing smarter than a smart one—we all know that. The war taught it to us if it taught us anything. John built bridges all over kingdom come: over the Allegheney, over the Monongahela, over Niagara Falls, the Ohio—each runs under a Roebling bridge. You'd think, sometimes, he was out to build a single bridge across the whole of the country. And the plans for this one were, yes, his. But I want to write the life of Washington. (Don't think it's an accident John named his son after our good first president!)" Again, he nodded deeply. "Roebling — Washington A. Roebling — *was* this bridge; this bridge was Washington Roebling. He was born into it, through his father: every rivet and cable you see around us sings of him. Write such a life? It shouldn't be too hard. To get the feel of it, all I have to do is to go into the back room, look out the window, and imagine... *this*, cable by cable, rising over the river."

When the man was quiet, Sam said with some enthusiasm: "The plaque says the bridge was opened to traffic in 1883. That's the year they started the first commercial electricity in New York City and Hartford, Connecticut!" because, along with and among his magic and tricks, Sam had lots of such informations—like the sixty stories of the Woolworth Building—and this was a man who might appreciate it.

"*Really*—?" the young man asked, conveying more surprise than was reasonable.

"That's right."

"In May it was—since you're being so particular—the very month we're in: on the twenty-fourth, that's when they started to roll and stroll across. Though your plaque doesn't say *that!* Nor does it say how, on the first day, when they opened the walkway here to the curious hordes, going down those steps there a woman tripped and screamed—and the crowds, thinking the whole structure was collapsing, stampeded. Twelve people were trampled to death. It's a strange bridge, a dangerous bridge in its way; things happen here. I mean things in your mind—" a wicked smile behind his glasses gave way to a warm one—"that you wouldn't ordinarily think of." The man held out his hand. "My name's Harold. Harold Hart. People call me Hart. A few folks—especially in the family—call me Harry. But I'm becoming Hart more and more these days."

Sam seized the hand to shake—in his own hand with their nails like helmets curving the tops of the enlarged first joints, their forward rims like visors. "Sam." He shook vigorously—let go, and put his hands down beside him. "My name is Sam." No, the man was not particularly look-ing at them. "My birthday's just coming up—" he felt suddenly expan-sive—"and it happens during the transit of Mercury."

"Does it now? And the last year of construction on this bridge, here —in 1882—took place under the last transit of Venus! A fascinating man," the man said, leaving Sam for a moment confused. "When you live in the same room as someone, realize when you go to the bathroom, or leave by the front door, or simply stop to gaze out the window, you're doubtless doing exactly what he did, walking the same distances, seeing what he saw, feeling what he felt, it gives you an access to the bodily reality of a fellow you could never get at any other way—unless, of course, you went out in a boat on the river yourself, and, underneath, stood up, pulled down your pants, and let fly into the flood!" Playfully the man hit at Sam's shoulder once more, then turned to the water, sniggering.

At contact, realizing what the man was referring to, Sam felt the anxiety from the bridge's Brooklyn end flood back. Perhaps, he thought, he *should* excuse himself and go.

But the man said, snigger now a smile and face gone thoughtful: "Sam—now *that's* the name of a poet. There's the biography I should *really* write."

A tug pulled out from under the traffic way's edge—as the dinghy had floated out when Sam had been nearer Brooklyn.

"Pardon?"

"A marvelous, wonderful, immensely exciting poet—named Sam. Another kraut. Roebling—John Augustus—was born in Prussia—Mühlhausen!" He pronounced it with a crisp, German accent, like some vaudeville comic (Mr. Horstein?) taking off Kaiser Wilhelm. "But Sam was born in Vienna. His parents brought him here when he was seven or eight. No grammar, no spelling, and scarcely any form, but a quality to his work that's unspeakably eerie—and the most convincing gusto. Still, by the time he was your age, Sam was as American as advertising or apple pie. He died about seven years ago—I never met him. But—do you know Woodstock?"

"Pardon?" Sam repeated.

"Amazing little town, in upstate New York—full of anarchists and artists and—" he leaned closer to whisper, the snigger back—"free lovers!" He sat back again. "It's full of all the things that make life really fine in this fatuous age. It's a place to learn the measurement of art and to what extent it's an imposition—a fulcrum of shifted energy! It's a town where, on Christmas Eve morning, leaves blow in a wailing, sunny wind, all about outside the house, over the snow patches. It's a good place to roast turkeys and dance till dawn. A good place to climb mountains, or to curl up with a volume of the *Bough*—though you can get bored there, sweeping, drawing pictures, masturbating the cat... Well, that's where I spent this past winter. That's where I discovered Sam—somewhere between making heaps of apple sauce and cooking the turkey in front of an open fire in a cast-iron pig! I've been growing this mustache since about then. How do you think it looks?"

"It looks fine." It looked rather thin for all that time—certainly thinner than Hubert's. "You found Sam's books?"

"Alas, poor Sam never *had* a book. But I found his notebooks and his manuscripts—a friend of mine had them. He let me borrow them so I could copy some of them out."

"He lived in Woodstock?"

"Sam? No, he lived right here in the city—within walking distance of the bridge." This time he gestured toward Manhattan. "Oh, Sam was very much a city poet. He lived just on the Lower East Side, there. Went to P.S. One-sixty at Suffolk and Rivington Street. Worked in the sweatshops—stole what time he could to go to the Metropolitan Museum, take piano lessons. He played piano just beautifully—that's what my friend said. And drew his pictures; and wrote his poems. He wrote a poem once, right here, while he was walking across the bridge with his oldest brother, Daniel—there were eight boys in the family, I believe." Again the man spread his arms along the bench back; one hand went behind Sam's shoulder. "Late in November — just a month before Christmas—they were walking across, from Brooklyn, talking, like you and me, when Sam pulled out his notebook and started writing." He closed his eyes, lifted his chin: "'Is this the river "East", I heard? / Where the ferry's, tugs, and sailboats stirred / And the reaching wharves from the inner land / Outstretched like the harmless receiving hand... / But look! at the depths of the dripling tide / That dripples, re-ripples like locusts astride / As the boat turns upon the silvery spread / It leaves strange—a shadow—dead…'"

Through the cables, the dark, flat, and—yes—dead green spread behind the tug. Ripples crawled to the wake's rim, like silver beetles, to quiver and glitter at, though unable to cross, the widening borders.

"The river's very beautiful," Sam said, because beauty was the aspect of nature and poetry it seemed safest to speak of.

"Oh, not for Sam the poet. If anything, for him it was terrifying. He was to die, looking out at it, from a window of the Manhattan Hospital for the Destitute, up on Ward's Island. They keep the dying there—and the insane. It's only an island away from Brother's, where the *General Slocum* beached after it burned up a thousand krauts and drenched them till they drowned, back in 'aught-four—makes you wonder what we needed a war for. It was the dust and the airless walls of his brother Adolf's leather shop where he worked that first seated in the floor of Sam's breath that terrible, spiritual, stinking illness—have you ever visited anyone dying of TB? They do stink, you know? Here in the city, you learn to recognize the stench—if you hang out in the slums. Nobody ever talks about that, but—*Lord!*—they smell. The lungs bleed and die and rot in their chests; and their breath and their bodies erupt with the putrefaction of it—in a way it's a purification too, I suppose. But before he was nineteen, Sam had already learned the rustle of nurses around his bed, like the husks of summer locusts. All the nuns—and he'd been reading Poe, the ghoul-haunted woodlands, that sort of stuff —once made our rogue tanton bolt St. Anthony's at Woodhaven, in terror for his life. That's where they first packed him off to die. For a while after that he stayed in New Jersey—Paterson—with Morris, another brother. But a few months later, he was back in another hospital— Sea View this time, on Staten Island." Without closing his eyes, again the man recited: "'And the silvery tinge that sparkles aloud / Like brilliant white demons, which a tide has towed / From the rays of the morning sun / Which it doth ceaselessly shine upon.' But that was written some years before, when he was well—walking across the bridge here with Daniel. Still: 'loud, brilliant white demons…'? He had a very excitable poetic apprehension—like any true poet would want to or—really—must have. Don't you think?"

By now Sam was feeling somewhat sulky there'd been no praise of his own eccentric bit of electrical information. He was not about to condone all this biography. "It doesn't sound all *that* good of a poem."

"Well, in a way, it's not. But it's what poetry—real poetry—is made of: '…The dripling tide that dripples, re-ripples…' Really, for any word-lover, that's quite wonderful! Words must create and tear down whole visions, cities, worlds!" (Sam was not sure if he was saying Sam—the other Sam—did this or didn't.) "And then, Sam was only a child when he died—twenty-three. I'm twenty-four now. A year older than Sammy. But I suppose he was too young, or too uneducated—too unformed to make *real* poems. But then, Keats, Rimbaud—all that material: you can feel its sheer verbal excitement, can't you?" He chuckled, as if to himself. "Twenty-four? In a moment I'll sneeze — and be *older* than Keats!"

Sam looked at the face now looking past his; at first he'd put it at Hubert's age. But there was a dissoluteness to it—the skin was not as clear as it might be, the eyes were not as bright as they should be; and, of course, just the way he spoke—that made the man seem older than twenty-four. Sam asked: "Don't poems have to make sense, besides just sounding nice?" A teacher down in Raleigh had once explained to them why Edgar Poe was not really a good poet, even after they'd all applauded her recitation of "The Bells." Apparently Poe had not been a very good man—and people who were not good men, while they could write fun poems, simply *couldn't* write great ones.

"Oh, do they, now? But there're many interesting ways to seem not to be making sense while you're actually making very good sense indeed—using myths, symbols, poetic associations and rhetorical gestures. I never wrote my mother about Sam—just as I never wrote her about Jean's scooting off with Margy. I haven't written her about Emil yet, either—but I'll have to do that, soon. I wonder if I'll write her about you? Grace proffers the truth in a regular Sunday Delivery, and I send her back lies—of omission mostly. (Can you imagine, telling her about some wild afternoon I had at Sand Street, skulking down behind the piled-up planks and plates beside the Yard?) So I just assume they can be corrected later. I dare say it's all quite incoherent to you. But it's leading up to something—a bigger truth. I just have to get my gumption up to it. At any rate—" he chuckled—"Sam was not only a poet. He drew pictures. He played the piano beautifully, as I said—at least that's what my friend who'd known him told me. You see, it was a poetic sensibility in embryo, struggling to express itself in all the arts. Do you play an instrument?"

"The cornet." Playing the cornet, Sam had always figured, was like knowing about electricity in Hartford and the number of stories in the Woolworth Building. Or maybe a couple of magic tricks.

"Well, then, you see?" the man said. "You and little Sammy Greenberg are very much alike!"

"He was a jewboy!" Sam exclaimed—because till then, for all he'd been trying to withhold, he'd really begun to identify with his strange namesake who had once walked across the bridge and had seen, as had he, the water dripple, re-ripple...

"Yes, he was, my young, high-yellow, towering little whippersnapper!" The man laughed.

Once more Sam started, because, though he knew the term—high-yellow—, nobody had ever actually called him that before. (He'd been called "nigger" by both coloreds *and* whites and knew what to do when it happened. But this was a new insult, though it was given so jokingly, he wondered if it was worth taking offense.) Sam put his hands on his thighs again, then put them back on the bench, to arch his fingertips against the wood, catching his nails in weathered grain. Was *this* man, Sam wondered a moment, Jewish? Wasn't there something Semitic in his features? Sam asked: "Do you write poems, too?"

"Me?" The young man brought one hand back, the slender fingers splayed wide against the sweater he wore under his corduroy jacket. "Do I write poems? *Me?*" He took a breath. "I'm in advertising, actually. Ah, but I *should* be writing poems. I *will* be writing poems. Have I ever written poems?" He scowled, shook his head. "*Perhaps* I've written poems. Once I found a beautiful American word: 'findrinny.' But no American writer ever wrote it down save Melville. And since it never made it from *Moby-Dick* into any dictionary (I've looked in half a dozen), I've finally settled on 'spindrift.' Go look *it* up! It's equally lovely in the lilt and lay of what it means. Believe me, if I wrote a real poem, everyone would be talking about it — writing about it. When I write a poem — find its lymph and sinew, fix a poem that speaks with a tongue more mine than any you'll ever actually hear me talking with — you'll know it! Boni and Liveright did *Cane* last year, *Beyond the Pleasure Principle* this year; I just wonder when they'll get to me. I can promise you — Crane," he said suddenly, sat forward, and scowled. "Isn't that endlessly ironic?" He shook his head. "Crane — that's whom they're all mad about now. Someone showed me the manuscript. And, dammit, some of them are actually good! They're planning to get endorsements from Benét and Nunnally Johnson — he lives in Brooklyn, too."

"A poet? Named Crane?" Sam asked.

The man nodded, glancing over. "Nathalia Crane. She lives in Flatbush, out where it builds up again and Brooklyn starts to look at least like a town; and she's in love with the janitor's boy — some snub-nosed freckle-cheeked mick named Jones."

"In the heart of Brooklyn?" Sam said.

"If Brooklyn can be said to have a heart. I wonder why, no matter how hard I try to get away, I always end up working with sweets — Dad makes chocolates, you see. Well, I've lived off them long enough. Personally, I think Brooklyn, once you leave the Heights, is a heartless place. For heart, you go downtown into the Village. Really, the irony's just beyond me. She's supposed to be ten — or was, a couple of years ago. They go on about her like she was Hilda Conkling or Helen Adam. And they actually gave me the thing for review! I mean, I told them — under no *circumstances* would I! Could you think of anything more absurd — *me* reviewing *that?* If I liked it, people would think I was joking. If I hated it, they'd think I was simply being malicious. *They* thought it would be fun. No — I said; I certainly wouldn't be trapped into *that* one. Poetry's more serious than —" Again he broke off and turned, to regard

Sam with a fixity that, as the silence grew, grew uncomfortable with it. "I mean, any poem worth its majority must pell-mell through its stages of love, meditation, evocation, and beauty. It's got to hie through tragedy, war, recapitulation, ecstasy, and final declaration. But sometimes I think *she's* got more of the Great War in her poems than I do. I wonder if that makes the geeky girl a better poet? No, I'm not going to be able to take these engineering specifications, instruction manuals, and giant architectural catalogs much longer — Lord, they're real doorstoppers! Soon, I'm going to leave that job — the only question is, at my behest or theirs?"

"You're quitting your — ?"

"*Nobody* can write poems and have a job at the same time. It's impossible!"

"You don't think so?" He wondered if he should mention that Clarice worked as a secretary to the principal in the school where Hubert taught — and seemed to turn out her share.

"Do you think I should quit my job because they — not the people I work for, but the people I sometimes write for — asked me to review that silly little girl's silly little book? Of poems?" He crossed his arms severely, hunched his shoulders as if it had suddenly grown chill. "And, of course, they're not silly. Really. They're quite good — a handful of them. But they're not as good as poems I wrote when I was that age. (But doesn't every poet feel like that?) And they're certainly not as good as the poems I could write now!" He rocked a few times on the bench, then declared: "Now who do you think it was who wrote,

"Here's Crane with a seagull and Lola the Drudge,
With one pound of visions and one of Pa's fudge.

"Do you think there's that much fudge — and does anybody ever really notice? Fidge, perhaps? Well, Lowell did in Poe…" He rocked a few more times, then began, softly, intensely, voiced, yes, but quiet as a whisper:

"And midway on that structure I would stand
One moment, not as diver, but with arms
That open to project a disk's resilience
Winding the sun and planets in its face.
Water should not stem that disk, nor weigh
What holds its speed in vantage of all things
That tarnish, creep, or wane; and in like laughter,
Mobile yet posited beyond even that time
The Pyramids shall falter, slough into sand,—
And smooth and fierce above the claim of wings,
And figured in that radiant field that rings
The Universe:—I'd have us hold one consonance
Kinetic to its poised and deathless dance."

He broke off, turning aside, then added: "No, wait a minute. What
about this." Now the voice was louder:

"To be, Great Bridge, in vision bound of thee,
So widely belted, straight and banner-wound,
Multi-colored, river-harboured and upbourne
Through the bright drench and fabric of our veins,—
With white escarpments swinging into light,
Sustained in tears the cities are endowed
And justified, conclamant with the fields
Revolving through their harvests in sweet torment.

"And steady as the gaze incorporate
Of flesh affords, we turn, surmounting all
In keenest transience to that sear arch-head,—
Expansive center, purest moment and electron
That guards like eyes that must always look down
Through blinding cables to the ecstasy
That crashes manifoldly on us when we hear
The looms, the wheels, the whistles in concord

Teathered and antiphonal to a dawn
Whose feet are shuttles, silvery with speed
To tread upon and weave our answering world,
Recreate and resonantly risen in this dome."

Again the man sat back, relaxed his arms. "All right—tell me: is that
the greatest—" he growled *greatest* in mock exaggeration—"poem you've
ever heard? Or is it?"

Sam looked up, where arch ran into arch, along great cables. "What's
it *about*?" he asked, looking back. "The bridge?"

"It's called…'Finale'!" The man seemed, now, absolutely delighted,
eyes bright behind his lenses.

"I get the parts about…the bridge, I think. But what's the dome?"

"Ah, that's Sam's 'starry splendor dome' — from a poem he wrote,
called 'Words.' 'One sad scrutiny from my warm inner self / That age
hath—but the pleasure of its own / And that which rises from my inner
tomb / Is but the haste of the starry splendor dome / O though, the
deep hath fear of thee….' It goes on like that—and ends: '…Another
morning must I wake to see— / That lovely pain, O that conquering
script / cannot banish me.' Conquering script—I like that idea: that the
pen is mightier; that writing conquers." His eyes had gone up to tangle
in the harp of slant and vertical cables, rising toward the beige-stone
doubled groin. "Yes, I think I'll use it, make that one mine—too."

"Can you do that?" Sam asked. "If you write your own poems, can
you just take words and phrases from someone else's?"

The man looked down. "Did you ever see a poem by a man named
Eliot—read it in *The Dial* a couple of Novembers back. No, you probably didn't. But his poem is nothing *but* words and phrases borrowed from other writers: Shakespeare, Webster, Wagner—all sorts of
people."

"Taking other people's poems," Sam said, "that doesn't sound right
to me."

"Then I'll link Sam's words to words of mine, engulf them, digest
and transform them, *make* them words of my own. Really, it's all right.

You said you grew up on a college campus?" Leaning forward, his face became a bit wolfish. "The word is…'allusion'!"

"I grew up there," Sam said. "But I didn't go to school there."

"I see. But look what I've managed to call up! Go on—take a look there, now." The man nodded toward Manhattan. "What's that city, do you think?"

Sam turned, about to say… But the city had changed, astonishingly, while they'd been sitting. The sunlight, in lowering, had smelted its copper among the towers, to splash the windows of the southernmost skyscrapers, there the Pulitzer, in the distance the Fuller, there the Woolworth Building itself.

"Risen from the sea, just off the Pillars of Hercules—that's Atlantis, boy—a truly wonder-filled city, far more so than any you've ever visited yet, or certainly ever lived in." Behind Sam the man lowered his voice: "I'm a kind of magician who makes things appear and disappear. But not just doves and handkerchiefs and coins. I'm one of O'Shaunessey's movers and shakers, an archæologist of evening. I call up from the impassive earth the whole of the world around you, Sam—stalking the wild nauga and bringing it all down to words, paired phalluses, bridge between man and man. I create and crumble worlds, cities, visions! No, friend! It is Atlantis that I sing. And poets have been singing it since Homer, son; still, it's amazing what, at any moment, might be flung up by the sea. So: *ecce* Atlantis Irrefragable, corymbulous of towers, each tower a gnomon on the gold afternoon, flinging around it its metric shadow! And you should see it by moonlight—! They speak a wonder-filled language there, Sam: not like any tongue you've ever heard. My pop—C.A.—thinks poetry should be a pleasure taken up in the evening —but not so in Atlantis! No! There, Raphèl maì amècche zabì almi makes as lucid sense as mene, mene tekel upharsin or Mon sa me el kirimoor—nor is it anywhere near as dire as Daniel. But we *need* Asia's, Africa's fables! In Atlantis, when I stand on the corner and howl my verses, no one looks at me and asks, 'Whadja say?' Because mine's the tongue they speak there. In Atlantis I'll get back my filched *Ulysses* with the *proper* apology. I tell you, all twenty of those dead workers are up

and dancing there with savage sea-girls, living high and healthy in gar-
den-city splendor, their drinking late into the dawn putting out Liberty's light each morning. And the niggers and the jewboys, the wops and
the krauts say hey, hi, and howdy—and quote Shakespeare and Ade-
laide Crapsey all evening to each other. And even if I were to pull a
Steve Brodie this moment from the brink of the trolley lane there—
watchman, what of the track?—, as long as that city's up, the river
would float me, singing on my back, straight into its docks at a Sutton
gone royal, no longer a dead end, and I'd walk its avenues in every sort
of splendor. You say you saw the empty boat of our dark friend a-dribble
over his gunwale? Well, if it was empty, it's because he's found safe harbor there. And he's happy, happy—oh, he's happy, Sam, as only a naked
stallion (may St. Titus protect your foreskin in these heathen lands)
prancing in the city can be!"

Sam said: "Wow...!" though his "Wow" was at the gilded stones, the
burnished panes, the towers before him, rather than at the words that
wove from behind through the woof of towers ahead. He glanced back
at the man, then turned to the city again, where, in a building he could-
n't name, copper light fell from one window—"*Oh...!*" Sam breathed—
to the window below. "Wow..."

"Atlantis," the man repeated. "And the only way to get there is the
bridge: the arched nave of this loom, the temple of this stranded warp,
the pick of some epiphenomenal gull among them as it shuttles tower to
tower, bobbin, spool, and spindle. The bridge—that's what brings us
exhausted devils, in the still and tired evening, to Atlantis."

"That's...I mean—"

"Atlantis? There, you can see it, when the sun's like this—the city
whose kings ordered this bridge be built. Better, the city grows, weaves,
wavers from the bridge, boy—not the bridge from the city. For the
bridge is a woob—orbly and woob are Sammy's words: a woob's something halfway between a womb and a web. Roebling's bridge, Stella's
bridge, my bridge! Trust me—it wasn't gray, girder-grinding, grim and
grumpy New York that wove out from this mill. Any dull, seamy era can
throw up an Atlantis—Atlantis, I say: city of mirrors, City of Dreadful

93

Night, there a-glittering in the sun! Vor cosma saga. Look at those towers — those molte alti torri, those executors of Mars, like those 'round
Montereggione. Vor shalmer raga. Look at them, listen: O Jerusalem
and Nineveh — among them you can hear Nimrod's horn bleating and
Ephialtes' chain a-rattle. Whose was the last funeral you tagged behind,
when the bee drowsed with the bear? What primaveral prince, priest,
pauper, Egyptian mummy was it, borne off to night, fire, and forever?
What mother's son — or daughter — was it, boxed now and buried? *Per
crucem ad lucem.* Everything living arcs to an end. Nabat. Kalit. The
hour to suffer. It's a dangerous city, Sam. *Et in Arcadia ego.* Anything
can be stolen from you any moment. But all you get bringing up the rear
of funerals in November is shattered by the sea — for death's as marvelous a mystery as either birth or madness. Go strolling in our city parks,
Caina, Ptolomea, Judecca. (The only one I don't have to worry about
getting frozen into, I guess, is Antenora — if only thanks to the change
of season.) *Li jorz iert clers e sanz grant vent.* Go on, ask: '*Maestro, di, che
terra è questa?*' No, not penitence, but song. I'm still not ready for re-
pentance. See, I'm looking for Atlantis, too, Sam — sometimes I think
the worst that can happen is that I'll be stuck with the opportunists in
the vestibule — maybe even allowed to loll among the pages of the virtu-
ous *Pagan.* But then I'm afraid you're more likely to find me running in
circles on burning sand, under a slow fall of fire — that's if I don't just
snap and end up in the trees, where harpies peck the bleeding bark.
Mine and Amfortas's wounds both could use us some of Achilles' rust —
if not a little general ataraxy. In Atlantis you spend *every* night carous-
ing with Charlie Chaplin — and celebrate each dawn with randy icemen
at your knees. In Atlantis, you can strut between Jim Harris and the
emperor every day, Mike Drayton squiring Goldilocks behind. In
Atlantis, all poets wake up in the morning *real* advertising successes —
and cheese unbinds, like figs. Step right up, sit down with your own
Sammy, drink a glass of malmsey, and share a long clay stem. When this
Orlando is to his dark tower come — when I split my ivory horn in two,
bleeding from lip and ear (you think my pop will be my Ganelon and
finally pluck me from my santa gesta?) — will they hear me eight miles

or thirty leagues away, the note borne by an angel? You're sensitive, boy — sensitive to beauty. I can tell from your 'Wow!' — it's a sensitive 'Wow!' So — *Wow!* — I know you know what I'm talking of. As well, you're a handsome boy—like Jean. Only *handsomer* than Jean; I'd say it if anyone asked me. But there—I *have* said it; and it's still true! That's the job of poets, you know—to speak the terrifying, simple truths, that, for most people, are so difficult they stick in the throat from embarrassment. I mean, what's poetry for, anyway? To write a reply on the back of a paper somebody slips you at the baths with their address on it whom you don't feel like fucking? To celebrate some black theft of goose, cigar, and perfume—rather than toss it out the window at Thompson's?"

Sam had been used to people down home saying, "The Bishop has some *fine* looking boys!" He'd even had two or three girls at the school get moony and giggly about him, fascinated with the silliest thing he'd say. But the notion of himself as *really* handsome...? He pushed his fingertips over the green bench planks, beneath his thighs.

"Actually," the man said behind him (again Sam looked at the city), "I'm probably as good a poet as I am because I'm quite brave. I'm not some Jonathan Yankee nor yet, really, a Pierrot. But I've trod far shadowier grounds than those Wordsworth preluded his excursion to cover— precisely because they are *not* in the mind of man. Sure. I mean, here a logical fellow must ask: okay, what finally keeps me from it? We have the river's flow — instead of certainty. I could be any old priestess of Hesperus — wrecked on whatever. Am I really going to sing three times? It's a pretty easy argument that, whether in Egypt or at the Dardanelles, with any two towns divided by water, one can always play Abydos to the other's Sestos: for every Hero somewhere there's a Leander, and every Hero has her Hellespont. There's always hope as long as he remembers how to swim. I mean what are you going to do with Eve, La Gioconda, and Delilah — replace the latter two with Magdalene or Mary? Do I covet the extinction of light in dark waters? Three Marys will rise up and calm the roar: sure—Mary Garden, Merry Andrews, and Mary Baker Eddy.

"But we have the bridge.

"Oh, surely, it starts with your having a satori in the dentist chair, and the next you know you're at work on your hieros gamos and giggling over what Dol Common said to Sir Epicure. There are some folks to whom the thunder speaks; but there are others who need poets to rend and read into it their own trap-clap. (I hope you're not sure, either, who that their own refers to.) It ends, however, here, with *me* talking to *you* — I certainly didn't *think* I would be, half an hour ago. Not when I first saw you. The ones who terrify me are always the short, muscular blonds — and the tall, dark, handsome ones. Like you. 'Tall, dark, and handsome'? That's trite for terror. But it's true. I live with a short, muscular blond. We have a nice, six-dollar a week room. Only, I confess, it's the eight dollar room I lust after. *That's* Roebling's room. My blond's a sailor. His old man's the building owner. Now *he's* got the view — but he tells me I can come in and use it whenever I want. They're nice, that way. You can't imagine what it took, getting up nerve to speak to him — but I said, his name's Emil — to talk with him; and really talking with someone is different from simply speaking. I mean, you and I are speaking. But are we *talking* yet? Perhaps we ought to find out if we can. Still, suddenly, Emil and I — my handsome sailor, my golden wanderer, off after his *own* fleece — we were talking — telling each other how we felt. About one another. About the world. We talked till the sun came up; then he kissed my eyes with a speech entirely beyond words, and I've been able to do nothing but babble my happiness since. We decided it really would be terrible if we ever left each other. So he asked me to move in with him. All life is a bridge, I told him. Even the whole world. He's like an older brother — it's like living with a brother. And once again I'm hearing things before dawn. I'm three years younger than he — and two inches taller! But sometimes, it's true, I feel like I'm the elder. His father can't imagine that anything could be going on that shouldn't be — if anything is going on at all." Sam *heard* him shrug... "It's a hoot. The last person to pick him up and suckle at his schlong was Lauritz Melchior. Now, because they both speak Danish, we get to lurk backstage at the Met, about as regular as *The Brooklyn Eagle*. But it's very pure. Very severe, between us — Emil and me. But he *is* a sailor — and he goes on voyages. He's away, now — in South America. But in Atlantis, I live forever, in my room with my Victrola and my love. It makes my dark room light and light." Suddenly the man leaned forward again. (Sam could hear him, not see him, closer at his back.) "Tell me, Sam: Have you ever tried to kiss the sun? I mean, deep kiss it — French kiss it as they've just begun to say. Maul it with your lips and tongue? Flung your arms around it, pulled it down on top of you, till it seared your chest and toasted the white wafer cheek of love, poached the orbs in your skull, even while you thrust your mouth out and into its fires till the magma at its core blackened the wet muscle of all articulation? Well, Atlantis is the town in which everybody, man and woman, can kiss the sun and still have the moon smile down on them — not this stock, market culture of the stock market. And believe me, sometimes when the sun's away, you'll find yourself needs reaching for the moon. All I do is sweat with imagined jealousies while he's gone — Emil, I mean. But someday, he's going to come home, just while I'm in the throes of it, down on the daybed, with you or some guinea fisherman's randy brat — does it matter which? And..." The man sat back. Sam couldn't see him for the city — though he heard his fingers snap: "That'll be it! But that's not for today. That's for another time. Do you want to come back to the place with me — have a drink? We could be alone. I'm a good man to get soused with, if you like to get soused — and what self-respecting Negro doesn't? Come on, relax. Spend a little time — come with me, boy-oh-boy, and we'll get boozy and comfortable."

Was it the mention of the fisherman? Was it the mention of the moon? Suddenly Sam stood and turned around. "Look," he said. "I'm going to get a policeman."

The man frowned, put his head to the side.

"I'm going to get a *policeman*. This isn't right — " He thought: How do you explain to this fellow that the boat was really empty, that a man had *really* drowned?

"But you don't have to do — "

"I'm sorry! But I have to tell *somebody!* Look, we just can't — "

The man was looking at Sam's hands — which, in his excitement, had come loose to wave all over the day.

"I know all about it — the force of the club in the hand of the working man. Really," the man added, with a worried look, "policemen are *so* dull. Laughter's what you want here. Celebration of the city. Beauty. Higher thoughts. Get yourself lost in that lattice of flame. Humor's the artist's only weapon against the proletariat — and, in this city, my friend, the police are as proletarian as they come. Hey, I'm not going to make you do anything you don't — I mean I only *asked*...only offered you a sociable drink — "

"I'm going to get a policeman," Sam repeated. "Now." He added: "Maybe we'll be back — !" He started away. "In a few minutes."

From behind him the man called out, almost petulantly: "*That's* not the way to Atlantis!"

Sam glanced back.

"And you're a damned fool if you think I'm going to wait around for *you*." The man stood now, one hand on the bench back, like someone poised to run. His final salvo: "Don't think you'll ever get to it calling the law on people like *me!*"

Sam started again. Really, the fellow was a fool! What in the world had made him sit there listening, letting the man drench him in his lurid monologue? Sam broke into a lope, into a run — turned and, practically dancing backwards, looked once more:

The man was hurrying off, into Brooklyn, into Flatbush, or wherever he'd said he lived, moving away almost as fast as Sam was moving toward the city. Sam turned ahead, in time to take the stairs down the Manhattan stanchion — two at a step. Three minutes later, he almost missed the narrow entrance down to Rose. He had to swing around the rail, come back, and, at the entrance, plunge in silence by gray stone.

He found a policeman coming along the black metal railing by City Hall Park, where tall buildings' shadows had already darkened the lower stories to gray — save when Sam passed an east–west street, gilded with sudden sun. He hurried up to the officer. "Excuse me, sir. Please." On the other side of the park's grass, light glinted on the edge of the sprawling trolley terminal's tin roof—where some of the green paint had come away...? "But I think someone's drowned—in the river, sir. I was up walking across, into Brooklyn, and—"

"You saw someone do a Brodie off the bridge?" Below the midnight visor, webbed in forty-plus years' wrinkles, river-green eyes were perfectly serious.

"Someone jump, you mean? No. He was in a boat. I could see it, down in the water. And later on, I saw the boat again—and it was empty. A green rowboat—I think."

The policeman said: "Oh. You saw him go over?"

Sam watched the man's dull squint and his ordinary thumb laid up against the belly of his shirt between his jacket flaps, like something inevitable. He thought about putting his own hands in his pockets, but kept them hanging by force. "Well, no—not really. I mean, I didn't actually *see* it. But later—I saw the same boat. The oar was floating behind it. And there was nobody in it."

"Oh," the policeman said again. The ordinary thumb rose, and the officer scratched ash-blown blond, cap edge a-joggling on the walnuts of his knuckles. "And how long ago was this?"

"Just a few minutes," Sam said, trying to figure how long he'd been talking with the man on the bridge. "Maybe twenty, twenty-five minutes." Probably it was over thirty. Could it have been an hour? "But, well, you know. It takes some time to get all the way back over, to this side, from Brooklyn."

"It was on the Brooklyn side?"

"It was closer to the Brooklyn side than ours."

"Then why didn't you try to get some help over there?" The officer dropped his hand to put a fist on his bullet-belt.

"I didn't see anybody over there. And I was coming back this way, anyway—I mean, I don't think there's anything anybody could have done. Not now. Even then. But I still thought I ought to tell somebody. An officer. That it happened—that it probably happened...I mean."

"Oh," the policeman said a third time. "I see."

Sam looked around, looked at the policeman, who seemed to be waiting for him to leave, and finally said a hurried, "I just wanted to tell you—Thank you, sir," and ducked around him, embarrassment reddening his cheeks, rouging his neck.

At the corner, Sam glanced back, hoping the officer would be marking it down on his pad—at least the time or the place or something—in case, later, it came up. (Above, incomplete construction marked the day with girders and derrick, flown against the clouds in sight of the sound; for a moment Sam recalled the white workers who, with saw and torch, would hang there, humming, through the week.) *Would* that white man remember? But the officer was walking on, crossing silver tracks in a fan of sunlight, one untroubled hand flipping his billyclub down, around, and up—now one way, now the other.

Starting purposefully uptown, Sam mulled, block after block, toward the twilight city, now on the disappearance of the fisherman, now on the ravings of the stranger on the bridge, now on the three girls coming down the steps when he'd arrived at the underpass, whose delicate descent had innocently initiated it all, now on the policeman who'd brought the afternoon to its inconclusive close. A knot had tied low in his throat—an anxious thing that wouldn't be swallowed, that kept him walking, kept him thinking, kept him rehearsing and revising bits of the day in their dialogue — till, stalking some greater understanding still eluding him, he got as far as Fifty-second Street.

Nestled in the grip of gilded tritons and swept round by cast nereids' metal drapes, up on the pediment of a bank, with its brazen disk, from arrow-tipped hands, down-cast, short one right and long one left (a wonderful water clock, he thought suddenly and absurdly, in which the water had all run out), Sam realized it was just after…twenty-five-to-five!

Along all four legs of the intersection, he looked with electric attention for a subway stop's green globes. He'd been due at Elsie and Corey's almost forty minutes ago!

e

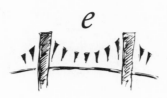

Mine eyes feel dim and scorched from grey,
The neighboring lamps throw grey stained gold—
Houses in the distance like mountains seem,
The bridge lost in the mist—
The essence of life remains a screen;
Life itself in many grey spots
That trickle the blood until it rots...

    —SAMUEL BERNHARD GREENBERG,
      "Serenade in Grey"

Shuttles in the rocking loom of history,
the dark ships move, the dark ships move...

    —ROBERT HAYDEN, "Middle Passage"

Sam got to Elsie and Corey's after five.

Elsie's school books—she was studying for her Master's in Education
—had been moved to the windowsill. The table had been carried from
the kitchen into the living room and the wings attached. The peach colored cloth was already spread. Knives, forks, spoons, and linen napkins
were laid—and in front of Lucius, in New York for the week, a bread-
and-butter plate was crummy with half a dinner biscuit, butter knife
propped on the rim. Lucius was saying: "Well, I certainly wasn't going

to wait for him. Where you been, boy? We've all been sittin' around here *hungry!*"

Originally Lucius's apartment, eventually (Sam knew) it had housed all his older brothers and sisters—getting in each other's way, helping each other out, arguing with one another, going out for the evening so this one might study or that one entertain, scuffling to get together the forty-five dollars a month rent, generating a thousand stories to tell on holiday trips back to Raleigh. Even Jules, during her year in the city, had lived here. (They'd all moved now, except Corey and Elsie.) Even Hubert.

"Well, he's here *now*," Corey said. "That's what's important. There's no harm done." (All had lived here — except Sam.) "Go wash your hands, Sam—then bring in those soup plates for Elsie."

In the hallway while Sam was heading for the bathroom, Hubert overtook him. At the mirror, a loop of palm still stuck in back from Easter, one gas lamp chuckled faintly against the wall; and Hubert, hurrying up to lean a hand on Sam's shoulder, said quietly, quickly: "Look, now—Corey had an emergency extraction this morning, and had to go into the office. So they didn't get a chance to do anything special for your birthday. They feel right bad about it, too. But I just didn't want you to be expecting anything—or say anything to make them feel worse than they do," while his mirror image leaned away.

"Oh," Sam said, from the chasm of his own forgetfulness. "Sure. That's all right."

In the bathroom, he turned the enamelled handle at the sink. From verdigrised brass the raddled stream chilled his knuckles, ran over the backs of his hands, dripped between his outsized fingers. While it warmed, he washed with the fresh bar of Jules' soap sitting in the clamshell soap dish: knifed, unblunted edges meant Elsie must have unwrapped and set it out that afternoon.

The bathroom window held a granulated pane. Though it splayed the tile across from it with early evening sun, it let through not a shadow of the city. At its leaded edges, in blobby tesselations, however, rectangles of red, green, yellow, and blue showed—if you got down to the border panes and looked — colored fragments of the fire escapes and trees and clotheslines in the lot outside. If you didn't, but only stepped in and out, say, it reminded Sam of the stained glass in the school chapel down at the college. (Sitting on the commode's wooden ring, or standing, listening to his water fall while gazing at the overhead flush box, he wondered sometimes if it were right for a bathroom to look like a church.) Diagonally on the sill sat a box of kitchen matches—for the gas lamps in the hall. *Lucifer.* Years ago Corey had explained to him that Phosphorus was Greek and Lucifer was Latin for the same thing. *Christos Pheros. Phos Pheros.* John, carrier of Christ. Venus, carrier of light. *Hesperus.* Were John and Lewy sitting down to their Saturday dinners? Outside in the back the Negro fellow was hollering, as if his voice were the city's plaint itself: *"Hang-a-line...? Hang-a-line...?"* — as he made his way through Harlem's alleys, to put up new clotheslines or clothesline pulleys for a dime, in time for Monday's washing. Somewhere in the past months Sam had learned to decipher the shrill exhortation. At some moment he'd seen the man with a coil of rope on his shoulder, a ladder under his arm, swinging his pail of metal spikes and wooden spools... Outside the glass, the line-man wandered away, litany fading, barely heard, *"Hang-a...?"*

Sam dried his hands on one of Elsie's white hand-towels, on which she'd appliquéd a spray of red and purple flowers among long leaves, that creased and uncreased about his fingers.

On the little step stool beside the commode lay a newspaper, dated back in April, whose headline he recognized from some two weeks ago:

WORLD RENOWNED ACTRESS

DIES IN PITTSBURGH

He picked it up, to see, on the newspaper beneath it, Mary Blair kissing Paul Robeson's hand. Might a white actress die from kissing the hand of a black man? He dropped the first paper and turned to the door.

103

"Boy," Hubert said, forearm on the table, when Sam came back into the living room, "you are *something!* This is your idea of getting here by four o'clock?"

"Sam's here at four o'clock," Lucius said. "It's just four o'clock C.P.T." — which made everybody laugh.

"What's *that* supposed to mean?" Sam asked, trying to smile.

They laughed again.

"What's C.P.T.?" he asked again.

"That's — " Clarice started. "That's *country* people's time!" Which made everybody howl.

"Well, if you're going to joke like that," Dr. Corey said, "you might as well tell the boy what it really means. C.P.T. is Colored People's Time."

"Why's it colored people's time?" Sam wanted to know, beginning to lose his grin at the joke he didn't get.

"Our people," Corey explained, with a deep and knowledgeable nod, "at least up here in the city, have a tendency to get distracted — especially if they're on their way to see you."

"Seven-come-eleven!" Lucius called out, and shook his fist, fingers up, over the table — pretending to shoot craps, like Negroes did in Raleigh's back lots and doorways. Lucius opened his fingers, snapped up his hand. (Imaginary dice danced, glittering white with black pips, over the tables of Atlantis…) "Distracted!" Lucius repeated, nodding emphatically.

Everyone laughed again.

"That's why I was so late getting here from the office this morning," Corey said.

"You got deflected?" Sam asked — only just hearing himself say the wrong word, even though, by now, he knew perfectly well that wasn't what Corey meant.

"*I* didn't get distracted!" Corey said, mocking indignation. "My *patient* did! He wasn't *quite* as late as you were — but he was almost. Now go get those plates, before Elsie has to bring them in herself!"

In the kitchen, Elsie stood at the sink by the brown, wooden ice box, its black rubber seal pressed out around the upper door. "Now they're

going to worry you to death for coming in so late for your birthday dinner. But don't you pay them any mind." Out the wooden washtub in the
sink, she pulled, rattling from among the utensils, a long-handled
wooden spoon and took a dish-towel to it. Although she wasn't really as
tall as Hap or Lucius or Hubert, Sam always had to see her standing
next to them to realize it. She was also the gentlest. "Lucius didn't get
here till four-thirty-five himself — and we weren't ready to serve till
quarter of. So, no matter what they say, you are *only* twenty minutes
late. And we aren't having anything that'll be spoiled by twenty minutes! You take those soup plates in for me, like a good boy?"

But once he came back in, handed out the china, and took his place
between Lucius and Clarice, it was as if Elsie's warning, even in the other room, had turned aside all further jibes at his tardiness.

Talk was of other things.

Elsie carried in the tureen from the kitchen, set it on the peach cloth,
and uncovered it. Steam puffed. Inside the tureen's oval cover in Elsie's
hand, droplets ran over white glaze. Elsie said: "Black bean soup...!" —
so dark it was nearly purple, red and green pepper bits throughout. She
sank the porcelain ladle: it flooded. Elsie was going to teach domestic
science, and her Master's had included a nutrition course, since which
Saturday meals had grown more varied, even exotic. (*And* nourishing,
Corey reminded them: beans — now beans were *very* good for you.
Plenty of protein. That's why poor people all over the world—in Africa
and Italy and Mexico—*ate* so many!) Elsie took the tureen cover back
into the kitchen while Dr. Corey asked: "Sam, when are you going to
start night school?"

"Soon, I guess." Indeed, the question was a relief. Though Corey always brought it up, once she'd asked it and he'd answered, it was over.
Corey said what she had to, but she didn't harp—and she'd told the rest
in no uncertain terms they shouldn't either. Harping would do no good
—not with Sam.

As Elsie, now without her apron, stepped back through the door, Dr.
Corey said: "You're the oldest here. Elsie, you want to say blessing?"

"Let Sam say it." Elsie took her seat at the table head around the corner from Corey. "It's going to be his birthday in three days — and we won't see him again before he turns eighteen."

So Sam bowed his head, folded his hands, and recited what, at home, he'd learned as a single polysyllable all but incomprehensible — but which, since he'd been in New York, coming to dinner Saturdays at his sisters', had begun to separate into individual words with meanings:

"Bless, we beseech thee, O Lord,
  This food of which we are about to partake,
  That it may nourish us and strengthen us
  To do thy service, for Christ our redeemer's sake…"

After the soup there was fresh ham; and peas and onions; and mashed potatoes—butter blurring yellow among white peaks and dells; and a gravy almost sweet that had prunes cut up in it—which Elsie said was not a gravy at all but a sauce.

"Well, then, you just pass that there gravy sauce right on over here," Lucius said. "This is some fancy eating we're doing today!"

They asked Sam what he'd done that afternoon.

"Sam went to see the Brooklyn Bridge," Clarice told them.

"Well?" Dr. Corey wanted to know. "What did you think of it?"

"It's a real nice bridge," Sam said. "It's big, too! But when I got over to the other side, it was all cornfields and meadows and little white houses — shoot, I thought Brooklyn was supposed to be part of New York. It's nothin' but country — just like down home!" — which made them all laugh again.

"Don't say 'shoot,'" Corey said. "That's not nice."

Clarice leaned toward him and said more quietly, "Don't say 'real nice' either. It's very nice — or really nice."

Not paying either much mind, Sam finished up: "You could see some real good skyscrapers from it, though!" He'd already resolved not to tell them about the Italian in the boat. That kind of thing could upset people. Everybody was having too much fun.

Afterward Elsie brought in a big salad with water cress and raisins in it.

"This is all so good!" Lucius declared.

"Well, I'm glad," Elsie said, considering. "I was just afraid it might be a bit tainted."

"Tainted?" Lucius asked in surprise; he sat back. "*Tainted?* Didn't the ice man bring ice for the weekend? What you mean, this food might be 'tainted'?"

"I was just afraid, maybe," Elsie said, "well, 'tain't enough of it!" which was a joke Sam had first heard Lucius and Elsie go through back home years ago. But Clarice had never heard it, and clapped her hands now, screeching like a bird.

"Really, Elsie," Lucius said, beaming bright-eyed about the table. "I do have to ask one thing: prunes, raisins, *beans?* Just what are you trying to do to us?"

Amidst more laughter, Corey's voice cut over: "She's just trying to keep you healthy—make sure you're nice and regular."

"Well, *I'm* going to be so regular," Lucius declared, "nobody'll be able to stand *next* to me!"

"That's a terrible thing to say!" Corey said. But, amidst more laughter, Elsie—and Dr. Corey—were laughing too.

Was there any way to tell them about the man on the bridge, Sam wondered, *without* telling about the man on the boat? Should he even try? If he was a friend of Toomer's, maybe Clarice knew him—

But here, in her enthusiasm, Clarice got to arguing with Lucius about something, and Sam was waiting for a lull into which to interject some mention of the strange fellow he'd met that afternoon, with his strange tales and talk — when Elsie, who'd slipped into the kitchen, came back in with a cake in her hands—with candles on it!

Dr. Corey and Elsie began to sing.

Hubert, leaning on his forearm again, and Clarice and Lucius—with his healthy baritone—joined them:

"...Happy birthday, dear Sa-am...!
Happy birthday to you!"

Why then, he wondered, as he stood to blow out the flames ("Make a
wish!" Clarice was saying, beside him. "Don't forget, Sam! Make a
wish...!"), had Hubert told him there *wouldn't* be any birthday for him?
Was it Hubert's notion of punishment for coming in so late? Or had
Hubert wanted him to think nothing would happen to make it more of
a surprise when it did? He glanced at his brother, leaning way back in
his chair now. With Hubert, sometimes, you couldn't tell.

But even as Sam looked up, Hubert brought his chair legs forward,
leaned down, and reached under to come up with a grin and a big box
wrapped in red paper, though there was no ribbon around it: "And this
is for you—though you don't deserve it...! Coming in here an hour-
and-a-half late the way you did!"

While Sam tore the paper off, Hubert explained:

"Now Mr. Horstein said to tell you that any one you already had, or
didn't want, you can bring back and he'll exchange it for another one
that's the same price."

It was a whole *box* of magic tricks!

While Sam was taking out the card deck with the shaved corners and
the metal hoops—some whole, some gapped—and the picture frame
with the secret compartment, other presents were coming out from behind the sofa, from the bedroom, from under the settee cushion: a
sweater (from Corey), gloves (from Elsie), a book of poems, with pho-
tographs of colored people down south sitting around the woodstove
playing banjos or walking to church (from Clarice)—and a fountain pen
(from Lucius).

"Is Sam going to do some magic tricks for us now? Hubert's been
telling us how you're getting all interested in magic. Are there any of 'em
you know already? Come on, you're going to put on a show for us...?"

But Corey said: "Now Sam has already told us, he needs to practice
his magic before he can perform it. Right now, he's just learning it—
exploring it."

Elsie said: "He just got it tonight. You have to practice before you can perform," and backed, with dishes, into the kitchen.

"Oh." Lucius glanced at Hubert. "I see."

Hubert didn't say anything.

Just then Sam looked down into the box of paraphernalia. The one trick Mr. Horstein had inadvertently duplicated (or had Hubert duplicated it maliciously?) was the false, metal thumb.

"Oh. I *have* this one—already!" Sam picked it up from the box, trying to sound nonchalant and accusatory at the same time.

Hubert sucked his teeth. "Hey—I *told* him you had that one and to leave it out! He must have misunderstood me."

"Oh." Well, he felt a little better knowing it was not, then (probably), maliciousness.

Lucius sat, drumming his big, manicured fingers on the peach cloth. Sam pictured magic dice, spinning and dancing between them.

Then Elsie came out of the kitchen again carrying a silver tray, mirror bright, on which stood half a dozen little wine glasses—and a dark bottle.

"Well," Dr. Corey said. "Isn't this a treat! This is Elsie's blackberry wine—that she made herself last summer. We picked the berries together, when we went out to Asbury Park."

"We certainly did," Elsie said. "And bottled it ourselves, too." She put the tray down on the table. "Now who would like a glass?"

"I'll have some," Hubert said, laying one forearm on the table. "You want some, Clarice?"

"Oh, yes," Clarice said. "Thank you."

"I'll have some," Sam said.

"I'll have some too," Lucius said. "But I do have to mention—I mean as a lawyer, now. Hubert'll back me up. You know this is—strictly speaking—*completely* against the law!"

"Against what law?" Dr. Corey said.

"The eighteenth amendment," Lucius said. "We got prohibition, I hope you remember!"

"This is *not* against the law," Elsie said. "This isn't moonshine. This isn't bathtub gin. This is homemade blackberry cordial—it's not going to hurt anybody!"

"When the revenue officers cart you off, you better tell *them* that!" Lucius laughed.

"Now, if you don't want any, Lucius, you don't have to have any. Maybe you think we shouldn't—?"

"Now I'm not saying that! I'm not saying that at all!" Lucius's large hands waved above the table. "I'm just saying—"

"We are not breaking any law," Dr. Corey said. "This here is medicinal."

"That's *right!*" Elsie said, as if the idea had just hit her. A smile replaced the moment of worry on her face. "This is medicinal wine. A glass of this after dinner will absolutely help with the digestion. You know, Papa always takes some after Sunday dinner—"

"Mama too," Dr. Corey said.

"Well, I can just see the police now, breaking in on one of them speakeasies around on Lenox Avenue and the doctors breaking out their prescription pads—"

"If it will make you feel better," Dr. Corey said, "I will *write* you a prescription for it—"

"No," Lucius said. "For me? No—you don't have to do that." And his arm, which had been moving to the laughter like a conductor's, dropped its pinstriped coatsleeve on the table—the original, Sam realized, of the gesture Hubert performed so frequently.

Beside the red and blue wrapping-paper-and-tissue ruins of his birthday, Sam looked at his twenty-nine-year-old brother, with whom he'd spent fewer days in his life than he had with any number of his friends. Leather gloves, magic tricks, book, pen: this birthday, because of Hubert, had been completely unexpected, and was now over—three days before it had actually occurred.

Lucius said he'd walk with them back to Hubert's—the argument with Clarice had quieted to an intense conversation over some fine point of the Jim Crow laws. When they came downstairs, they found there'd been an unexpected shower that, because of their laughter inside, they'd missed. But the sidewalks were wet—or, at any rate, drying in patches now. Tall Lucius and diminutive Clarice strolled together under a street lamp, over glimmering, puddled pavement, her skirts swinging back and forth below her calves, the heat of their conversation enough to keep the two of them twenty paces ahead.

The box of tricks under his arm (with the other presents inside it), suddenly Sam said: "...I get it now!"

Hubert said: "Get what?"

"Nothing," Sam said. "It wasn't anything. Just something that...well, nothing."

"What was it?"

"Really," Sam said. "It wasn't anything at all. Just something—that Corey said."

"Come on. What *was* it?"

"It was just..." He knew Hubert wouldn't let it rest. "I get the joke, now. About C.P.T." Which was a bald lie—to make Hubert stop questioning.

"Oh." Hubert said. "That."

But what had come to Sam was the reason the man on the bridge had gotten so upset when Sam had said he was going for a policeman. He hadn't realized Sam had meant for the man in the boat. And the fellow had just asked Sam back to his place for a drink...!

Well, Mr. Harris kept a bottle in his store. Hubert even had a bottle at the house. Not to mention Elsie and Corey's homemade wines. Sometimes it was hard to remember prohibition was really in force—especially here in Harlem.

But, Sam reflected, the fellow probably thought I was going to have him arrested for possession of liquor!

"Hubert?"

"What?"

"Do you remember, back home, going into downtown Raleigh, with a bunch of guys, and standing on the corner, across from the park, at the trolley stop—waiting there, and watching the women get on the trolley car?" Sam reached around to pat his pockets for cigarettes. But he'd been in such a hurry to get to Corey and Elsie's that he hadn't stopped to buy any. "They'd step up on the step of the car, and their skirts would swing up, so that you could see their shoes, the buttoned kind that went up over their ankles? You remember how we'd nudge each other—or try to keep a straight face. And sometimes, if there was a breeze or something, and the skirt blew up just a little more, you could see the stocking at the top of the shoe—then, boy, you'd *really* seen something! I did it. You must have done it, too."

"Yeah," Hubert said. "What about it?"

"Well, we all used to like it—me, John, and Lewy all did it. But some of those boys, out there doing that, were really sent out of sight by it. You must have known one or two of those—the ones who were always *suggesting* that you go down and do it. You remember?"

"What if I do," Hubert said. "What's the point?"

"Well," Sam said, with a feeling in his throat he knew would have been assuaged with the first draw on a cigarette, "now, here, in New York, with skirts up above *everybody's* ankles, suddenly it's nothing to see some lady's legs. Isn't that funny? When you're twelve, thirteen, fourteen—it's the most exciting thing in the world. Then, you come to a different city—and it ain't anything anymore. But you remember when it was, don't you?"

"Sam," Hubert said, "why do you want to talk about things like that?"

"Hubert," Sam said, "that stuff was important to us. You can't forget stuff like that."

"Like you said, skirts are up now—and in ten or fifteen years, *everybody's* going to have forgotten it. You should forget it too. Stuff like that's nasty, Sam!"

"Well, *I'm* not going to forget it," Sam said. "I had too much fun doing it. I bet you did too."

"Boy," Hubert said, "you are a country nigger to your soul. You better think about gettin' civilized—that's what coming up here was supposed to do for you!"

But, hefting up his box, Sam laughed—though he had already forgotten the brilliant city at one end of the bridge and the empty skiff at the other.

As he lay in bed, drifting, a summer's walk returned to Sam, along the south field's dusty edge-path. Shirtless, John walked ahead. Behind John, his shirt open and out of his pants, Lewy talked heatedly: "John, you can be the White Devil," Lewy explained. "And Sam — " whose long sleeves were still buttoned at his wrists, with only his collar loose — "will be the Dark Lord. And I'll be the Ancient Rabbi who understands the Cabala's secrets and can speak them backwards—"

John said: "Why you always want to take things back to the Jews, Lewy? Why you do that? Take 'em back to somewhere else, now — Egypt. Or Africa. You should take 'em back to Africa."

"You some *kind* of redheaded African," Sam gibed, but it would not, this time, break what tensed between his friends.

"You don't *really* want to originate with the Jews, do you?" John asked, turning around to wait, as Lewy, then Sam, caught up.

"I think," Lewy said, "with Christianity we already do."

Two weeks after his (pre-) birthday dinner — and after a birthday that seemed less like a birthday than Christmas had seemed like Christmas—, Sam dreamed. Papa's interpretation of the dream certainly would have been that it came from Sam's sneaking off to read those magazines that lied so about Egypt and the darker races. Before dismissing that interpretation, however, we should remember that the sneaking was — for Papa — as constitutive as the stories; which put him not so far from the Viennese doctor whose book on the death instinct had been translated into English two years before by the redoubtable C.J.M. Hubback, published first in England and just reprinted in the United States by Boni and Liveright—and who, for his interpretation, would have erected an elaborate structure of authority and transference, language, sexual guilt, and wish fulfillment: Papa and the Viennese doctor had, neither of them, heard of one another; but both were educated men of a single age and epoch, so that

"Well," John said, "that's *different!*"

"I don't see why," Lewy said. "Now, me—I'm going to originate everywhere...from now on. I've made up my mind to it."

"Lewy's doing that," Sam said, "just to get your goat—"

"No," Lewy said. "From now on, I come from all times before me — and all my origins will feed me. Some in Africa I get through my daddy. And my momma. And my stepdaddy. Some in Europe I get through the library: Greece and Rome, China and India — I suck my origins in through my feet from the paths beneath them that tie me to the land, from my hands opened high in celebration of the air, from my eyes lifted among the stars—"

"Some in Egypt and Arabia," John said, "you got through the magazines.... He's gonna try an' out-preach your daddy." John grinned through his freckles at Sam.

But the tension was all in Sam's listening now.

"—and I'll go on originating, all through my life, too," Lewy said. "Every time I read a new book, every time I hear something new

they shared a number of ideas. Doubtless the Viennese doctor's younger Swiss-born rival would have added that the dream indicated a surge of the creative in Sam, frightening in its implications and quite possibly to be repressed, but that still must be reckoned with. And the medical wisdom of half a dozen decades on would have suspected in it the first sign of an apnœa, directly related to smoking, that very likely would get worse — though probably not for years.

Night. Night the terrible...

Carefully, Sam the Spy walked down the steps into the strange cellar. The light behind him dimmed. He glanced back — someone had just closed the wooden doors up to the street. Moonlit chinks along the ceiling's edge by the ends of the great beams were winking out, here and there. Outside, he realized, things were toppling over the small openings. Something shook the whole building. Behind, the cellar doors flapped up a moment—but only dirt and darkness tumbled down the steps — before they closed for good under the weight above. Water began running about history, every time I make a new friend, see a new color in the oil slicked over a puddle in the mud, a new origin joins me to make me what I am to be—what I'm always becoming. The whole of my life is origin—nowhere and everywhere. You just watch me now!"

"But you don't *know* where you came from in Africa," John hazarded. "I don't. And Sam don't—because the Bishop don't. You remember, 'cause you asked him if he did."

"They didn't keep records of all that." As they walked through the summer dust, Lewy grew pensive: "They should have — but that's how they kept us slaves. You know what I think? I think it's those deprived of history who create the world's great histories." Then he repeated, "I...originate, everywhere!"

"How you gonna stay a nigger," John asked, "if you come from so many places?"

"Look," Lewy said. "Knowing all I really come from, that won't stop anybody calling me a black bastard," which startled Sam. (Though nobody really knew *who* Lewy's father was, people were

through the single upper window, suddenly to gush — while trickles rilled the walls.

The subterranean chamber was descending into the sea!

The pressure grew intense; it was becoming harder to breathe. What light there was in the weedy water dimmed as they sank; but in the last of it, he realized, behind him, beside him, something — formless and dark — was in there with him. It splashed toward him through the darkening flood. He had to get out, get away, only in the enclosing blackness his breath was stifled in his chest—

Sam tore his face from the pillow, punching and pushing himself up into light. He gasped as the quilt fell to his lap. He sat, gulping. In the middle of the room, the tall figure turned toward him: chills encased him — the thing splashing in the submarine black had transfigured into this moonlit form...? The drape was back over the wing chair. Moonlight sluiced the room.

As Sam got his orientation back, the figure — frowning Hubert, in his pants, shirtless now but wearing his carpet slippers, and surely on his way out to pretty sure he'd been a lot blacker than Lewy's stepfather.) "That don't stop anybody from calling you a nigger, calling Sam a black boy, calling me colored, calling you a redheaded African, calling Sam a Negro, calling me black. And I guess we're what we're called, no matter where we're from. That's what calling means — that's all. It isn't no more important than that."

"Well," Sam said, "it's pretty important, what they call you, when it means where you got to live, got to go to school, even what you got to work at."

Considering, their shoulders neared with the seriousness of it, to touch each other's under the sky.

Then, as if the energy or the anxiety of the closeness became too much, John, hand up and head back, ran into the hip-high grass, to begin imitating a bomber, banking here, swooping there, shouting Vrummmmmmmmmmmmmm into the sun...

In half-sleep Sam recalled the insight of his walk home from work on wealth and power and art. Was this prior summer's amble the origin of that peripatetic revelation? Or had the winter evening's revelation been the origin of this

the hallway's chilly commode — asked: "Sam...? You all right?"

"Yeah..." Sam was breathing hard.

The frown fell away before a chuckle. "What were you dreaming about?"

But in the moonlight, the tomblike dark of the submerged and suffocating crypt was already slipping away.

"Hubert...?"

"Yeah?"

Sam ran his hand around his bare neck, down his naked chest. Nothing was wrong with his breathing now. He took three more breaths to make sure. "Hubert? Back when you were about fifteen — or sixteen, you did something. And Papa got so mad, he chained you to the water pump in the backyard, and he was shouting at you that he was going to leave you chained up in the yard all night— only then he must have gotten even madder, because about ten minutes later, he got this orange crate and came back and began to beat you with it, beat you 'til the slats broke all up, and you were bleeding and crying— and Mama was scared. I think she thought he was going to kill you."

memory of summer, which, without it, would never have returned?
But even as he wondered, both,
with sleep, began to slip away.

A city, Sam thought, turning
over, that was everywhere and nowhere, where we all come from,
where we all go...

"Yeah," Hubert said. "So
did I."

"Hubert — what did you do?"
The question asked, the last of
drifting, of dreaming, vanished.
Sam was icily awake, electrically
alert.

Hubert shifted his weight,
then shifted it again. "Just... stuff.
That's what you were dreaming about?"

"No—well, maybe I was. I'm not sure. But I woke up thinking about
it." Outside the window, clotheslines hung like lapping lariats that, beyond the frame, would encincture night to day. "Can't you tell me what
it was, Hubert? So I'll know? I was just nine or ten, and Jules or Laura
wouldn't tell me anything. Jules—I don't think she really knew what it
was about either—but she said if I was that curious, I should ask Papa.
But I was afraid to. I thought if it was that awful, if I asked about it he
might do the same thing to me. At least that's what I thought then."

"Yeah, maybe he would have — no." Hubert humphed. "It was just
stuff...with a girl." He pursed his lips, debating whether to say more.
"You remember Alina, Reverend Fitzgarn's daughter?" Hubert took a
breath, the moonlit admission clearly difficult. "I stole some of Papa's
money, to go out and get a bottle and be with her. And then Reverend
Fitzgarn caught the two of us, doing it—or, least ways, just *about* doing
it. And he came raging to Papa that he would have me locked up by the
police if Papa didn't do something himself—and Papa was embarrassed
as all get out, at least at first; then he got real mad because I'd shamed
him. Then, when he got back to the house, he found out I'd stolen from
him too. Five dollars."

"Alina Fitzgarn?"

"*Um-hm.* Look—just a second, I got to go to the toilet. You be all
right?"

Sam nodded.

His arms and back gone from ivory to—with his next step—cadaverous gray, Hubert went out through the hall door. Limen to lintel, like a species of mystery, black filled the space ajar. Sam's fingertips tingled on the quilt. He moved his foot over, beneath the covers, from where it had thrust, on his waking and turning, into cold bedding. Outside in the hall, water gushed into the commode.

Hubert came back in and pushed the door closed behind him. "I'm gonna have to get me a chamber pot—this getting up and having to go out to pee in the morning *every* morning at—" he reached into his pants to pull out the pocketwatch Mama had sent him for Christmas (but it had arrived three days late), and held it up—"nearly ten to four!—just isn't going to make it. At least not in this weather." He dropped the watch from its chain—so that it swung in the light, turning and unturning—and burlesqued a shiver. "It's cold out there! I guess—" He swung up the watch and caught it, white-gold flashing in the moon, and dropped his hand toward his pants pocket—"I'm starting to turn into an old man!" (Hubert liked that watch, Sam knew. But each time Hubert took it out, Sam felt not so much jealous of the object as he did simply at sea, himself not knowing the hour.) Hubert had stopped in the middle of the floor on the same spot he'd stood before. In moments he seemed to have settled back into the same discomfort. Hubert took a long, considered breath. At last he said: "Papa didn't let me stay outside all night, you know. He turned me loose—after he wore himself and that orange crate out. He made me come inside and sit in his study—my nose was bleeding, my arm was sore—and he talked to me. I can remember it, I can see him just as clear, behind his desk. He said we had to call a truce, him and me. He said we had to call a truce between us—that if we didn't, he was going to kill me or I was going to kill him. If I didn't drive him to his grave with shame and sorrow, I was going to do it with a gun or my hands. Or worse, he'd have to kill me first. 'You want to go to New York,' he said, 'with Hap and Corey?' I hardly heard what he was saying, when he said it. I mean, after he'd just about murdered me, it was like he'd turned around and offered me a present. What I'd expected him to say was that I wouldn't be allowed to go out of the house and had to stay in my room and eat bread and water for the next three months—or something like that. He said, 'You want to go to New York…?'" Hubert reached up across his bony chest to rub his arm with his hand. "You see, Papa's a strong-headed man. I guess he had to be, to do what he's done—working at the school, be a minister to all those Negroes down home, get himself elected bishop. But he's got some strong-headed children too. And he's smart enough to know you can't have all these strong-headed people living under one roof—not ten or twelve of us. Not *that* many. So that's why I came up here. He loves us, you know. It's taken me a while to figure that one out. But he does." Hubert dropped his hand, took a breath. "Look—if you want to talk about this some more, let's do it in the morning. Is that all right?"

"Sure," Sam said. "All right."

As Hubert walked into his own room, Sam settled back down in the bed. Very much awake, he pulled the covers to his chin. Even if he didn't know what might happen in the vestibules of subway cars during rush hour, or what was worse than passing water or doing your business, though some of his ideas about it might have surprised Hubert, Sam *did* know—more or less—what "doing it" was. And he knew it was a pretty bad thing even to think about, especially for a bishop's son—and even more so with a minister's daughter. Alina Fitzgarn? He could hardly remember what she looked like, except that she was dark and quiet and had been a good friend of Milly's, till her parents had sent her away. Did her going away have anything to do, Sam wondered suddenly, with Hubert?

For a while Sam thought about getting out all his magic tricks, new and old, to look them over in the moonlight. But the rectangle of light, that had flooded the rose rug like white oil and lay half on the wall, did not touch the bed. Maybe he should put on his long johns, turn on the light, take *Weird Tales* from the top drawer, sit over in the wing chair, and read the first installment of Houdini…? (But would he remember it clearly enough when he got the next issue? Lewy read everything right away, then read it again and could tell you all the contradictions between the various parts and didn't mind at all if you told him what happened next in the story. Sam reread the stories but couldn't spot the contradictions to save himself. And John wouldn't let you tell him anything, though he could get real excited and had a hard time not telling *you*.) Finally Sam pushed back the covers, stood up, and stepped—naked—to the window.

For four, five, ten seconds he looked at the black windowframe across the alley. Then he pulled the drape and curtain from where he'd put it back over the wing chair's edge (odd that Hubert had never commented on it; but then, in his family, there were so many things they somehow didn't talk about) to let it swing before the glass, cutting out most of the light.

Then Sam turned, bent his knees, and jumped for the bed, to land in a crouch on the thin mattress, springs shrieking beneath (from inside Hubert said: "*Sam…?*"), grabbed up the covers and shoved his feet under the quilt, to slide down between the sheets' pools and puddles of warmth and chill, shivering on his back for seconds, clutching the covers to his chin, grinning. (Suppose she'd been awake, in her dark room, looking toward her window. Had she seen him in his, in the moon-light…naked?) He lay awake a long time, in wait for morning.

A month later, Sam had lost much of the business about the building of the bridge—though, for a while, working in Mr. Harris's basement, he tried and tried to recall it. In September, Lewy sent him another letter, apologizing for not having forwarded the next two installments of *Imprisoned With the Pharaohs*, though he was certain by now it wasn't really by Houdini at all. That same week Sam started night school. Mr. DeCourtenay, his English teacher, went on at such lengths in the first class about how important it was that they expose themselves only to the finest and greatest of what had been written in English literature, Sam was pretty sure Mr. DeCourtenay didn't want them reading anything written in America at all—and certainly not if it had been written since nineteen hundred. But why go to school if—this time—he wasn't going to take it seriously? So he put all ideas of adventure magazines out of his mind—which seemed to be featuring less and less of the Eastern, Egyptian, and Arabian stories he liked, anyway.

Eleven years later in the sixth year of the Depression, a partner in his own floundering Harlem haberdashery, Sam found a book about the construction of the Brooklyn Bridge and, reading it, recalled a surprising amount about it; but, a week after, had forgotten much of it again; and again tried to remember. After eighteen years, when, in his second marriage, he would have his first son, also named Sam, he finally forgot the last fragments of what had happened on the bridge in between—the young man with his ravings, the rower in the boat below.

For a while, though, he *did* remember sitting naked on his bed, cross-legged, late at night, the curtains pulled back, fingering magic tricks in the moonlight, after Hubert had come home from arguing with some friends after classes and Sam had finally asked him about what had happened back home, all those years ago, when Papa got so mad he'd chained Hubert to the water pump. But, by then, of course, he'd confused that first evening with another several months on.

Well before that, however, he forgot the white woman on the train. He forgot the black woman across the alley.

But, as he always remembered the fields at the bridge's Brooklyn end, he always remembered

VII. three brownskinned girls coming down between narrow-set stones, with their yellow coats, black shoes, white socks, a blue feather in the straw hat of the oldest: three inhabitants, delicate as fire, of another city entirely,

though, during the rest of his life, he spoke of them only seven or eight times, all when visiting cities in which he did not live, and only if talking to strangers.

—Amherst / Ann Arbor / New York
November 1992–June 1993

ERIC, GWEN,

AND D.H. LAWRENCE'S

ESTHETIC OF UNRECTIFIED FEELING

"It has never bothered me a bit when people say that what I am doing is not art," Rauschenberg told me. "I don't think of myself as making art. I do what I do because I want to, because painting is the best way I've found to get along with myself."

Well, so much for euphoria.

—Calvin Tomkins, *Post- to Neo-*

I remember standing beside my father's knee, while, in his blue-black suit, he sat at the mahogany kitchen table and taught me to sing, *"Mairzy doats and dozy doats an' little lambsy divey. A kidledy divey too — wouldn't you?"* It came out, when you actually sang it, "Mares eat oats and does eat oats and little lambs eat ivy..."

And at her club meeting, for the assembled women in their hats and long-sleeved winter dresses sitting about our living room, my mother would urge me, with my boy soprano, to Rose Murphy's "I wanna be loved by you, just you and nobody else but you...*Poo-poo-pa-doop!*" till held-in laughter broke out along the green couch and wooden bridge chairs, among the gloves and hat veils.

Was I the same age? From black, twelve-inch 78 rpms, slipped from the brown wrapping-paper envelopes in their colorful book-like album covers (unlike my father's extensive jazz collection, from *Rhapsody in*

Blue unto the real thing: *their* covers were blue or maroon, every one, with white or pink dots), I lay on the living room's rose rug and memorized *Peter and the Wolf* and (on the rag rug before the fireplace up at our country place) *Tubby the Tuba* and (back in New York) a children's opera, *The Emperor's New Clothes*. But all this was driven from current obsession when, in the city one autumn, Mom took me to see a little theater production of Gilbert and Sullivan's *Pirates of Penzance*. An obsessed month later I'd talked Dad into buying me the D'Oyly Carte album with Martin Greene as Major General Stanley (the *first* thirty-three-and-a-third rpm long-playing records we owned); and I'd sing along with the verbal intricacies of the very model of a modern major general's patter.

Years before, from among many on the radio, I'd learned a song. It went:

> Younger than springtime are you.
> Gayer than laughter are you.
> Angel and lover, heaven and earth
> Are you to me...

A year or so after my trip to hear the Gilbert and Sullivan, an afternoon radio program called *Spot the Hits* became popular for a season. New songs aired on it, and a "panel of experts" discussed, with the composer, its chances of making the Hit Parade. While I was playing in the upstairs nursery one day, *Spot the Hits* was on the radio, and, from the three-piece orchestra and studio tenor, a pretty song wafted over the blocks and erector-set pieces spread around me:

> Maid of music are you.
> Maid of starlight are you...

When it was over, several of the experts (in those pre-rock 'n' roll days) allowed as how it was lyrical, engaging, and likely for success.

"But," objected one, as it struck him, "the melody is identical to 'Younger than Springtime'!" He sang the opening lines from first one song, then the other.

It was.

The composer who'd written the tune spluttered that he'd been entirely unaware of the similarity. The program's moderator spluttered; and there was a minute of that awkward confusion which occasionally plagued live radio and, later, live TV. I was convinced then, and still am, that the plagiarism was inadvertent. But despite my conviction, or perhaps because of it, the moment has remained indelible.

And that winter my cousin Betty and her boyfriend Wendell took me to an indoor ice skating rink somewhere in the city. After renting skates, with Wendell and Betty at either elbow, I made fair progress around the rink while the electric calliope played "Buckle Down, Winsockie," to which Wendell sang the lyrics, till finally I could move about the ice on my own.

My father's friends and family often spoke of Dad as someone who could get music from any instrument. Back then I had no idea what it meant to pull even a note from trumpet, clarinet, or transverse flute, each with its different mouthpiece—much less to get tunes from them, each with its different fingering.

But, however haltingly, Dad could play them all.

When I was eight, a few glimpses through the living-room arch at my aunt's home in New Jersey, where my cousin stood before the fireplace with his instrument at his chin, under the wire-framed gaze of his young, balding, black-suited music teacher, grew in me, a year later, to a passion for the violin. (Boyd's teacher was white; and, before my grandmother shooed me away to play upstairs and leave them alone, it was one of the few times in childhood when I was oddly aware that my family and I were not—possibly because Boyd wore, on his brown oval face, the same wire-rimmed glasses as that pale young man.) My mother nursed the passion on. And when it did not go away, I inherited Boyd's old instrument: he had given it up for college and medical school. To ensure that the passion was not a whim, Dad purchased four beginner violin instruction books.

We also got Boyd's music stand.

During breaks between funerals, my father would nip upstairs to give me a lesson. Sometimes he would set me up with stand and book in the evening before the dining room fireplace. By staying a lesson or two ahead, he proceeded to teach me violin — having decided he'd like to master a stringed instrument himself.

My father may have been a natural musician, but he was not a natural teacher. A wholly dogmatic man, he wanted things done his way—now. He had no sense that four-fifths of all meaningful instruction is the attentive silence teacher must proffer student, during which silence, among his or her own fumblings, the student actually learns—a silence in which teacherly attention must all be on which errors *not* to correct. Therefore the tension between us was high. It speaks well for us both that we were still at it three months on: I was still putting in an hour or two a day of practice on my own. In those months my father taught me to read the treble clef and got me more or less comfortable with up to two or three sharps, two or three flats. (Somehow, in the midst of it all, I also learned how to renotate all the music for B-flat cornet, that had been Dad's first instrument.) But these lessons were not pleasant. Then the short-haired woman who wore green felt skirts and taught stringed instruments at my downtown elementary school rescued me.

In the sixth-floor music room Mrs. Wallace gave real violin lessons— a room in which, years before, with colored paper patterns and black and white magnetic dogs, along with questions and answers that a squat, graysuited, white-haired woman with an Irish name (Mrs. Mac-Dougal?) had written down, smiling, on her clipboard, I'd been tested for reading and found lacking. My first hope at beginning the violin had been that I'd take lessons with Mrs. Wallace, like my schoolmate Jonathan, who was a bully, very handsome, called his judge mother and lawyer father by their first names, and never wore underwear — for which fact alone, I think, I tried to become his friend and got so far as to be invited for the weekend with him and his parents to their summer house on an island in Lake Placid, which you reached, across overcast evening waters, by motorboat.

But Dad had intervened.

After two months of Dad's lessons, I'd brought my violin into school and reported for practice with the Middle School orchestra. For the simple pieces we played, I did well enough. But after another month Mr. Ax detected something in my playing…idiosyncratic? Or perhaps I just told him how I was learning. He spoke to Mrs. Wallace, who called my parents in. Both of them—quite unusual—came. I stood outside the open door and overheard Mrs. Wallace explain that there were certain things that could only be taught by an experienced teacher—that, indeed, to follow a book without real instruction could, for an instrument like the violin, do more harm than good.

Since I'd stuck to it as long as I had, it was possible I had real talent.

So real lessons began—just in time, too: my father and I had had a falling out over the interpretation of a single phrase in a song which, between the two of us, we'd been working on by ear. "The Autumn Leaves…" It came over the radio enough times so that we both knew it pretty well. But—

"*No* — *!*" I'd insist, grabbing for the violin, while Dad turned, with the instrument under his chin, out of my reach, as if protecting it with his body from my eager hands. "It doesn't drop down again, there. It stays up, on the same note—the fourth. *Then* it drops down, only *half* a step!"

"Well, isn't that what I'm doing?" he protested, turning back.

"No, you're not—!"

Whatever it was, my father honestly couldn't hear it. And, as an ear musician, what he couldn't hear, he couldn't play—even if you wrote it out.

It led to loud and insistent declamations from him—and tears from me, till my mother looked in from the kitchen. "*What* are the two of you going on about so? It's only a song!"

"Look!" Dad insisted, "I'm going to *show* you you're wrong! I'm going to get the sheet music!"

"Okay," I said. "You'll see!" while I tried not to cry anymore.

The third time he told me he'd been to a music store and couldn't find it, I began to think some kind of shuck was going on. The song was still popular enough on the radio that, now and again, it would lilt into the living room.

"...Don't you hear that, Dad?"

"And I tell you, that's what I'm doing!"

Then one afternoon he announced: "Okay, I found it. It isn't called 'The Autumn Leaves.' The title's 'September Song.' That's why the man at the music store kept telling me he didn't have it in. You'll see now."

We set the sheet music up on Boyd's old music stand in front of the mantel.

I got out the violin. Dad put on his glasses, which he needed to read music, took the instrument from me, and began to play. I looked over his shoulder—

"No!" I shouted, when he reached the passage. "That's not what it says! You didn't play what the notes are—"

"Yes, I did!"

"No, you *didn't!* See—it *does* stay up on the fourth. Like I said. And there—only a half step down..."

"...to E."

"To F. That's an F!"

"Well, yes, but—"

"Here, let me play it."

I did.

And messed up the questionable phrase.

"See, that's just what—"

"But I made a *mistake!* I've been listening to *you* do it wrong so many times, I just did it the way—"

"Now watch your tongue! Don't you get insulting!"

"Let me do it again."

I did.

"And *that's* what the notes say, too!" I dropped the bow from the strings—to take the instrument from my chin. Perspiration left a shiny crescent inside the ebony chin rest.

"Well, then," my father declared, which was pretty much his way in an argument, "the music's just *wrong!* And so are you! Look, I've been trying to tell you all along: I *know* how the damned song goes! *You're* just too pig-headed to listen!"

"But look, the music even says—!"

"Well, I don't *care* what it says!"

"But...!" And, like a mountain climber who has suddenly had the foothold struck from beneath the toe carrying the weight, I tumbled from the heights of logic, reason, and evidence into the pit of steaming tears, which rose about me, to scald my eyes. Putting the violin down on the varnished table twice as dark as it was, I stalked from the dining room.

Angrily Dad called after me: "Come on back here! Don't you walk out on me like that! You've got your practicing to do!" Then, in a moment of total frustration, he added: "You are one hard-headed nigger, is what *you* are!"

"Sam!" my mother called, outraged, from the kitchen: but it was both my father's name and mine.

Dad shouted after me, in what—today—I suspect was an emotional plea rising wholly outside the realms of reason: "Can't you ever admit you're wrong about *anything?*"

What I heard, though, as I stood in the hall, quivering by the entrance to the walk-in closet (in which, at Christmas, I could never find the presents that must be hidden behind the winter coats or somewhere on the upper shelves with the eight-millimeter movie camera and the stenotype machine—from the unimaginable time before my birth when Mom had been a stenographer—and the piled-up hat boxes) was the absolute and obscene, to me, contradiction with all reason, so that when tears and words broke out together—*"Why can't you!"*—I'm surprised that, back in the dining room, he even understood what I'd said.

He shouted: "Don't you talk to me like that—!"

131

Maybe it was because we'd shouted it so many times before.

But that's what Mrs. Wallace's lessons rescued me from—rescued us both from, really.

At school, in the small sixth-floor room at the end of the hallway, with its green walls and its tan shade lowered over the wire window guards, Mrs. Wallace, sweater mottled with the sun outside, ambled about the little space, attending to my scales, tunes, and, finally, at our twin stands, my duets with her. With her own violin against her hip, her estimate of what my father had been able to do with me ranged from the professional musician's disdain for all things amateur to real surprise at what he'd accomplished. On the one hand, I was already comfortable with the circle of fourths (for the flatted keys) and the circle of fifths (for the sharped ones) that she did not usually give to students until they were much more advanced than three months. On the other, that most important arch of the left hand, as it supports the violin neck, that allows the string player to turn strength into speed when moving among the higher finger positions, was something neither Dad nor I had ever paid much attention to.

"The violin," Mrs. Wallace would explain, her face near mine, forcing back my hand beneath the slim neck's shaft (she was almost without chin), "is not a dagger that you clutch. Nor are you trying to cut your throat with it. Here. Pretend there's a hard rubber ball in your hand, between your palm and the instrument. Don't ever let your hand close through that ball. Come on, now. You're a violinist. *You're* holding it like a country fiddler!"

And sometimes, when I would make a mistake, she'd say with the faintest smile: "Did your father teach you that, too?" which, as he was no longer there to badger me, I was now free to resent, however silently: without him, of course, I wouldn't have been there at all.

My father was also a fairly good artist. When, as a four- and five-year-old, I would come to some adult and ask, "Draw me a bird...? Draw me a lady...?" Dad would take the paper, and the figures he'd sketch would have form, dimensionality, even personality. Once he showed me, for a cat I'd requested, the basic geometric forms I could build it from, that later might guide the modelling of more detailed features.

Dad never tried to teach me to draw. Had he, I'm sure we would have had the same conflict as we did over music. But, in 1951, we acquired our first television set—a huge console Zenith that also contained a record player and a radio. Once I'd finished watching *Pat Michaels and the Magic Cottage, Kukla, Fran, and Ollie, Howdy Doody, Buzz Corey and the Space Patrol, Tom Corbett — Space Cadet, Captain Video*, and *Bobby Benson and the B-Bar-B Riders*, the Saturday morning show I always caught on the black and white screen was *Draw with Me*, a Basic Art Course led by "internationally known artist John Nagy." The day I first tuned in, in the middle of the program, right up there on the screen were Dad's basic forms—John Nagy might have even been, that show, drawing a cat.

Nagy was the perfect television artist: he wore plaid shirts, dress slacks—never jeans. Often he made his entrance smoking a pipe. Sometimes he even rolled up his sleeves. He had a beard—a small, neat one. Everything about him was redolent of autumns on Provincetown beaches. He had an oboe of a voice, and his bearing was that of your most sympathetic summer camp counselor. The show was aimed wholly at making pictures that *looked* like something. Weekly he went over those principles that have organized Western figurative drawing and painting since the Renaissance: vanishing points, horizon lines, one- and two-point perspective. ("For objects sitting on the ground or parallel with it, the vanishing point—or points—are *on* the horizon, which is always at about eye level, even if it's behind a hill or a house. Always sketch it in, however lightly. And even if you don't, always be aware of *where* the horizon line is in your picture…" What a revelation for the nine-year-old sketcher of city streets and Central Park paths!) The program's teaching plan was wholly imitative. Nagy had his sketch pad, his pencil, his eraser, and—mysteriously and most importantly—his paper stomp. (Could anyone draw anything without a paper stomp? Apparently Nagy didn't think so.) You had *your* sketch pad, pencil, eraser— and used your fingertip for the stomped-in shading (then got prints all over the rest of the page). Nagy would draw a line or a shape; you would draw that line or that shape. ("If it doesn't look exactly like mine, don't worry. Just relax and do the best you can. You'll still be surprised at the results.") And at half an hour's end, both Nagy and you would have a basket of flowers on a table, a boat hulk beached against a grassy dune (like I said, P-town), a dog sitting before a fireplace, or a small house at the end of a path among the trees and hills.

Two or three times, Nagy actually had a young woman sit and model for him, while he, I, and how-many-thousand-more New Yorkers spent Saturday morning "trying for a likeness." There was much analysis of the young woman's head into those eternal basic forms; and he would point out how the rectangular solid that made up the lower part of *her* jaw was much longer than the one that made up the lower part of his.

By program's end, we both had faces on our sketch pads. But neither was much of a likeness. "Well," Nagy mused on the screen, regarding his sketch, clearly with dissatisfaction, "to get a likeness in a half an hour —with ten minutes out for commercials— *is* difficult." (His show, too, was live.) "If you want to do this kind of thing, figure on spending an hour, an hour-and-a-half at it. Maybe even longer, at least when you start."

Another revelation!

Now, beginning artists throughout the city had an idea of the *duration* of the task we'd undertaken—and an example from the internationally known Nagy himself of what would happen if you rushed it.

After the show, my younger sister and I would chase each other up and down the stairs, from the second to the third floor, bawling at one another, "*Salagodoola! Menchicka Boola Bibbidi-Bobbidi-Boo — !* " unaware that the song's writer was the same Walt Disney staff musician who, twenty years before, had written "Mairzy Doats."

Our art program at school was, however, entirely different. The move from Third Grade to Fourth Grade — from the heights of the Lower School to the bottom rung of the Middle School—was, at least for me, primarily the move from art classes with Miss Dorothy Andrews, a tall, black-haired woman with a bun, who wore dark turtlenecks and long gray jumpers, but with a wholly open and experimental policy as far as the art room was concerned (whose limits I only strained once when, in my earliest years, I took off my shoes and socks and painted both my feet blue: it was reported to my parents), to art classes with Gwendolin Davies, an irrepressible woman with an English accent, bright red hair, cool-colored sweaters, and frequently some enormous piece of free-form aluminum jewelry. Older students had storied her eccentricities to us by then, so that on our first day in the new art room we were all expectant.

"No, no!" Gwenny said (we already knew we were to call her that), as some of us made tentative moves toward the paper piled on the shelves and the paint cans on the counter — as would have been proper the year before, upstairs with Miss Andrews. "We're going to talk a bit, first. Find a seat, now. That's right, you can sit over there. Up on the counter with you. And you lot can sit over there under the window — that's right. No talking now; we're big Middle Schoolers and quite grown up, all of us — aren't we? So let's have some attention here!"

Here, apparently, not only were we going to *make* art; we were going to *discuss* it.

Once the dozen of us were seated and silent, Gwenny clapped her hands together with the sober-eyed satisfaction of someone who had just created a masterpiece. "Now —" (We were perched around the room, some on the shelf running under the window, some on the waist-high table with cabinets beneath, down the room's center.) "I have a question for you. What is a picture *made* of?"

On shelves to the side were rows of clay and wire sculptures, piles of finished watercolors.

"Has the cat got your tongue?" she demanded of one of us. "It must. You're not saying anything. Now, tell me. What goes into a picture?"

The gravity with which she put the question made it clear that she did not want an answer such as *dogs, cats,* or *flowers.* From my seat under the ridged wire window guard, I raised my hand.

"Yes...?"

I ventured: "The horizon line—?"

"Absolutely *not!*"

The crisp denial startled me. However tentatively I'd given my answer, I'd expected praise.

But Gwenny went on. "Horizon lines, one- and two-point perspective, incident light, reflected light, isometric projections — that sort of thing: that's precisely what we are *not* interested in, in *this* class!" She glared at me. "And I never want to hear you mention them in here *again!*" Then, incongruously, she smiled: "All right?"

Bewildered, I nodded.

"Good!"

Today I wonder whether Gwenny had ever caught Nagy's Saturday morning show, to loathe it for the anti-art experience it was.

At the time, though, I was only awed by her knowledge: Nagy had never mentioned anything so complex as "isometric projections." "Incident light...?" What, I wondered, could they possibly be; and why were they not for us?

"Now." She turned to the rest of the room. "Can somebody do a little better than that? What goes into a picture? Someone else. Tell me... What? *No* idea? Well, it's not an easy question. But, here—I've got a piece of paper, all tacked up. And I'm going to make a picture." She picked up a crayon and rapidly drew an informal amoeboid line that came back to close on itself. "What's that?"

Was it Debbie, with her pale blond hair, who volunteered from where she sat cross-legged on the central counter: "It's...just a kind of... shape?"

"Very *good!*" Gwenny whirled about to practically incandesce! "*What* was that word again?"

But Debbie was as nonplussed by her success as I'd been by my failure.

"You had it right!" Gwenny declared. "Just say the word once more!"

But it was someone else who finally offered: "...shape?"

"Correct!" Gwenny turned back to the paper. "And here's another one!" She drew a circle. "And another!" She drew a triangle. "And another!" The outline this time, drawn with a sureness that shamed Nagy, was of a child: we laughed. "And another!" This one was of such an intricate complexity, with so many inroads and curlicues, peaks, dells, and harbors, it made both child and amoeba look circle-simple. "And another!" Another circle, but with two points near the top. Adding a few whisker strokes and some eye dots, Gwenny turned it into a lopsided cat's face. We laughed again. "Shapes. Lots of different shapes, all there in my picture." She stepped back from the paper tacked to the painted wall board—galaxies of tack holes across its gray enamel. "So—*what* is one thing that goes into a picture?"

We smiled, but we were still—at least I was—confused.

"After all this," Gwenny said, "you must have figured it out. I've told you ten times, now."

So, very tentatively, someone said: "Shapes..."

"Absolutely!" She closed her eyes and breathed in as though she were scenting a fire—that suddenly turned to roses. She opened her eyes again. "It's *very* hard to make a picture that doesn't have *any* shapes in it at all. So, let's all say it together. What is one of the things that makes a picture?"

This time, we cried out, emboldened by unison: "Shapes!"

"Well, then, you're *not* just a bunch of little wooden noggins after all! *I* was beginning to wonder." It wasn't like a Nagy lesson at all. We were grinning now. "At least one of the things that makes up a picture is...shape." She turned back to thumbtack up another yard-wide piece of drawing paper over the first. "But what *else* goes into a picture?"

We were silenced again. I couldn't think of anything else of the same basic import.

Suddenly Gwenny raised her crayon and put a diagonal slash across the off-white sheet. "What's that?"

Wanting to redeem my previous failure, I raised my hand.

"Yes...?"

"That divides the picture up into *two* shapes," I said with analytic certainty.

"Oh, I can tell," she said. "You're going to be a scientist. But you're in an art class now." She looked at me sternly. "You see, what I want to know is: what is it that *does* the dividing?" And she was looking around for another hand.

I'd failed again.

But nobody else answered either.

"Well," she said, making another slash across the paper, "what's that?" She made still another—only this one was a wavery curve. "And that." It was kind of a squiggle. "And that." The next was a longer, softer curve.

Someone had apparently gotten the idea and called out: "Lines!"

Gwenny loped across the room, grabbed the very startled boy by both cheeks. (For an instant I thought she was about to strike him for some unimaginable infraction!) She kissed his forehead loudly. "*Yes,* my little strawberry-custard confection! *Lines!*" She stepped back to clasp her hands again. "That's *exactly* what they are!" For a moment, the rest of us were as startled as he. Then, once more, we laughed. But Gwenny had our attention, and as soon as she spoke again we fell into (anxious) quiet. "So, we have *two* things now that go to make up a picture: *shapes* and *lines.* But there *must* be something else." She furrowed her face, began to pull at her chin. Walking slowly by the low counter where the gallon cans of watercolors stood on their ledge, circled with stalactites of lazuli and alizarin, she gazed into them. "I wonder...what...it... could...*be?*"

The stripped-down quality of her esthetic had registered. (I had my own suspicion as to the answer, but I'd failed twice and wasn't going to be caught out a third time.) Someone called out: "Paint!"

"Paint?" Gwenny pondered the paint pots. "But what do we put the paint on a picture *for?* What do we use the paint to achieve?"

Why I blurted it through my initial hesitations I don't know: "*Color...!*"

Gwenny looked up at me, scarlet-nailed hand splayed across her mouth in glaring astonishment. Then the hand swung out toward me, over the class's heads, and the gesture became a grandly blown kiss, as flamboyant as any by fat, black Rose Murphy. *"Color...!* Yes, color! I kiss you too, my little mocha eclair!" (In my seat under the window I went tumbling down into the pools of hopeless devotion to this brazen-voiced redhead.) *"How* could we have pictures without colors! So—" she addressed the whole class once more—"we have *three* things that make up a picture. What are they, now—?"

Shape, line, and color...

"What are they, again?"

Shape, line, and color!

"Once more..."

Shape, line, and color!

What I knew was that we were chanting and having great fun doing it. What I didn't know was that we were inscribing the tenets of a formalist esthetic on the pedestal of our souls.

In the essay from which I've taken my epigraph, Calvin Tomkins locates the same three terms in the same order to describe the esthetic of minimalism — that austere outgrowth of abstract expressionism that came to the fore in the late sixties, once the first furor over pop art had died down. But it was back in September of 1951 that these three terms rang out in the art room on the sixth floor at 89th Street—as they had rung for a handful of Septembers already.

"But there's still one problem," Gwenny returned to the tacked-up paper. "How do we put the shapes, lines, and colors *together* in our pictures?"

"With a brush!" someone volunteered, brightly.

"With a brush!" Gwenny declared, darkly.

Then she repeated, "With a brush..."

Now she made a sour face: "With a *brush...*"

Breathlessly we waited to see what these accents meant.

It was disdain, but what sort none of us knew.

"With a brush...?" Gwenny shook her head. "Oh, you're just too clever by half!" Again she took up the crayon. "Pay attention now. Because this isn't easy. I'm going to put a shape in my picture. But do I put it up here, like this—?" She drew another amoeboid, but it began in the corner, and in a moment she was drawing off the paper and on the wall itself.

"No!" we chorused.

"Well, why not?"

Someone called: "Because it goes off the paper!"

"Yes," Gwenny admitted. "But I want you to say that in another way."

So we tried for a while. Pretty soon we came up with, "It goes over the edge."

"And *what* edge is that?" Gwenny prompted.

A minute later, we'd ascertained that it was the *outside* edge of the picture that was her perimeter of concern.

"So, once more. What is it that makes up a picture?" *Shape, line, and color!* (We knew we were to chant it with her and came in on cue.) "And how do we arrange them, in order to make it a picture?" (By now we knew the second part of it too.) "In relationship to the outside edge! That's wonderful. Now, go, loves, and spend the rest of the period making just the most *beautiful* paintings in the world!"

We broke from our seats for the paints and papers around us that, for the last ten minutes of Gwenny's lesson, I, for one, had been itching for.

I was a little surprised just how single-minded Gwenny was about her formalism. While I was looking at my own edge, looking at my paints, and arranging blue, green, and brown expressionist blobs as carefully as I could, Debbie came up to her and asked for help in painting a…cat. As I overheard and watched from my eye's corner (while I worked on my own abstraction), I wondered if cats were not as forbidden here as horizon lines. But before the paper spread out on the counter next to mine, Gwenny stood beside Debbie's shoulder and said, "Now, you've got your color. You've got your paper. You want to paint a cat. But basically, you're going to put a *shape* on your paper—if it's a cat shape, that's certainly all right with me. But run your eyes all around the outside edge—go ahead, do it, look at it. Now think about the shape you're going to put there. Is it going to be a little tiny shape like this…?"

Gwen balled up her knuckle and put it down in one corner of the paper.

"No...!" Debbie laughed.

"Is it going to be a great big shape like this...?" With both hands Gwenny outlined a form even bigger than the paper.

"No!" Debbie protested; she was really a very serious girl. "I won't get it all in!"

"Well, you just look at that outside edge, think about your cat shape. Then you put it down."

Debbie bit her lip—and looked up, down, sideways. A moment later, she turned her paper around ninety degrees, so that it was the long way, and began to paint a large green tabby.

Soon I learned, though, that despite her formalism, Gwenny would acknowledge talent even when it came in late-romantic terms. I did the required abstract pictures and got a fair amount of praise for them. But a year later, without prelude, I turned to a figurative subject: my own, I thought. But the technique was pure Nagy, supplemented by what I'd learned of color modeling from a thick book that sat on my cousin Boyd's desk in his refinished attic bedroom out in New Jersey. *Illustration*, by Andrew Loomis, was full of color charts and composition diagrams. It was *called Illustration*, but what Loomis really wanted to teach his readers was how to paint pin-up girls and athletes, neither of which, as picture topics, particularly excited me. Still, it was only a step away from the comic book art of Frazetta, Williamson, Krenkel, and Wood that *was* my first, visual love. So, in one corner of the busy art room, with just a little sketching that only one student noticed, I began a picture of a mighty-muscled potentate, seated on his throne, turned three-quarters face—which Loomis had explained was far more dramatic than a full front or full profile—chin on his fist and looking stern. His robes trailed the throne steps. Rising columns and smoking braziers loomed in the foreground.

"What are you drawing it first for?"

"Nothing." But I was sketching it first because that's what Loomis *said* you should do (emphasizing that you not put in much detail, but only basic forms), though I was sure Gwenny, who by now had also told us about "love of the materials," wouldn't have countenanced it.

The setting had come from one of Mr. Loomis's harem scenes, odalisques banished and replaced by a hulking body builder I'd glimpsed inside a newsstand muscle magazine, where, somehow, the focus on the gleaming shoulders and shadowed belly had been sharp enough for me to notice on the great blocky fist that the lowering Hercules bit his nails. From my terror of homoerotic sexual discovery, in this school version I'd clothed him a bit better. But the background was Loomis's arches, windows, and steps, only with his bevy of busty, gauzily-veiled maidens removed. The foreground columns and braziers were Loomis's as well. (Probably he'd swiped both from Parish or Alma Tedema.) Emptied of Loomis's sexual symbols (and replaced, yes, with my own), the picture was one I'd tried in my sketchbook half a dozen times over spring vacation back in Jersey. But now, in the sixth-floor art room, as I painted at my wholly borrowed amalgam of visual clichés, not only did the students crowd around, but finally Gwenny pushed up to see what I was doing and pronounced with some surprise: "That's really very beautiful!"

From then on I was treated as someone talented at art. But I had been as prepared for her to be as dismissive of the whole counterfeit pastiche as she had once been of the horizon lines, the vanishing points, and the basic forms that, now hidden behind layers of gouache, had made that pastiche draftable.

Our science teacher was also an artist. Some years before, he'd married the woman who had been my teacher in the five-year-olds, magically changing her name (I never quite understood how) from Rubins to Robus.

If both last names had not been initial-R trochees, I probably would have understood the process. But for me, it was a transformation, rather than a replacement, and thus remained mysterious.

Hugo, as we called Mr. Robus, had a sculpture — *Woman Washing Her Hair* — in the permanent collection of the Museum of Modern Art. I had pleaded to have him as my homeroom teacher ("to be put into his

House," in the school's idiosyncratic jargon), and, with my friend Robert, I *had* been. In a way, Gwenny was too much a total surround for me to think of her as a favorite teacher—though she was certainly my most influential. But the title of favorite went to Hugo. He didn't look in the least like John Nagy. He was clean shaven. When he taught, he always wore a white shirt and, usually, a tie. If the lab, with its wooden tables, glass-cased cupboards, and chrome gas jets, was warm, sometimes he left his sports jacket off. Whenever I came physically near him, I always thought of (but never once mentioned) *Woman Washing Her Hair*. Yet the little electric lights, the single-pole/double-throw switches, and the voltmeters and ampmeters Hugo taught us to wire up, the Lyden jars and Bunsen burners he taught us to operate, the test tubes, retorts, and pipettes he showed us how to fill and empty to precise measure, were all he ever spoke of. For me he was a scientist, and when I was around him, that's what I wanted to be, too.

Oh, maybe, like Hugo, I'd have something in a museum somewhere, or a novel that you could buy in a bookstore, or a concerto that, while I was working with a hydrogen bubble chamber in an atomic lab someplace, was, even that same evening, being performed by a major symphony orchestra.

But science was my center.

Robert was among my best school friends—often my *very* best. Blond and round faced (yes, the strawberry custard confection), *he* was an inveterate nail biter and a general oddball. He tended to become splutteringly overexcited about things, and in many ways he was an immature and, often, an awkward boy. An early motor difficulty, which had caused him to clutch his pencil or pen in both hands when he wrote or to steady one hand with the other when he pointed at something, had settled into a slight clumsiness, most of the time unnoticeable. And he was as goodhearted a friend as you could want. *Freddy the Pig* books had been our early shared enthusiasm. Now it was Heinlein's science fiction juveniles and amateur electronics. Our friendship dated from our first weeks together in the five-year-olds, when, on the first day of school,

Robert had been the object of some truly vicious teasing. Sometimes I would pull away from him, but when I had been betrayed by Jeff or bullied by Jonathan (and Robert's and my friendship had survived its own betrayals), Robert was whom I came back to.

In Robert's penthouse apartment, just a block down from the school, a year before we got our own, I saw my first television set. The show we watched that evening was Burr Tillstrom's *Kukla, Fran and Ollie.*

Then, a few months later, we were *on* television—together!

It was a cowboy show, where three or four children sat around on a corral fence, while, for five minutes at the beginning and five minutes at the end of the program, the chapped and Stetsoned star talked about the ancient Republic Pictures serial that filled the bulk of the airtime. Robert's mother had arranged it and was to take the two of us to the studio. Robert wore jeans and sneakers, as we always did at school. But in light of my public appearance, Mom had sent me in that day in a suit and tie. As we didn't have a TV yet, she didn't know what the other kids on the show usually wore—and certainly wasn't about to let me tell her: "But Mom, it's a *cowboy* show—"

"Just because it's a cowboy show doesn't mean you can't look nice. You put on your tie, now!"

At the studio, the director's assistant, a young woman in a purple blouse, slacks (not that common on women in the '50s), and glasses, frowned at me, then told me to take off my suit jacket, in order to "dress me down." Then someone said I'd have to put it back on, since my white shirt, even *with* the jacket covering most of it, would glare. (More than anything else, TV was responsible, during the '50s, for the ascendancy of the Oxford blue shirt.) They asked me to take my tie off. I did; and decided they were really nice people. Then they opened my shirt collar as wide as they could under my tightly buttoned-up suit coat— and gave me a ten-gallon hat to make me look "more informal."

Several times my mother had taken me to see radio programs. Although I'd been disappointed that the shows were not really acted, but simply read out from sheaves of flimsy paper by ordinary men and women standing around on an empty stage, one had been in a full-sized theater with balconies and the other in a hangar-like space that had seated at least three hundred. But this was a one-camera show, done live, in a studio only a hair's breadth bigger than our bathroom at home. In his soiled white shirt, the cameraman chain smoked (like my father), and when I asked, "Won't his cigarette smoke get in front of the lens and make it cloudy?" the assistant laughed and said, "If his cigarette bothers you, I'll ask him to put it out. He's not supposed to be smoking in here, anyway."

"No!" I said, abashed at not being taken seriously. "It doesn't *bother* me! I was just wondering about the camera, that's all!"

But my greatest, silent astonishment there was that the desert background which, on Robert's television only the night before, had stretched infinitely far behind the length of corral fence, with a couple of cactuses standing among distant dunes and sagebrush, was only painted cloth, a foot higher than the star's head, and with a sag along the top! The whole desert (not to mention the prop fence before it) was not as wide as Robert and I laid together, toe to head!

But the very bright lights were already on.

Already we were more or less positioned.

My next surprise was one that has surprised me all over, every time I've been on a talk show or guest interview since: the unruptured continuity from non-air time to air time.

We four kids had been on monitor for fifteen minutes now and had gotten used to it. (Or would never get used to it: the other boy, who'd come with his father, kept staring back and forth from the TV screen in the studio corner to the camera in the middle of the room, unable to understand why, when he turned to look at himself, his image on the screen looked away, so that he could never get his screen self to look directly at his own face.) Standing beside the camera, wearing earphones and a green, open-necked shirt, dark as the sea, the director gave all his attention to his clipboard.

Only the red light coming on above the camera lens told us that the studio had changed from a cramped cell with flaking gray paint on the walls and a very shiny clock with a red second-hand jerking about it above the door, to a dream presentation vaster than Arizona and replicated unto gray thousands. It was a transition wholly without emotional weight, thoroughly technological, hidden within some nacelle of wires and timed to a clock in another room we couldn't see.

In the same voice with which he'd been asking us if we were comfortable, was I secure on the rail there, if the party dress of the girl who sat beside me was caught under her leg ("No sir! It's fine!"), the star in his chaps and cowboy hat said, as though he were continuing to talk to us or to people like us who, for some reason, weren't quite there: "Well, boys and girls, it's good to see you all back again. This evening, as our guests, we have Billy and Suzy and Bobby and Sammy..."

I'd never heard anyone call Robert "Bobby" before. And I loathed the name "Sammy." Yet, before the metallic lights like white-hot holes in the walls, in almost no time he was saying (in the same voice in which he'd been addressing uncountable ghost children), "All right, that's all there is to it. For now, anyway. Or at least for the next fifteen minutes."

The red light was off.

The dream was on hold—or had switched beyond us to another of its infinitely malleable, endlessly linkable segments.

"You can get down. Just don't go too far, so we can all get back together for the closing part of the show."

Suzy (if she was any more "Suzy" than I was "Sammy" or Robert was "Bobby") climbed down from the fence. I got down too. Billy was still staring from camera to monitor. Robert just jumped. "Can we go watch the movie now?"

"Aw...!" The star leaned back and folded his large, clean hands before his silver buckle, as though this were the single sadness in his generally joyful job. "I'm sorry! But that's done from an entirely different building, way over on the other side of town. And we aren't hooked up to that cable. But we'll be back on the air in just a while..."

I took off my ten gallon hat and looked for the director's assistant to give it to. She was at my elbow a moment later. "Don't you want to keep that," she said as I turned to her, "till the show's over?"

Though my family did not yet have a TV, the Hunts, who lived in a cramped apartment on the second floor in the building next door to our private house, did. (Their daughter, Laura, a girl six months older than I, was supposed to be "engaged" to me, so ran the joke among the other black children along the Harlem block.) Dad and Mom and my sister were all going over there to watch.

Robert's mother stopped in with us at a coffee shop after the show and we got hamburgers. So we didn't get back to my house till about seven.

"What in the world happened to your *tie?*" Mom demanded when I walked in.

"I've got it on...?" I looked down at myself in conscientious bewilderment. (How carefully I'd knotted it again before the mirror above the sink in the studio's blue phonebooth of a bathroom.)

"But you didn't have it on the show!"

And I was surprised all over: I actually *had* been on television! Thousands of people really *had* seen me!

"They made me take it off," I said, wondering now if it wasn't really me who'd made the suggestion. What was it they'd said about the glare from my shirt? Maybe I'd just looked silly in a suit and an open collar... But Mom seemed to think it was more funny than not. And when Dad came upstairs from the ground-floor funeral parlor, *he* didn't say anything — maybe he hadn't actually gone over to the Hunts' and seen me...?

A year or so later Robert provided me with the most sexually exciting few hours of my childhood.

I had met Robert's father a few times. A physically vast, gray-haired man, the elderly and successful Scotsman was notably senior to his German-American wife. Then, one year, just before school started, my mother put down the phone to tell me: "Aunt Kay just told me that Robert's father died this summer! That's so sad for his mother. And the boy, too. He's had such a rough time." She meant Robert's motor problems that had, by now, all but vanished and whose faintest lingerings I never noticed anymore.

When I saw Robert again in school, I was a little scared for the first minutes, wondering if his having a dead father would make him any different. But he looked just the same as before. And soon—almost—I'd forgotten it.

That spring vacation, for the first time, Robert invited me to come up to *his* summer house. (April's cruelties, as Chaucer knew, have a certain thread of generosity woven through them.) His family had a farm outside New Paltz, and his mother—who'd gone back to work as a nurse in a hospital—would drive us up there.

Our own family's summer place in Hopewell Junction was a small affair. But it was *sort* of a farm—at least for several years my father had grown a field of corn behind it. We had a dozen acres of woods. And one summer Dad had raised a matte-black coop of chickens and, another, stilted up five feet from the guano-splatted ground and walled with octagonal wire, a house full of turkeys.

But what Robert's mother (us in the back seat of the station wagon) finally pulled up to was, after our two-hour drive, a sprawling three-story farmhouse, with an even more sizable barn set off from it. There were several fields, a forest, a sloping lawn, and even a pond on the property. There were a number of cows, some ducks, and a rambunctious dog, who lolloped out of the barn to leap on and lick all over us as we got out of the car. His name was King, after the dog on the *Sargeant Preston of the Yukon* radio show, Robert explained. Robert and I both listened to it each week at home (a booming, slightly anglicized baritone, which meant Canada in the 1950s: "On, King! *On*, you huskies…!"), along with *Superman, The Green Hornet*, and *The Lone Ranger* — television was still, at that time, an expensive novelty more than anything else.

How the farm was managed when Robert and his mother weren't there, I don't recall. But the system of live-in hands and visiting caretakers was explained to me satisfactorily enough at the time.

That first afternoon, Robert's mother had to drive into town. A little later, the hand who was about had to go off in his own car. Being left alone fit in perfectly with a plan I'd had in mind for some time now.

Though Robert was my friend, he was not a part of the pre-adolescent afternoon sexual carryings-on I engaged in in the showers of our school basement after swimming. That circle of initiates included Raymond, Wally, Vladdy, and—sometimes—Jonathan. There was another tall boy in our class, Arthur, another bully, who knew *something* was happening and, when Jonathan wasn't there to tell him to get lost, would occasionally barge naked into our gray marble changing booth and threaten to tell: the menace from Arthur far outweighed any threat from the Phys. Ed. teacher or his assistant—who simply wanted to stay as far as possible from the wet, naked, screaming, towel-snapping Sixth and Seventh Graders.

But I couldn't see why Robert wouldn't like it as much as the rest of us. Awkward as he was, though, I decided it would probably be better if I broke him in myself *before* I brought him to the others. These sexual explorations were carried on almost wholly without words—only partially because of Arthur. So you had to know what to do, or at least be able to figure it out without making noise.

When, once, Arthur finally did confront our regular Phys. Ed. teacher with an accusation, the t-shirted man put his hands on his hips, looked at the tall, belligerent boy, and, with a contemptuous jerk of his head, asked, "How come *you're* so interested in stuff like that? Nobody likes squealers—about anything. But *you* keep on talking about *this* kind of stuff, somebody's going to start wondering why *you're* so curious and concerned about it all…" which left the boy surprised, silent, and probably confused.

But the rest of us were miraculously off the hook.

Today I suspect this was just our gym teacher's (wholly homophobic) way of dealing with a situation he'd probably encountered many times in ten or fifteen years of teaching athletics.

But more recently, a male history teacher had been temporarily assigned to supervise the afternoon swim activities, and, wandering through the labyrinth of marble-walled shower and changing stalls, he must have overheard something, so waited outside ours for a good five or ten minutes, listening. Finally, still in his bathing suit, he stepped around, where three of the five of us had completely abandoned ours, and announced nervously: "What you're doing is sick!" He was a tall, sunken-chested man, who never looked very happy. "You know, that's very sick, now. I should report this. You just don't understand how dangerous what you're doing is. This is much more serious than you think— you don't understand it. What you're doing is *very* sick…!"

We froze in naked guilt. Then Wally, the most aggressive of us, suddenly declared, mockingly: "Well, I think *you're* sick!" Then he let an ululating hoot, that ended in a kind of grunting, idiot laugh. Was he returning the intimidation to the teacher the way our gym coach had done with Arthur? Wally was the class clown anyway and, probably from nervousness, had simply blurted the most outrageous thing he could think of. Still, maybe he had *some* notion that moving our actions from the simply sinful into the truly insane — certainly the effect his words, wail and cackle had on me — might, somehow, save us. The history teacher blinked, said nothing, then—suddenly—walked away. And for the next anxious week, I wondered if we were to be punished. But in the end there was no more fall-out from his discovery than from Arthur's. And so, after a hiatus of three or four days, we resumed.

But this was why you had to be on your toes to join in. And had to be quiet. On your toes was *not* the place Robert ordinarily stood—unless he had some coaching. But he was a smart kid and learned quickly. This country visit, now we were alone on the farm, seemed as good a time as any for me to start him out.

Our shoes and socks off, we were wandering around the grass. We'd been told we weren't supposed to go into the livestock part of the barn barefoot. So we didn't. But I started horsing around with Robert. Wrestling together on the hem of a haystack, I made a couple of grabs for his crotch. Once I got my hand down his baggy corduroys and made tickling motions between his legs.

"Don't *do* that!" Robert protested.

"I'm not going to hurt you," I said. "That doesn't feel good?" I grinned.

He frowned. "It doesn't feel anything," he said. "It's just *silly.*"

So much for my attempt, positioned (as are pretty much all early acts of desire, however clumsy) so ambiguously between the selfish and the compassionate, to introduce Robert to our puerile pleasures. But he was not very physically developed anyway. That seemed to be the end of it. So I didn't try again.

Now we threw sticks for lolloping, golden King. And got tired of it.

Then Robert brought me over to show me his ducks. With King nosing up at his elbow, Robert leaned over the half door in the barn's side, pointing around in the indoor duck pen. He told me that the fat, white, waddling birds had been given him that summer. During their stays on the farm, they were his responsibility. When they were sold, in a few months, Robert was going to get a third of the money. They had to be kept very calm and quiet, he explained, or they'd get all tough, and you wouldn't be able to eat them.

At some point, we decided to let the ducks go for a (calm and quiet) swim in the pond down the slope. But to do it, we'd have to tie up inquisitive King—otherwise, Robert explained, he'd kill them.

Between us, we decided to hold the dog, let out the ducks, then put King in the duck pen and leave him there while the ducks enjoyed the water. I held onto King's collar, while Robert opened the lower half of the door—King nearly yanked me over.

Ducks flapped, fled, and quacked.

"They're not supposed to *do* that!" Robert cried. But once they'd scurried off a few feet, the birds turned placidly toward the pond and started over the grass, while Robert and I got King into the pen and closed the bottom half of the door.

The ducks seemed to know exactly where the pond was, and went ambling, amiably and loudly, toward it.

Robert had locked the bottom half of the Dutch door; but he'd only pulled the top half closed. It must have swung in a crack. King nosed it open—at a bark I turned to see brown and gold rise up, arch over, and out! With another bark, there were dog and ducks all over the grass.

Robert cried, "Oh, Jesus *Christ* — !"

We ran after them. I wasn't too sure how you were supposed to pick up a terrified duck, and didn't want to learn by trial and error. I hadn't had much experience with barefoot running, and did it gingerly in the cool grass. Friendly enough before, King was practically as big as we were and didn't *want* to be stopped!

Nearly in hysterics, skidding after one of his frightened charges, Robert slipped in the grass, then clambered to his feet, yelling, "No…! No…!" He tried to chase the dog away from the honking ducks, grabbing one of the earthbound birds. "No…! They're not *supposed* to run…! They'll be all ruined…! *No…!*"

I ran around as much as I could, wishing that Robert wasn't so upset and that we could treat it more like a game. Once, when he finally got hold of one, I ran over to see. The yellow web raked repeatedly at Robert's belly (duck's feet have claws, too), where his blue t-shirt had ridden up from his pants. Once, behind its beak, a dark red eye turned to sweep mine, not seeing me or Robert (my sudden panic insight) as any less menacing than King—who leapt and leapt, trying to bite the bird, while Robert turned away to protect it with his body from King's eager jaws. Near them, for one moment I saw, among the snowy feathers, cushioned around Robert's scratched-up hands, a single and, in the midst of the hysteria, scary smear of duck blood.

"Get him away…! Get him *away!* Bad King! *Bad* dog! Get him away…!"

So I chased King back—

—who careered off, down to the pond, where two ducks had already reached the water. King went splashing right in, throwing up a steel-bright sheet that angled above the grass and fell as spray.

Running down, I stopped at the lake's edge. Robert went splatting in, fell, coughing and crying, got to his feet, and leapt on King, while pushing a flapping white bird away over the water.

Once I saw it wasn't deep, I waded in after them and helped Robert haul King back to the grass.

The ducks clustered, honking, at the pond's far side.

Holding onto the wet dog collar with Robert, while sopping King pulled against us, I realized—as I tugged, shoulder to shoulder with him —how upset Robert was. *"Bad* King...!" He hiccuped and cried, even as we got the dog up on the bank. We had to haul King back to the barn. "You *damned* dog — !" Once Robert kicked at the beast with his naked foot. King tried to dash away again.

"Come *on,* Robert...!"

Then King decided to shake himself.

Robert let go and started crying again.

But under the splatter I pursed my lips, turned away my face, tightened my hold and, knuckles deep in wet fur, with the smell of dripping dog all around me, pulled King forward again.

As he clipped the dog onto the leash that he'd tied to one of the barn posts, Robert started crying once more. (We were still barefoot and were in the barn against orders, but there hadn't been anything else to do.) "They're all ruined and tough, now! Nobody'll eat them...!"

"I think we better get them back into the pen anyway, huh?"

King barked a few times as we walked away. We stepped off the straw- and pebble-strewn planks and onto soil, patterned with tire tracks and packed down, now, with our footprints, then onto the grass.

With King out of the way, it was fairly easy to herd the ducks out of the pond, up the slope, and back to their pen. The duck that had been bleeding seemed to have gotten washed off by her swim and was okay now. None of them looked too much the worse. I thought that would be the end of it.

But Robert was still desolate.

"Look—" I tried to be practical—"nobody was around and saw us. You don't have to tell anybody it happened, do you?" We were standing under a tree. The sky was overcast, and I thought we should go inside. "You could always pretend that it didn't—"

"That isn't the *point!*" Robert's face was dirty. His hair was wet. Tears still streaked his cheeks. "They were my responsibility! And now nobody'll be able to *eat* them!"

"Well, maybe," I said, "since they were only running around five or six minutes—" It had seemed to take hours while it had been happening; but it hadn't, I realized now, been *all* that long—"it won't make them *that* tough."

This seemed to be an argument that he could partially accept. He wiped his nose.

Then he turned and shouted: "That *god*-damned dog!" The profanity fit in Robert's mouth as awkwardly as it would have in mine.

I said: "Let's go inside until your mom gets back."

As we walked across the grass toward the farmhouse's white steps that went up to the kitchen porch, occasionally Robert would sort of quiver—and now and then sniffle as though he were going to start crying again. Through the whole thing, I hadn't really been upset. But, once more, lost between compassion for my friend and a selfish worry that his state would ruin the rest of my visit, I decided I had to say something that would change things.

"Robert," I said. "Your father's dead—"

He turned to me and blinked—either because what I'd said was true, or because I'd voiced the fact that, certainly, no one else among our classmates had yet dared speak to him of.

"—you probably feel like you're responsible for *everything!*"

He stopped.

We looked at each other.

We were both wet. Our shirts were out of our pants. Buttons were missing. Our clothes and faces and arms were stuck all over with grass blades, duck down, and leaf bits. Robert had more cuts and scratches than I did. But I had a bruised knee, and there was a tear in my shirtsleeve where King's tooth had torn it, raking down my forearm to leave the smallest trickle of blood—which I'd decided not to mention to anyone, since back at school Hugo had told us about rabies injections directly into the stomach wall and how much they hurt. It *just* didn't seem necessary.

"You didn't do it on purpose, Robert," I went on. "It wasn't your fault. And it's probably not going to be as bad as you think, anyway."

Robert blinked, sniffed, then shook his head, with small quick motions, as if to say I just didn't understand at all.

"A duck gets tough from running around and exercising and things the same way a...a body builder's muscles get big and tough." I had no idea *what* made a duck tough—or tender. But it sounded good, even scientific.

"I know," Robert said. "I've got a lot of responsibility, now. My mom says so." There were still tears in his voice, but they were not the tense, terrified tears of someone fighting the descent into deeper and deeper misery but the easier tears of someone rising at last toward reason—a distinction children can all make, though sometimes adults forget it.

"Robert, a duck would have to run around a lot more than five minutes to grow *that* kind of muscle!"

He actually smiled a little. The notion of those quacking pillows with muscles like the pictures in the Charles Atlas advertisements on the back of the comics we traded *was* funny.

Inside we got washed up. Looking in the medicine cabinet, I volunteered to put mercurochrome on his scratches, but Robert decided against it.

"It's iodine that stings—"

"I know. I still don't want it. I'll be all red and look funny."

That evening, after his mother got back, and we were at the kitchen table eating hot dogs and baked beans (both of us still barefoot, but cleaner and drier), Robert, with a mouthful of frank, told her:

"The ducks got out this afternoon. King almost caught them. But we got them back in."

"That's good," his mother said. "You know, Bill told you, when he said you could take care of them, they're not supposed to run around too much—or they won't be fit to eat!"

That was all there was to it.

I could hear, neither in his words nor hers, no trace of the physical exertion or moral despair the adventure had put Robert—and me—through.

That evening Robert's mother told us she had arranged a trip for us

155

the next morning. The farm's cows generally produced two full milk cans a day. When the milk driver came to pick up the farm's milk, we would join him and ride the rest of his run to the dairy. We were to be up and ready by five.

Robert told me he had been on the trip before and that the milk truck driver, Eric, was a great guy. Robert's mother added that Eric had worked on the farm back when he was a teenager. Her husband had always liked him. Then Eric had gone away for a year — into the armed forces. But he'd been back a while now, and for the last few months he'd been just as nice and as helpful — well, she didn't know what she'd have *done* without him! So that night, I went to sleep in a small room with a sloping ceiling, and Robert went to bed in his own room — "Because you two can't talk all night if you have to get up at four-thirty in the morning," Robert's mother told me, turning out my light.

I'd wondered if I should make another stab at introducing Robert to sex once we were in bed — Robert *could* be slow about things. But since we weren't in the same room, I decided — again — to forget it. I turned over under the country comforter, and went to sleep.

Getting up in the middle of the night was kind of interesting.

"Oh, don't worry," Robert's mother said. "It won't be dark for long."

Down in the kitchen, by the time we finished our cornflakes, the windows had lightened to an indigo as deep as evening's.

Robert got in an argument with his mother about whether we could go on the ride barefoot.

"Running around the farm is one thing," she told us. "But you don't know where you're going. So I want you both to put some shoes on. Now!"

"But I *know* where I'm going!" Robert insisted. "I've been there before!"

"And *I* don't want to argue anymore! Put your shoes on, or I will phone Eric right this minute and tell him that you're not coming!" She stepped toward the phone — which got a capitulatory squeal from Robert.

She was angry, too.

Robert's mother actually had a pretty short temper—shorter than my mom's, anyway. I wondered if that came from having her husband die.

We sat at the table, bending down, Robert to tie his sneakers, me to lace my shoes.

Then, outside, we heard a truck.

"That's Eric!" Robert cried. We were both up and out the door, with Robert's mom behind us.

The milk truck was just a little bigger than a pick-up. The back was open, and there were a dozen upright milk cans already standing in it from previous farm stops. A lanky guy was already hoisting up our two (filled by the electric milker Bill in the barn had shown us working the evening before).

"Mornin', ma'am. Hey, Robert — this your little friend from New York City? Howdy, there!" Squatting on the open tailgate, Eric grinned. "You two fellas ain't gonna give me no trouble now, are ya'?" He pushed up his red cap, and reached over to shake my hand.

Robert's mother said: "I've told them they have to do everything you say."

As I took Eric's hand to shake, I saw that for all his hard, country-soiled calluses, he was as bad a nail-biter as Robert. It gave me a kind of start.

Twenty-three or twenty-four, with a pleasant smile but not a whole lot of chin, Eric was a gangling, good-natured, upstate farmboy. His jeans were frayed at knee and cuff. His high-laced workshoes were big, scuffed, and muddy. His plaid shirt was rolled up from forearms show-ing an anchor and an eagle from his Navy stint. "Don't worry, ma'am," he said to Robert's mother, standing now and pulling his cap visor back down. He jumped to the ground: "I'll have these little guys back here by eight-thirty, nine o'clock in the morning—at the latest." He pushed up the tailgate, clanked it to, and stuck in the iron bolt on its jingling chain that held it closed, hammered on it once with his big hand's hard heel, then walked us around to the cab, where the door—the truck sat on a slant—hung open. "Come on, now, you two. Get on up in there. Bye, now, ma'am."

"Bye, Eric. You two be good, now, and do what Eric tells you!"

That milk run through the paling New Paltz dawn was the most wonderful thing that had ever happened to me.

As Eric grasped the wheel (the top arc covered with oil-blackened carpet, fixed at the ends with electrician's tape), to haul us round onto the road, one wheel *chunked* down and up, into and out of, a pothole. "*God*-damn, if that ain't some shit!" Eric broke out, then glanced over. "Now you ain't gonna tell on me, huh? You let your mom know I'm cussin' around you little fuckers like this, an' you'll never see *my* ass again! You two remember that, you hear me?"

Yeah, sure. We nodded vigorously. Oh, his friend would never say anything about something like that, Robert spoke for me — as if his own assurance had been given long ago.

Over the next thirty yards of bumpy road, however (we were still not off Robert's property), by the time we reached the highway, I'd realized that, while — if he *had* to — Eric could maintain country decorum with farmers' wives and mothers, turned loose in a truck with a pair of boys he became the *most* foul-mouthed man I'd ever met!

Of course I'd heard "bad words" shouted in anger on Harlem streets. But this open joviality was as heavily weighted with profanity and scatology as speech could bear. Nor was it bawled in the anonymous urban distances. It was directed, without an ounce of ire, straight at Robert and me — "How you little shit-asses doin' in that fuckin' school you fuckin' go to down in that ol' shit-ass city?... You messin' 'round with that science-crap, huh? I never knowed shit about no fuckin' science. Or pretty much about no school-shit either. But you bastards are probably pretty smart little sons of bitches about all that fuckin' shit now, ain't ya'?" Then, when he would gun the truck to pass a rare car out on the early road, he'd grunt toward the window, "*Suck* my fuckin' asshole, cocksucker!" Then, back to us with mock frustration: "What do these early mornin' fuckheads think they're goddamn doin' anyway, this fuckin' early, on the fuckin' highway, gettin' in shit and everybody's fuckin' way besides? Trippin' over their goddamn dicks like they left their fuckin' flies open!"

I and I guess Robert, too, were in ecstasy!

We had to stop at one more farm to pick up a last milk can before going on to the dairy. "A fuckin' little one-can shit hole — and that can ain't *never* fuckin' full. I'm not supposed to take the fucker if it ain't fuckin' full. But I'm a soft-hearted son-of-a-bitch; so I do it. Now your daddy —" this to Robert — "he always kept a *hell* of a good-lookin' farm. And your mom's done pretty well by it since. But this ol' shit hole we're goin' to now ain't worth a damned dog turd!" The farmhouse we came up to, though, looked as neat as it could — if a lot smaller than Robert's. Unshaven, with bib-overalls and long johns beneath them, a heavyset, elderly man came out; and without noticeable transition Eric managed once more to put his profanations aside. "Hello, sir. How you doin' this mornin', sir?"

"Hi, there, Eric. You want me to give you a hand up with that can — ?"

"No, sir!" Opening the door, Eric leapt from the cab. "No, sir — you don't have to do nothin' with it, sir. I'll get it — that's what they pay me for. So you just relax."

From our seat in the cab, we heard Eric in the back, the can first rolling across gravel, then rasping on the truck bed.

From inside, we heard Eric call down from the truck, "How's Bubba doin'?"

And from the ground the farmer answered, "Why, he's doin' just fine."

"You tell 'im," Eric said, "not to get in no trouble with that motorcycle."

"Now, I'll tell 'im *just* that."

This apparently was some joke that set the two of them off laughing.

"You tell 'im," Eric declared. "You tell Bubba that Eric said you was to *tell* him that!" (Eric pronounced his own name as one diphthongized, down-swung syllable that, for all the slurring of the Negro speech around me in Harlem I could sometimes assume, would have been beyond me.) "You tell 'im, I say!" They were still laughing. "Tell 'im! Don't you forget it, now, neither!"

159

"Oh, I'll tell 'im!"

Eric's boots scudded on gravel. (In my mind I saw him vault.) A moment on, cap in hand, he swung up into the cab and slammed the door. "Bye, now, sir!" With one hand back and the other front, he tugged it over spiky hair the color of light coffee. "Bye, now — so long, sir!"

"Bye, Eric!"

Eric grabbed wheel and gearshift.

The motor revved beneath.

We started again.

"Now we're fuckin' outta here, boy — like pig-balls on butter! Let's get the *fuck* on the road!"

We jogged along awhile. Eric kept up his banter. I remembered Robert's awkward curses yesterday. By now Eric's sentences seemed just as awkward when curses were missing. For, during this stop, I'd heard, as I hadn't at Robert's farm, the faint halts and false starts you couldn't really write without burlesquing, that nevertheless told where a *fuckin'* or a *shit* dearly yearned to fall.

"You know —" We went round another curve, with Eric's near elbow getting my ribs and me pushing Robert against the door (tools rattled in metal below the seat) — "when I throwed up the goddamn Navy an' come the fuck home (Oh, they fuckin' wanted me to stay but I told 'em to get fucked, I knew where *I* fuckin' lived!), I shoulda gone the hell to Texas and been a goddamn cowboy, herdin' fuckin steers and ropin' fuckin' calves — *then* I bet you little scumbags would *really* like shittin' around with a wild-ass bastard like me!" He put his head back and sang out: *"Whoopie-Fuckin'-Tye-Yi-Yippy-Shit-Ass-Yay!* Well, now, *hey —"* His gold-stubbled cheeks filled with air as he whistled, then his chin came down as we bounced over another stretch of broke-up macadam — "I bet I'd be a fuckin' movie star by now, with fuckin' *fine* music every time I turned the knob — that would be a goddamn sight better than rustlin' fuckin' milkcans for a bunch of shit-machine cows, you better *believe* your fuckin' balls when they spit on ya'!" We bounced down the straightaway. "But it ain't that fuckin' bad around here, now, is it? You an' your ma keep comin' the fuck back."

A few minutes later Eric pulled over again.

"Now don't you two little peter-heads get all excited — we ain't got there yet. I'm just takin' a fuckin' break to do somethin' you can't do for me." He opened the cab door, dropped down to the shoulder, strode a few feet into the undergrowth, half squatted, then stood again. Rasping down his zipper, he hauled himself out, testicles and all, and began to spray grandly, goldenly, over leaves and logs and paired birch saplings. "Pick up the fuckin' milk, then have to jump out an' take me a fuckin' leak — I do it ever' mornin', and ever' mornin' I'm goddamned for a sinner if I don't fuckin' forget." Swinging his stream around, he turned to us, grinning.

The amber arc glittered through coppery leaf-dapple.

"You two assholes wanna come down here and have us a pee fight? I'll drown the both of ya', one ball tied behind my fuckin' back!"

"No!" declared Robert, happy as I was. "You'd win!"

"I fuckin' wouldn't!" Eric protested as his stream lost its arch. Like Vladdy back in school, Eric was uncircumcised. Unlike Vladdy's though, Eric's cuff hung loose down over his knuckles, so that as it slid forward, the top interfering with his water, he splattered like a bright umbrella. Then the umbrella closed. Urine dribbled from his fist, wet his grimed fingers, dripped to the dried mud on his boot toe. "Cause I just ran out of fuckin' piss, an' I don't got me no more!" Shaking himself, he stuffed himself back in his pants. "Come on now, the two of you little bastards. Get on down here and irrigate some trees. I don't want you sons-o'-bitches havin' to go when there ain't no fuckin' place to do it at."

So we got down and left our puddles in the ditch beyond the shoulder, then returned to the cab, where Eric sat, elbows on the wheel, sucking at his knuckles, biting at his cuticles. He glanced down at us from under his red visor.

"*Get* the fuck back on up here, now, 'fore I wail the piss out of you little shit-asses!" His grin held not a jot of aggression.

We climbed back into the cab, and Eric drove again. He talked about "...Jew-bastards. I guess some of them is as bad as ever'body says. But

SAMUEL R. DELANY

I knowed some that weren't a hell of a lot worse than anybody else —
though if I said that in the fuckin' bar, some guy'd wanna pull me apart
and shit on the pieces." He talked about "wops." There were, I guess, a
lot of them in the Navy with him, "I just never understood the fuckers,
is all. They all them Catholics an' stuff," and he shook his head. He
talked about "niggers — Ooops!... *Oh*, shit! I done forgot. His momma
told me, yesterday on the phone — you a nigger too, now, ain't you? — to
get me all prepared, so I wouldn't start talkin' no nigger-shit: like this.
Well, you sure as hell don't look it — you *could* be a little wop kid,
though. Or one of them Puerto Ricans. Well, now, it's gonna always be
like that with me: I open my fuckin' mouth an' I'm gonna stick my big
toe — cowshit an' all — right in it, till that ol' fucker come out my fuckin'
ear like ya' goddamn dick left hangin' out ya' pants and you don't even
know it!" He hauled on the wheel, went round a leafy curve, and leaned
over to show us the side of his head. "See it there, that fucker wigglin'
out my ear? You look, you can see it. There it fuckin' goes! Wiggle, wiggle, wiggle!" But, whether it was a penis or a toe, Robert and I were beyond offense and simply howled.

I wonder if the man thought it was his inane jokes that kept us in
hysterics, or if he realized it was his scabrous vocabulary tickling us to
our boyish cores. Could, indeed, we have made the distinction? Eric
cussed out more potholes, more drivers, and speculated at length on the
sexual habits of the waitress at the diner who'd served him breakfast that
morning. ("Shit on a fuckin' shingle, that's what she gave me, I swear.
Goddamn, it's a fuckin' miracle I'm still fuckin' alive!") His invective
involved her with toothless octogenarians and several large barnyard animals, at a specificity quite beyond our nine-year-old minds to follow:
"I'm sittin' at the goddamn counter, being fuckin' polite and thinkin'
'bout my face full of pussy..." evoked a picture of Eric on a counter stool
with a kitten trying to climb down from his head — while his specula-
tions on whether the waitress was or wasn't the sort who'd "...give a
fuckin' donkey head with rusted-out braces an' rotten teeth till the hairy
bastard he-hawed for mercy..." sailed by in an image worthy of *Chien
andalou*, but devoid of information for Robert or me — though enough

162

big monster-mule and little wormy pig dicks got sucked off, cut off, and rammed down this or that cocksucker's throat, Lord knows, to make up for it. We couldn't stop laughing anyway, as it all swirled around us in phallic confusion, a surreally mis-imagined haze.

Nor was it entirely monologue. Eric asked us more questions about life in the fuckin' city, professing to each answer we gave his own smilingly indulgent terror of *that* fuckin' place:

"When I was in that goddamn Navy they wanted to put me on a fuckin' plane. I told them right the hell out, there was no fuckin' way they was gonna get me up in one of them fuckin' things! Well, I feel the same way about fuckin' subways. I want the wheels *on* the fuckin' road. Not twenty feet under it, or half a mile above it. *On* it. An' that's fuckin' *it!*"

When the truck crunched onto the gravel beside the dairy, a guy in a blue uniform with white piping across the pockets and down the sides came out and, as Eric opened the cab door, called:

"Well how the hell are *you?*"

For a moment, as Eric climbed out, I thought we were entering some unimaginable world where *all* males talked like this. ("Got some kids with ya'," the uniformed guy observed. "Yeah, I remember Robert, from last time." And, to both of us, as we dropped down: "Hi, there.") But the occasional *hell, dang, damn,* and *goddamn* we heard from the rest of the dairy workers as the morning rolled on were no more than ordinary, civilized slips, that vanished against the profane transgressions of Eric's dithyrambic scatology.

Standing in the sun, I looked down at the gray stones graveling away before the building, thankful for my shoes as only a city child can be.

Grinning, Eric motioned to me. "Get over here, ya' little shit-ass bastard." Beside me, he bent and put one hand on my shoulder. "You stay the hell back, now, while me and a couple of these other cocksuckers unload them shit-ass milk cans down onto that fuckin' chain-linked conveyer, right there — see?" He pointed with the other. "They carry the shit —" clinking and wobbling, half a dozen, already on it, moved by the red brick wall — "till they go right through that fuckin' archway, over

163

there — you see it, now?" He smelled of earth and machine oil. "So you stay the fuck outta the way." Then he dropped his hand, stood up, and went around to the truck back. "*God*-damn, get that big ol' shit-ass fucker!" he'd shout, standing in the truck bed, leaning a can out to one of the men below — till finally one of the loaders objected:

"Come on, now! You better quit talkin' like that, Garbage Mouth. You got *kids* around here! And they ain't even yours. Maybe they haven't been brought up to hear that kind of thing!"

From the truck, Eric grinned over at us: "Sorry, there." He went back for another can. "Whyn't you two go look around. We don't want your goddamned little ears to wither up and fall off from the fuckin' heat, listenin' to our shit."

"*Your* shit!" the other loader said sullenly, standing below. "Come *on*, now!"

So Robert and I went off to explore inside the building.

Robert had been here before and explained to me how everything had to be kept real clean — then let me wander off to see something on my own that didn't much interest him. I strolled past tall aluminum equipment, slanted with salmon sun through high levered-out windows, to amble over the red, tessellated flooring slurred with milky spills — wondering what it *would* be like to walk through the white puddles barefoot. I probably looked like any ordinary kid, loafing around, gazing at the pasteurizing tanks, the homogenizing tubs, the cooling vats, the angled pipes and arching hoses that ran between gauges like clusters of clocks. I was still in a kind of profane trance, separated from the overtly sexual, at least in me, by a barrier no more substantial than a misty breath breathed out on a chill April dawn.

Once, in an empty corner (other than a few loaders and a foreman or two, all outside now, the workers didn't come in till eight-thirty: so the dairy proper was deserted), I stopped by bare brick. Asbestos-covered pipes ran up to the high roof. Then I felt down inside my pants. What, before, I'd suspected, now I confirmed: back in the truck, about when Eric had scorched the Texas plains, I'd wet my underpants with that mysterious discharge that came more and more frequently these days —

and which sometimes I could even make happen by various pleasurable frictions.

Immune in his youth to genital joy, could Robert have undergone a less sloppy, if similar, reaction?

Eric did not have an iota of the child molester in him. (I've known a number of Erics since: all heart and mouth.) He would have been outraged by any such idea. In a sense, the man who kept his cussedness under control with respectable women and men probably gives a better picture of him than his verbal excesses of the road. But if he *had* been so inclined, the sad and simple truth (at least I thought so then) is that I would have been the happiest, most willing, most gratefully molested child one might have asked for.

There was simply no sexual act, whether or not I'd tried it already with the guys after swimming, I wouldn't have happily performed with him.

Soon I was in the truck again, between Eric and Robert.

The ride home was equally glorious, obscene, and innocent. Back at the farm we got down from the cab, said hello to Robert's mother, who came down the kitchen steps drying her hands on a dish towel, while Eric swung the empty milk cans from the truck bed. We called our thoroughly inadequate goodbyes to the amazing man whose cussing caused such marvels.

He called back: "Bye, Robert. So long, little guy." (I realized he'd lost my name on our trip.) "We had fun, didn't we?" Then he slammed the cab door after himself. "Hope you come up and we do it again. They were real good, ma'am. Both of 'em, real good. Bye, now, ma'am. Weren't no trouble at all!" Then he pulled his head back inside the window and the truck rolled off.

But I was still in a transgressive haze — that, frankly, if it had come down to it, I'd have traded my after-swim pleasures for any day.

"I told you Eric was a great guy," Robert said, while his mother waved after the rattling tailgate.

All I could do was nod, and remember Eric's big hands, his dirty boots, his cap — and his wondrous cussedness.

I never saw him again.

A few days later, I was back in the city.

And at school.

Robert wanted to be a scientist.

I wanted to be a scientist.

In Hugo's classes we worked wonderfully hard at it. Or at least Robert did. I wanted to work hard. But it was so easy, especially with Robert around, in the midst of some lab experiment to get into talking about some fancified possibility, some speculative what-if…

Hugo's assessment of me, once our first year together was over? In one of his biannual reports to my parents, he wrote:

"Sam is bone lazy."

He was right.

I still am.

That's probably why I've never been able to work at more than one thing at a time. And while — sometimes — I worked at my science, in those years art was something I didn't work at but merely imitated from other people, other books, other pictures—even if, because of an imitative knack, occasionally, in or out of Gwenny's class, I got more than my share of praise for it.

A year or so after my father's death, I, my wife, some cousins, and some friends all went for a last weekend to our own country house — just before Mom sold it. In the attic's evening nostalgia, from a small green table set up against the chimney brick, I picked up some dusty sheet music: "September Song" — though when and why my father had brought it up here, I didn't know. But this time, what I saw was not a contested progression of notes. As I turned back through the gritty pages to the opening, what I noticed now was that the French lyrics, running between the speckled staves in italic type, were by the poet Jacques Prévert, whose little volume *Paroles* had been published in part by the Pocket Poets series and, back during my high school years, had joined, along with Ginsberg's *Howl*, Corso's *Gasoline*, Ponsot's *True*

Minds, and Williams' *Kora in Hell*, my most cherished volumes.

"*Les feuilles mortes qui nous ressembles...*" Prévert had written; just as surprising, the translator and crafter of the American lyrics had been (I read at the music's top) the humorist poet Ogden Nash: "The autumn leaves drift by my window, the autumn leaves of red and gold..."

The piece of music beneath it on the table, that showed the yellowed right angle where, a bit askew (for how many years), "September Song" had lain, was as great a surprise: a frothy tune, wildly popular during some season of my childhood, it was, "If I Knew You Were Coming, I'd Have Baked a Cake!" The writer of *this*, I learned for the first time from the name at the top, was the playwright and popular essayist, William Saroyan.

Had my father been aware of any of this? And how, now, could I ever know?

But—as I said—that was later.

Gwen had been our art teacher for several years.

What goes into a picture?

Shape, Line, and Color...

How are they put together?

In relationship to the outside edge.

By the time I reached the Eighth Grade we'd repeated it so often it had almost no meaning. As happens with all dogmas, sometimes we'd laughed at it. Frequently we'd mocked and made fun of it. But, as dogmas will, sometimes it had astonished me with its explanatory force. There were even moments when it seemed to relate as much to music (Mrs. Wallace had only that week handed me the solo score to the Mendelssohn Concerto: "This is probably hopelessly outside the realistic frame of your abilities. But there're parts in it I'd just like to *hear* what you did with...") as to the most functional architecture, to theater, to dance (Wendy was already telling me all about Martha Graham, José Lamon, and that there was a wonderful choreographer at the City Center Ballet named Balanchine, some of whose works a few people liked to say they couldn't understand, though they certainly made sense to me!)

— as to sculpture (the easy transition) and to art.

Then there were those odd moments down in the third floor library — which, with permission, the Eighth Graders were allowed to use. The world globe stood beside me in one corner and the scrolled dictionary stand sat across from me in the other. (The dictionary did not contain, I knew because I'd looked them up, a number of the words Eric had used three springs ago — though some surprising others it did.) I looked over the analytic geometry and calculus text I was pursuing on my own, and for seconds Gwen's dictum seemed to explain the more amazing parts of mathematics and science as well…though that insight I could only hold in my mind for a heartbeat.

That must have been the year, when we were working in the art room one April afternoon, that Robert became wholly, intently, and surprisingly involved in one of his pictures. He painted with his brush held in both hands, the way he used to hold his pencil when he was six or seven, and he seemed to fight the paper — rather than paint it. Blues and reds and grays swirled around each other, the colors getting angrier and darker as he got closer to the center, where, in his energy, he'd already torn the paper once — and was *still* painting at it.

We used the tops of the old paint cans for our colors. Robert's brush swept down across the one, licking up red, the other, lapping up blue. Then brush hairs smashed again into the saturated paper.

Gwenny happened to walk by in her paint-speckled smock. She looked over Robert's shoulder — and made a sound as though she'd been hit. Recovering herself, she let out a breath: *"Pure* sex!"

The half dozen of us, who'd been glancing from our own projects to watch or whisper, went into mindless, paralyzed silence (except Robert, obliviously at work). If Eric had stepped from springtime, through the door, and into the art room to call out some innocent and astonishing excoriation, it couldn't have been more shocking. Teachers just didn't *say* things like that in those years. After another moment, however, we began to laugh.

Because Gwenny had always been a *very* different teacher.

Robert looked around, gave a sheepish smile.

Gwenny blinked at him — at us. "Well, it *is!*" she exclaimed. "Pure sex — that's *just* what it is! You may not see it now — but you will, eventually. It's quite marvelous. Go on!"

When school let out that afternoon, I went back up to the art room, let myself in, and spent a couple of minutes looking at Robert's painting, still drying on the wall. Robert — who, while the rest of us had gotten taller, leaner, and stronger, had just gotten bigger and pudgier, and was mad about science fiction and amateur radio, and was still, on any scale I could read, the *least* sexual of children — had painted a picture in which no single shape, line, or color had retained its identity over an entire brush stroke. Rather it was all process, energy, movement... Was that, I wondered, what "pure sex" was? I don't know whether it was beautiful. If anything, it seemed just a breadth away from a truly troubling ugliness — a quality that no figurative painting could have manifested without having been deformed, distorted, grotesque. Nor was it particularly sexy — to me. But it was powerful. Was "pure sex," I wondered, something that *ought* to inhabit a painting (though Gwenny clearly thought it should), since its purity seemed to subvert the very esthetic — of shape, of line, of color — that allowed it to manifest itself in the first place? And how did it relate to the outside edge? Robert's paint over-spilled all four sides and corners. The edge contained his painting no more than a photograph's edge contains the whole of the reality around the camera. Arbitrarily, it delimited only a fragment of that roiling energy. *Pure* sex? And how did the "pure" variety differ from the tentative, frightened, half-hidden (and presumably impure) sort I'd tried to sneak into paint years ago with my borrowed muscle-builder hulking on his borrowed throne in his borrowed, orientalized throne room? With a lot of questions in my mind, I went home.

I must say it here.

Something about this account bothers me, because its topic finally lists toward the estheticizing of *everything* — and that way, as Benjamin first suggested and Sontag more recently reminded us, lies fascism.

But that's the way the feeling world was presented, unrectified, to me. For better or for worse, that's how it became mine. And by now we knew that Gwen lived in Greenwich Village. We knew her acquaintances were de Kooning, Bourgeois, Pollock, Nevelson, Frankenthaler, and Francis…

We also knew she was a committed and serious artist—serious enough that, when the school's three art teachers (omitting Hugo) had an exhibition in the school lobby, several of our other teachers let it be known they did *not* like her work.

For the week of the show, Gwen's three two-foot-wide, seven-foot-high canvasses hung with the paintings of the others, on the wall behind the maroon rail where, each morning, we marched by the nurse, Miss Hedges, to show our tongues and make sure we were all without stain.

Diagonally across from where the teachers had put up their paintings, under several arches, were some old wall murals. In blue and pink pastels, their style suggested the WPA: in the foreground, wearing long dresses, with bare feet showing from under their hems, highly stylized women picked up sheaves of wheat, while, in the background, in overalls and workmen's caps, equally stylized men held aloft wrenches and hammers against a configuration of gears, smokestacks, and clouds. A faded rainbow arched over it all. The murals were, indeed, all shape and line (and ideology; though I couldn't have read that then). They weren't much on color, though. And they were simply wiped from the eye by Gwenny's dynamic fusionings across the lobby.

Impastoed with massive horizontal strokes (wide enough to make you *see* her six-inch housepainter's brush), rectilinear umbers, ochres, greens, and browns overlapped like amazing stairs, up the long surfaces, leading, in layered steps, to some apotheosis very *much* beyond that sacrosanct, upper, outside edge. Among the ochres and earths, squares of metallic gold recalled the utility of apartment radiators daubed over in winter, but with, as well, a patina of spirituality, like icons—the only objects that might justify such gilding. At once immediate and holy, their compositions were as solid as stone forts, energetic, sensuous, joyful, and vigorous — like the abstract passages in the lower-left-hand corners of Vermeer, as austere as non-figurative Klimt, as rich as Titian or Tiepolo.

To one side of them hung some impressionistic flowers and a painting of children — was Miss Andrews still at the school that year...? On the other, the high school art teacher had put up *his* several pictures of geometrically precise and vaguely surreal picket fences.

"Now that," said our new, young history teacher — who, as a stab toward tradition, insisted we call her "Mrs." — "I can relate to, at least a little." As I stood beside her in my snow suit, not quite ready to go outside, still wet from swimming downstairs, she went on: "I mean —" she bent her head to the side — "that's obviously taken some *skill* to paint."

I liked their skill, too.

But for me, Gwen's was the only *art* in the show. To see it, you merely had to stand before one of her scalar, desiring towers, letting it pulse and suck and glimmer at you, while its tans, mochas, golds, and strawberries lifted you through the awful ascent of its lapped verticalities. Its sensuous awe, along with the average, uninformed, and uncomprehending disdain that the other teachers used to fight off its troubling intensity (one, in her gray suit, with her handsome gray hair: "I'm afraid I just don't see them. What in the world are they supposed to be pictures *of?*" And one other, in heady purple: "They just look dirty, to me. Like what you'd expect from a child playing in mud." And, as I did and do so often, I remembered Eric, the spring dawn, and the marvel the muck of his language had loosed) — surely that was the *most* important of Gwen's formal lessons.

— *Amherst*
October 1988

CITRE ET TRANS

I

...all that we have been saying is as much a natural sport of the silence of these nether regions as the fantasy of some rhetorician of the other world who has used us as puppets!

—Paul Valéry, *Eupalinos, or The Architect*

"All Greek men are barbarians!" Heidi jerked the leash.

Pharaoh's claws dragged the concrete.

I laughed, and Pharaoh looked around and up, eyes like little phonograph records.

"Heidi," I said, "you just can't talk about an entire population that way."

It was too bright to look at the sky directly—even away from the sun. The harbor was blue, not green. And if I stared into the air anyway, it was as though I were watching the water reflected in some dazzling metal, brighter than, but equally liquid as, the sea.

"Half a population," Heidi said. "I like the women. They don't have any style. But I like them." She wore her black and white poncho — which, only after I'd been living with her in her Mnisicleou Street room two weeks, I realized was because she thought she was fat.

"Barbarians—*hoi barbaroi*—" I pronounced it the way my classics professor back at City College would have, rather than with what had been the surprising (for me) Italianate endings, despite spelling, of modern

Greek: "It's already a Greek word—the Greeks gave it to us—for people who aren't Greek, who spoke some other language—*ba-ba-ba-ba-ba!* — like you and me...Germans, Americans—"

"They also wrote Greek tragedies." The green ferry sign's painted wood was bolted to the two-tiered dock rail. "From the way they behave today, though, *I* don't think they still have it." HYDRA, SPETZA, and AEGINA were painted in white Roman capitals. Below, the same names were printed in smaller upper-/lowercase Greek. Heidi shrugged her broad shoulders as we strolled by.

Once, when I'd commented on how strong she was, Heidi told me that, six years before, when she was nineteen, she'd been women's swimming champion of Bavaria. She also told me she'd recently graduated from Munich University with a degree in philosophy and a minor in contemporary Hebrew literature: she'd arranged to study for the year in Tel Aviv, with special papers and letters of introduction. But because she was German Protestant, in Israel they wouldn't let her off the boat. She'd ended up in Athens. Then, when we'd had some odd argument, tearfully she'd explained—while I showered in the pink tiled stall in the room's corner—that she suffered from a fatal blood disease, not leukemia, but like it, that left no sign on her muscular, tanned torso, arms, or legs. But that was why she'd left the American artist she'd been living with in Florence to come to Athens in the first place: likely it would kill her within three years.

That last one kind of threw me. At first. And I wrote my wife about it—who wrote about it in a poem I read later.

At various times I believed all of Heidi's assertions. But not all three at once.

"I don't know whether to kiss David or never to speak to him again for getting me this job—baby-sitting for the children of rich Greeks is just not that wonderful."

"The parents want them to learn German. And French."

"And *English!*" she declared. "Believe me, *that's* the important one for them. Are you still mad at John—" who was this English electrical engineer—"for taking that job away from you at the Language Institute?" Heidi's French, Italian, and English were about perfect; her Greek was better than mine. And one evening I'd sat with her through an hour conversation in Arabic with the students we met at one in the morning in the coffee shop in Omoinoia.

"I was never mad at him," I told her. "He thought it was as silly as I did. His Cockney twang is thick enough to drown in, and he can't say an 'h' to save himself. But they wanted 'a native English speaker'; as far as they were concerned, I was just another American who says 'Ya'll come' or 'Toidy-toid Street'. John would be the first one to tell you I speak English better than he does."

"And you've written all those beautiful books in it, too. He said he'd read one."

"Did he? English John? He never told me." We were halfway along the pier.

"I really don't know which is worse. Rich Greek children, or that museum stuff I was doing..." Suddenly she closed her eyes, stopped, and shuddered. Pharaoh sat and looked up, slathering. "Yes I do. I hate German tourists. I hate them more than anything in the world—with their awful, awful guidebooks. All they do is look at the books. Never at the paintings. I used to be so thankful for the Americans. 'Well, that's reeeal perty, Maggie!'" Heidi's attempted drawl on top of the German-ic feathering of her consonants produced an accent that, I knew she knew, belonged to no geography at all. But we both laughed. "Even if they didn't know what they were looking at, they looked at the paint-ings. The Germans never did. If I'd been there another week, I was go-ing to play a trick—I swear it. I was going to take my dutiful Germans to the wrong painting, and give them my little talk about an entirely different picture—just to see if any of them noticed. You know: in front of a Fifteenth-century Spanish Assumption of the Virgin, I'd begin, with a perfectly straight face: 'And here we have a 1930 industrial land-scape painted in the socialist realism style that grew up in reaction to Italian Futurismo...'" She started walking again, as though the humor of her own joke had rather run out. "Rich Greek children it will be."

"Heidi," I said, "I think I've spotted a German national trait: you

Germans always talk about everybody, even yourselves, in terms of 'national characteristics'. Well, it got you in trouble in that war we had with you when you and I were kids. I wouldn't be surprised if it ended up getting you in trouble again."

Heidi took my arm. "It isn't a German trait, dear. It's a European trait — and you Americans, who are always fighting so hard against generalizing about anyone, look terribly naive to the rest of us because of it. I'd think you American Negroes especially, with your history of oppression from white people, ought to realize, of all Americans, just how suicidally — no, genocidally, there's the nasty word — naive that is. If you pretend you can't know anything about a group, how can you protect yourself from that group — when they're coming to burn crosses in your yard; or to put you in the boxcars." She seemed suddenly very unhappy — as if that were just not what she wanted to talk about.

"Well, I like the Greeks, myself. There's a generalization. Is that okay for you? Did I ever tell you that story about David and me, when I first got back from the islands? You know how David is, every time he spots a new international: coming over to say hello and have a glass of tea. Then, somehow, he was going to show me where something was, and the two of us ended up walking together down Stadiou Street, him in his jeans and t-shirt, and that blond beard of his. And me, right next to him with my beard."

"A cute little beard it is, too." Heidi leaned over to ruffle my chin fuzz with her knuckles.

With one arm, I hugged her shoulders. "Cut it out, now. Anyway, I didn't know how the Greeks felt about beards back then — that the only people who wore them — here — were the Greek orthodox priests —"

"Yes, I know," Heidi said. "David's told me — they all think that bearded foreigners are making fun of their priests, which is why they get so hostile. Frankly I don't believe it for a minute. Greece is only two days by car away from the rest of the civilized world. And there've been foreigners coming through here — with beards — for the last hundred years. If you'd have cut yours off just for that, I'd have been very angry at you. Remember, dear: David is English — and the English love to make up explanations about people they think of as foreigners that are much too simple; and you Americans eat them up. The Greeks are just angry at foreigners, beards or no. And a good deal of that anger is rational — while much of the rest of it isn't. I'd think you were a lot cleverer if you believed that, rather than some silly over-complicated English anthropological explanation!"

"Well, that's why I was going to tell you this story," I said. "About the Greeks. We were walking down Stadiou Street, see — David and me — when I noticed this Greek couple more or less walking beside us. He was a middle-aged man, in a suit and tie. She was a proper, middle-aged Greek wife, all in black, walking with him. And she was saying to him, in Greek (I could just about follow it), all the while glancing over at us: 'Look at those dirty foreigners — with their dirty beards. They mess up the city, them with their filthy beards. Somebody should take them to the barber, and make them shave. It's disgusting the way they come here, with their dirty beards, dirtying up our city!' Well, even though I knew what she was saying, there was nothing I could do. But suddenly David — who's been here forever and speaks Greek like a native — looked over and yelled out, *'Ya, Kyria — ehete to idio, alla ligo pio kato!'* Hey, lady — you have one too, only a little further down! Well, I thought I was going to melt into the sidewalk. Or have a fight. But the man turned to us, with the most astonished look on his face: *'Ah!'* he cried. *'Alla milete helenika!'* Ah! But you speak Greek! The next thing I knew, he had his arms around David's and my shoulder, and they took us off to a cafe and bought us brandy till I didn't think we could stand up, both of them asking us questions, about where we were from and what we were doing here, and how did we like their country. You know 'barbarian' isn't the only word the Greeks gave us. So is 'hospitality'."

"No," Heidi said. "You never did tell me that story. But I've heard you tell it at at least two parties, when you didn't think I was listening — for fear I'd be offended. It's a rather dreadful story, I think. But it's what I mean — about the Greek women having no style. If someone had yelled that to *me* in the street, I would have cursed him out till — how might you say it? — his balls hoisted up inside his belly to cower like frightened puppies." She bent down to rub Pharaoh's head and under his chin. "Then —" she stood again — "*maybe* I'd have asked him to go for a brandy. Ah, my poor Pharaoh."

Heidi pronounced "Pharaoh" as three syllables — Pha-ra-oh — so that, for the next twenty-five years, I really didn't know what his name was, even after I saw her write it out in a letter; only then, one day (twenty-five years on), looking at the written word for the Egyptian archon, suddenly I realized what she'd meant to call him. But because we were in Greece, and because in general her faintly accented English was so good, I always thought "Pha-ra-oh" was some declension I didn't quite catch of *pharos* — lighthouse.

"Here in Greece," she said, "you really do lead a dog's life — don't you, dog?" She pulled the black leather leash up short again. The collar buckle was gleaming chrome — from some belt she'd found in the Monasteraiki flea market; she'd put it together herself on the black leather line. It was unusual looking and quite handsome. Under the poncho she wore black tights and black shoes, with single white buttons on the front. "I take him for a walk in the city — they run up on the street and kick him! You've seen them. Don't say you haven't. And he's so beautiful —" She grinned down at him, slipping into a kind of baby talk — "with his beautiful eyes. It was your beautiful eyes, Pharaoh, that made me take you in in the first place, when you were a puppy and I found you limping about and so sick in the back of that old lot. Ah," she crooned down at him, "you really are so beautiful!"

"The Greeks just don't keep pets here, Heidi. At least not house pets."

"I know," she said. "Costas told me: you have a dog on a rope in the city. They think you're probably taking him off somewhere to kill him. They run up and kick him, they throw a stone or a bottle at him — and think it's great fun! They give him meat they've spent twenty minutes carefully sticking full of broken glass! I take him on the subway, and the police say I have to put a muzzle on him!" She made a disgusted sound. "You see somebody with a dog on a leash like this — you would have to be stupid not to realize it's a pet! They don't like foreigners; they don't like dogs. It's just their way of getting back at both. And even so, on the underground out here this morning, you saw how everyone cowered back from him—they think my little dog is a terrible and vicious beast! I had to put that awful muzzle on him. And he was so good about it. Well, you don't have it on now—my darling Pharaoh!"

Pharaoh wasn't a big dog. But he wasn't a little one either. He was a broad-chested coffee-colored mutt with some white patches as though a house painter had picked him up and maybe shaken one of his forepaws before washing his hands. Heidi'd had him about six months—which was twice as long as she'd known me. One of his ears and the half-mask around his left eye were black.

"They're just not used to dogs, and he makes them uncomfortable."

"They're uncomfortable with him because he's a dog. They're uncomfortable with you because you're a Negro—"

"They're uncomfortable with you because you're German."

She smiled at that. "Well, *that's* barbaric! When I go to David's silly baby-sitting job, are you going to be all right?"

"I told you, DeLys said I could stay at her place up in Anaphiotika, while she's away. I'll be off to England the day after tomorrow. And then back home to New York."

"That odd old Englishman, John, from Turkey, is staying at DeLys's too, isn't he?"

"He's not that odd. When I was in Istanbul, DeLys gave me his address so I could look him up. After Jerry and I hitchhiked there, I hadn't had a shower in a week and was a total mess—he was just as nice to me as he could be. He fed me all one afternoon, till I was so full I could hardly walk. He told me all about places to see in the city, the Dolma Bocce and the Flower Passage. And what Turkish baths to go to."

"Did he feed Jerry too?"

"No. Jerry was scared of him because he knew John liked guys. DeLys had told Jerry about him before we left. So Jerry wouldn't go see him."

"You like guys. You like Jerry, I think."

Which was true. "But Jerry," I said, "and I are the same age. And we were already friends. I told Jerry I thought he was acting silly. But he's a southerner, and he's stubborn."

"That was a lovely letter Jerry wrote you." She quoted: " 'Don't step on any low flying birds.' I always thought he was just another stupid American, too tall, and too awkward, with nothing very interesting to say — even though you liked him. But when you read me his letter, I really began to wish I'd gotten to know him better while he was here. You're very sensitive to people, in ways I know I'm not. But sometimes, I suppose, we just miss out. Because, as you Americans say, of our prejudices.

"But he is odd," she went on, suddenly. "Turkish John, I mean—isn't that a funny name, for an Englishman? Cosima says he gives her the creeps."

"He's a little effeminate — he's a queer," I said. "But so am I, I suppose." Though I didn't really think I was—effeminate, that is.

"I wonder why so many women like you." Pharaoh went around behind her and, when she jerked him, came back between us, drawing black and white felt one way and another across her shoulder. "DeLys, Cosima, me... Even Kyria Kokinou likes you." (Kyria Kokinou was the landlady Heidi had decided not to risk angering by having me stay in the room while she was away with her Greek children.) "Do you think there's any particular reason for that?"

"Probably *because* I'm queer," I said. Then: "I wonder why we didn't have more sex, you and I?"

Now she leaned away with an ironic sneer, backed by her big, German smile. "*I* was certainly ready!" Heidi and I had slept in the same bed for two weeks; but we'd only made love twice. "I think you were just trying to prove a point," she said. "That you *were*...'queer', as you say." Suddenly she straightened. "I'm really not looking forward to this trip. The ferry will have to go out by the paper mill; and it's going to stink. And I won't ever see you again, will I? Look, if you can stop for a day in Munich, you must visit the Deutsches Museum. I used to go there when I was little. It's a science museum. And they have almost an entire real mine in the basement, that you can walk around in and watch it work—that was my favorite part, when I was a little girl. And wonderful mechanical toys from the Eighteenth Century—you can see actually functioning. I know you'll love it. You like science, I know it. From your lovely books—that you write so carefully. I'd love to know I shared that little piece of my childhood with you. So go there—if you possibly can." She looked around at the ferryboat. "Well, you have a wonderful trip home. And write me. You'll go home—you'll see your wife again. And everything will work out between you. I bet that'll be so. It's been an awful lot of fun. I hope you and your wife get back together—or something good happens there, anyway." She leaned forward and gave me a kiss. I gave her a hug back, and she came up blinking. And grinned once more. Then she turned and went up the plank onto the deck, Pharaoh dashing first ahead, then suddenly back as if he'd forgotten something, so that, with a few embarrassed smiles at me, she had to drag him on board.

At the gangplank's top a man in a gray suit and an open-collared shirt, lounging against the rail like a passenger, suddenly stood up, swung about, and became very official, pointing at Heidi, at Pharaoh: an altercation started between them, full of "...*Dthen thello ton skyllon edtho...!*" (I don't want the dog here) and much arm-waving on his part, with many drawn-out and cajoling *"Pa-ra-ka-looo!"*'s and *"Kallo to sky-laiki!"*'s from Heidi. (Pleeease! and, He's a good puppy!) It didn't resolve until she went into her black leather reticule under her poncho to pull out first the John O'Hara paperback she was reading (it ended on the deck, splayed and spine up, by the rail post), some tissues, a pencil, and finally Pharaoh's muzzle, waving the leather straps at the boat official, then stooping to adjust them over patient Pharaoh's mouth and ears —while the other passengers stood close around, curious.

At last she stood up to blow me a kiss.

I waved back and called, "Get your book!"

She looked down and saw the upended, thick black paperback, laughed, and stooped for it.

"Ciao!" she called. "Bye!"

"Ciao!"

I walked back through the Piraeus market, under the iron roofs with their dirty glass panes above tomato and sea-urchin stalls, eggplant and octopus counters, through the red-light district (where, for a week, on my first return from the islands, I'd stayed with Ron and Bill and John), past blue and white doors and small wooden porches, to the subway that would return me to Athens.

II

"By all the gloom hung round thy fallen house,
By this last temple, by the golden age,
By great Apollo, thy dear foster child,
And by thyself, forlorn divinity,
The pale Omega of a withered race,
Let me behold, according as thou said'st,
What in thy brain so ferments to and fro."

—John Keats, *The Fall of Hyperion*, Canto I

"I may be bringing someone home with me," [Turkish] John said. "A man, I mean." John had a long nose. "You won't mind, will you? We'll use the bed in the kitchen; I promise we won't bother you. But…" John's blond hair was half gray; his skin was faintly wrinkled and very dry—"it probably isn't a good idea to mention it to DeLys."

"I won't," I said. "I promise. By the time she's back, I'll be gone anyway."

"I meant in a letter, or something. But believe me," he said, "I only pick up nice men. Or boys. There won't be any trouble."

And later, on the cot bed in the front room of the tiny two-room Anaphiotika house, set into the mountain behind the Acropolis, I went to sleep.

In 'Stamboul, just off Istiqlal, John had had a sumptuous third-floor apartment, full of copper coffee tables, towering plants, rich rugs and hangings. When I'd been staying at the Youth Hostel, one afternoon he'd fed me a wonderful high tea at his place that had kept me going for two days. A pocketful of the leftovers, in a cloth napkin, had—an hour later—even made dinner for timid, towering Jerry.

I woke to whispered Greek, the lock, and two more Greek voices. One laughed as though he were coughing. *Shhh*ing them, John herded two sailors, in their whites, through the room. The squat one halted in the door to the kitchen (in which was DeLys's bed that John used), to paw the hanging back. He had a beer bottle in one hand. He laughed hoarsely once more. Then the tall one, towering him by almost two heads, shoved past, with John right after.

I turned over — then turned back. Frowning, I reached down and pulled my wallet out of the pocket of my jeans where I'd dropped them over the neck of my guitar case sticking from under the bed; it was also my suitcase. I sat, slipped the wallet behind the books on the shelf beside me. Then I lay back down.

John came back through the hanging. All he wore now was a blue shirt with yellow flowers. He squatted beside me, knees jackknifed up, to whisper: "There're two of them, I'm afraid. So if you wanted to entertain one—just to keep him busy, while I did the other one—really, I wouldn't mind. Actually, it would be a sort of favor."

"I'm sorry, John," I said. "Thanks. But I'm awfully tired."

"All right." He patted my forearm, where it was bent under my cheek. He smelled drunk. "But you can't say I didn't ask. And I certainly don't mind sharing—if you change your mind." Then he said: "I haven't spoken Demotiki with anyone in more than a year. I'm surprised I'm doing as well as I am." Chuckling, he was up and back into the kitchen, thin buttocks grinding below blue and yellow shirttails. He disappeared around the hanging, into the lighted kitchen, Greek, and laughter.

I drifted off—despite the noise...

Something bumped my arm. I opened my eyes. The little lamp in the corner was on. The squat sailor stood by my bed, leg pressed against my arm. Looking down at me, with one hand he joggled his crotch. Then he said, questioningly, *"Poosty-poosty...?"*

I looked up. "Huh...?"

"*Poosty-poosty!*" He rubbed with broad, Gypsy-dark fingers. A gold ring hugged deep into the middle one's flesh. Pointing at my face with his other hand, he began to thumb open the buttons around his lap-flap. Once he reached over to squeeze my backside. Hard, too.

"Aw, hey...!" I pushed up. "No... No...!" I made dismissive gestures. "I don't want to. *Dthen thello. Phevge! Phevge!*" (I don't want to! Go away! Go away!)

"*Ne!*" Then he repeated, "*Poosty-poosty,*" emphatically.

The flap fell from black groin hair, that, I swear, went halfway up his belly. His penis swung up, two-thirds the length of mine, but half again as thick. His nails were worn short from labor, and you could tell his palms and the insides of his fingers were rock rough.

"Hey, come *on!*" I pulled back and tried to sit up. "Cut it out, will you? *Dthen thello na kanome parea!*" (I don't want to mess around with you!)

But he grabbed the back of my head to pull my face toward his groin — hard enough to hurt my neck. For a moment, I figured maybe I should go along, so he wouldn't hurt me more. I opened my mouth to take him—and he pushed in. I tasted the bitter sharpness of the cologne he'd doused himself with — and cologne on a dick is my least favorite taste in the world. Under it was the sweat of someone who'd been drinking steadily at least two days. While he clawed into the back of my neck, I thought: This is stupid. I tried to pry my head from under his hand and push him out with my tongue. And thought I'd done it; but he'd just moved, fast—across the bed, on one knee.

It was a hot night. I hadn't been sleeping with any covers.

He grabbed my underpants and, when I tried to dodge away, ripped them down my legs.

"Hey—!" I squirmed around, trying to pull them back up.

But he pushed me, hard, down on the bed. With a knee on one buttock and leaning full on my shoulders, he shouted into the other room— while I managed to lift myself (and him) up first on one elbow, then on the other.

I was about to try and twist him off, so I didn't see the tall one come through; but suddenly he loomed, to grab my arms and yank both, by my wrists, forward. I went off my elbows and down. The sailor on top began to finger between my buttocks. "Ow!" I said. *"Ow* — stop!... *Pauete!"* That made the sailor holding my arms laugh — because it was both formal and plural; and it probably struck him as a funny time for me to be asking him formally to stop.

The tall one let go one wrist and made as if to sock me in the face. He had immense hands. And when he did it, his knuckles looked like they were coming at me hard. I jerked my head aside, squeezed my eyes, and said, *"Ahhh...!"*

But nothing connected — it was only a feint. Still, I hit my jaw on the bed's iron rim.

When I opened my eyes, the tall one grinned and said: "Ha-*ha!"* — then shook one finger, in a slow warning. Still holding my wrist with one hand, he moved to the right, grabbed my leg just above the knee, and yanked it aside.

The one on top got himself in, then. Holding both my shoulders, he pushed, mumbling in Greek.

The tall one moved back to take my free wrist again and squatted there, his face very close. He kind of smiled, curious. His breath smelled like Sen-sen. Or chewing gum. He had very black hair (his white cap was still on), hazel eyes, and tawny skin. (By his knee, the other's cap had fallen on the rug.) Cajolingly, he began to say, now in Greek, now in English: "You like...! You like...! *Su aresi...!* Good boy...! *Su are-si...!* You like...!"

I grunted. "I *don't* like! It *hurts,* you asshole...!"

This pharmacologist, who'd first fucked me, told me that if I pushed out as if I were taking a shit, it wouldn't sting.

But not this time.

The one on me bit my shoulder and, panting, came. The one kneeling glanced up at him, then sighed too, let go, stood, and grunted down at me, as if to say, "See, it wasn't *that* bad...?"

The one behind got off the bed and stood, pushing himself back into his uniform. Once he said to me, in English: "Good! See? You like!"

like the tall one had. He picked up his cap from the floor—and (he'd missed two buttons on his lap) pulled it carefully over his head, then pushed one side back up to get the right angle.

I sucked my teeth at him and tried to look disgusted. Frankly, though, I was scared to death.

In Greek the squat one said: *You want him now? I'll hold him for you* —
The tall one said: *You jerk-off! Let's just get out of here!*

The squat one bent down again, picked up my jeans, and began to finger through the pockets.

Then the tall one drew back his hand with the same feint he'd used on me: *Come on! Forget that, jerk-off! Let's get out of here, I told you!*

The squat one threw my jeans back down, and they went through the kitchen hanging. There was a back door, but I don't remember if I heard it or not.

I lay on the bed a minute, without moving, propped up on one elbow. Then I reached back between my buttocks. When I looked at my fingers, there were little pads of blood on two fingertips. I got up and went to the stall toilet in the corner—

Urine covered the stone floor. On DeLys's blue rug, it had darkened an area three times the size of someone's head. John must have sent one of them in to use the toilet while I was still sleeping—before the first guy woke me.

I reached inside, holding the jamb with one hand, and got some paper from the almost empty roll. Still standing, I wiped myself, but with a blotting motion. It hurt too much to rub. When I looked at the yellow paper, there was a red smear, with some drops running from it, and slime on one side. My rectum stung like hell.

I felt like I had to take a crap in the worst way; but the other thing the pharmacologist had said was to wait at least half an hour before you did that.

When I went back to the bed, I saw the light in the kitchen had been turned out. As I sat down, gingerly, on the edge, on one cheek more than the other, from the dark behind the hanging, John asked: "Are you all right in there?" He sounded plaintive. For a moment I wondered if he was tied up or something.

I called back: "I think so." Then: "Yeah, I'm okay."

A moment later: "Did they take anything from you?"

I pulled my jeans back across the floor toward the bed with my foot. Then I looked at the bookshelf. Between fat volumes by Mann and Michener was a much read Dell paperback of Vonnegut's *Cat's Cradle*, a quarto hardcover of Daisy Ashford's *The Young Visitors*, a chapbook of poems by Joyce Johnson, and Heidi's copy of *L'Ecume de jour*, which every few hours I'd taken out to struggle through another paragraph of Vian's playful French.

"No," I said. "My wallet's safe."

At the very end were the paperbacks of my own few novels—and the typewritten sheaf of my wife's poems, sticking up between two of them. Wherever I stayed, I'd always put them on a shelf so I could see them, to make me feel better. They were the books I'd stuck my wallet behind.

"Good," John said. Twenty seconds later, he said: "I don't think they'll come back." And, a few seconds on: "Goodnight."

After a minute, I got up again, went to the kitchen door, and switched off the lamp. I didn't look behind the hanging. (The big light, still out, you had to stand in the middle of the room to reach up and turn on.) But John wasn't asking for help. So I went back and lay down.

I tried to think of all the reasons I hadn't called out. They might have beat me up, or hurt me more than they had. What would neighbors—or the police — have thought, coming in and finding me like that? Or thought of John? I might have gotten DeLys in trouble with Costas, from whom she rented the house. Or I might have gotten Costas in trouble with the police: he was a nice guy—a Greek law student at Harvard, home for spring break, who probably wasn't supposed to be renting his house out to foreigners anyway. But, lying there, I couldn't really be sure if any of those thoughts had been in my mind while it had been happening.

Again, I pushed out like I was trying to shit.

The stinging was just as painful. Then a muscle in back of my left thigh cramped sharply enough to make me cry out.

III

Oh, man is a god when he dreams, a beggar when he thinks;
and when inspiration is gone, he stands, like a worthless son
whom his father has driven out of the house, and stares at
the miserable pense that pity has given him for the road.

— Friedrich Hölderlin, *Hyperion*

At five-thirty, since neither of us was asleep, John got up to make coffee.
The sun came sideways through the shutters. Birds chirped. John kept
touching a bruise on his cheek with three fingers pressed together.
"Now they were not nice boys at all!" In his light blue robe with the
navy piping, he shook out yellow papers of grounds, of sugar, into the
long-handled pot on the Petrogaz ring. "Why I brought home two, I'll
never know! You'd think I hadn't done this before. But when I first met
them, they were both so sweet." He turned on the water in the gray
stone sink. "One of them hit me." He turned it off again. From the shelf
he took down a jar of marmalade, examined the green and gold label,
shook his head, then put it back. Again he touched his cheek. "Scared
me to *death!* Once he hit me, though, I decided I'd just let the two of
them do anything they wanted." He fingered his bruise again. "He took
money from me, too," he said, confidingly. "I don't like it when a boy
takes money from me. I don't mind giving a boy a few drachma, a few
lira, especially if he's in the army—or the navy. Nobody could be expect-

ed to live off what they pay you there. That's why the entire Greek army hustles." He touched the bruise again. "You know, you really didn't have to clean the piss up off the toilet floor this morning." The near corner of the bed with its ivory crocheted cover, the ancient refrigerator with the circular cooling unit on top, and the blue table with the three blue chairs with flowers decaled on their backs made a kind of crowded triangle on the red tile. "I would have done it myself if you'd left it. That was just rudeness. Believe me, they weren't *that* drunk! You know?" Moving about on bony feet, he pulled out first one chair, then the other. "I really thought, because you were colored, they weren't going to bother you and isn't *that* —" he went on, as though it were the same sentence—"the dumbest thing I could possibly have said this morning! But that's what I thought. Come, sit down now. And have some coffee."

I stepped away from the doorway where, just inside the hanging, I'd been leaning against the jamb. I'd put all my clothes on, including my shoes. For all the dawn sunlight, the house was still nippy.

"But when that boy struck me—who'd been just as sweet as he could be, an hour ago—the chunky one...?" Pouring little cups of coffee like liquid night from the brass pot, John took up his apologia again. "A perfectly dreadful child, he turned out to be. The other, I thought—the tall one — was quite nice, though. Basically. I don't think he would have done anything, if his friend hadn't put him up to it. But I was as scared as I've ever been before in my life! I'm awfully glad somebody else was here. Not that it did much good."

IV

This vast irregular sheet of water, which rushes by without respite, rolls all colors toward nothingness. See how dim it all is.

— Paul Valéry, *Eupalinos, or The Architect*

I got my ticket for London that morning. When the man behind the brass bars said I'd be taking the Orient Express, it was kind of exciting. There'd be no problem, he explained, my stopping off in Munich.

Back up in Anaphiotika, I came in to find an ecstatic John: "Really, I *don't* carry on like this when I'm at home. But you know, in 'Stamboul, because, I guess, it's part of the culture—every father of a teenaged son is busy negotiating which of his wealthiest friends is going to get his boy's bum—you just don't find it running around in the street, the way you do here. You'd think, after last night, I wouldn't be back in business for at least a fortnight. But it's like getting up on the horse as soon as you fall off: here, it's not even one o'clock in the afternoon, and I've already had three—and three very nice ones, at that!"

I laughed. "Once, about six or seven weeks ago, John, I had three before nine o'clock in the morning."

"With your looks and at your age—? I just bet you've had a bloody dozen since you left here!"

Actually, it had only been two. But I thought I'd better not say any-

thing to John, in case his own conquests were more imaginary than real
—to make him feel better about last night. "Are you doing anything this
evening?" I asked. "Some friends of mine and I are going to go out."

"Out to do what sort of thing?"

"Go to a concert—sort of."

John shook his head and his hands. "I'm afraid every free moment I
have is booked. I've got half a dozen moviehouses to explore. I need to
make an official inspection of at least eight public loos. There are parts
of several parks, here and up town, I haven't come anywhere near examining. No—I'm afraid my social calendar is filled to overflowing. But it
was sweet of you to ask."

I laughed, relieved. Five minutes before, I'd decided not to invite
him. He was so flamboyant, I could see him causing something of a
problem with the others.

I'd agreed to meet Trevor at sunset behind the wire-mesh fence along
the top of the Theater of Dionysus—the big outdoor theater on the side
of the Acropolis hill. Stravinsky was conducting his farewell concert
that night. Lots of students and poor foreigners would gather there. You
couldn't see very well, but the famous acoustics of the Greek amphi-
theater easily lived up to their reputation.

Earlier that month, I'd gone from being twenty-three to twenty-
four; which meant Trevor had gone from being a towheaded English
guitar player three years younger than I to a towheaded English guitar
player four years younger. It seemed to make a difference.

The sky out toward Piraeus was purple, flooded through near the horizon with layered orange. On good days you're supposed to be able to
see the sea from the Acropolis's rim. But here, half a dozen yards below
it, the waters beyond Piraeus were only a pervading memory.

The white lights down on the stage told me for the first time that the
platform there was gray-painted wood. During full daylight, just glancing at it when I'd passed, I'd always assumed it was rock. About ten of
the orchestra had come out to take their chairs. Sloping down from the
fence, the tiers of stone seats were filling. In silhouette, scattered before
me, were hundreds of Athenian heads.

Trevor let go of the hatched wire and glanced back. In its canvas case beside him, his guitar leaned against the metal web. Trevor wore two denim jackets, one over the other — though it was a pleasantly warm evening. In the quarter light, his cornsilk mop made his face look smaller, his gray eyes larger. "Hello," he said. "It's his last concert, tonight. I didn't know that."

"Whose?" I asked. "Stravinsky's?"

"That's right. He's retiring. I knew he was conducting, but I didn't know that this was it."

"I think I read something about it."

"The Swiss Bitch is supposed to come by, too. I hope she gets here before they start. I mean, you either hear him tonight or you don't. It's really quite special."

The Swiss Bitch was Trevor's nickname for Cosima; I never saw anything particularly bitchy about her. I don't think Trevor did either, but something about the euphony had caught him. And the first time he'd referred to her as that, Heidi, who was Cosima's best friend, had burst out laughing at the kafeneon table, so that it almost sounded as if she approved. Trevor had kept it up. "Cosima told me you were staying up at DeLys's with some English poofter."

"John?" I asked. "I don't know anything for sure about his sexual preferences — but he's really quite a nice guy." Although Trevor knew perfectly well I was queer, I liked generating ambiguity about anyone else who came up.

"God," Trevor said, "almost all DeLys's friends are faggots! I can't stand them — most of them —" which I guess was for my benefit — "myself. I wonder why that is, with some women?"

Then, behind me, Cosima said: "Hello, you lot."

We moved aside, and Cosima stepped up between us to gaze through the wire. "I think they're about to start. Is that the whole orchestra? — my, there're a lot of them tonight." Cosima was twenty-six and had black hair. She wore a gray jacket with a black fur collar. And a gray skirt. Now she said: "Well, how have you been, Trevor?"

"All right." He pretended to pay attention to something down on the platform.

A few feet away from us, two Greek boys wore short-sleeved shirts. One, with his fingers hooked in the wire above his head, swung now this way, now that, his shirt wholly open and out of his slacks, blowing back from his stomach.

I had on my once-white wool island jacket — too warm for the evening. But we internationals — like the Paris clochards, in their two and three overcoats even in summer — seemed to wear as much of our clothing as we could tolerate, always ready to be asked over, to stay for a few days, or at least to spend the night. That way, I suppose, we'd have to go back for as few remaining things as possible.

On the other side of us, half a dozen schoolgirls in plaid uniforms kept close together, to giggle and whisper when another arrived.

"This is his last time conducting," Cosima said.

"So I read and so Trevor told me. Robert Craft is conducting the first half of the concert."

"Who's Robert Craft?" Trevor asked.

Cosima shrugged — a large, theatrical shrug. Often that's how she dealt with Trevor.

"He's sort of a Stravinsky person," I said. "He writes a lot about him; and he did a wonderful recording of Anton Webern's complete works—about five or six years back."

"Who's Webern?" Trevor asked.

Cosima laughed. "Have you ever heard him conduct before? Stravinsky, I mean?"

"Yes," I said. "Once, one summer when I was about fourteen—back in the States. It was at a place called Tanglewood. There's a big tent there, and the orchestra plays under it. They did two programs that afternoon. Carl Orff had written some new music for *A Midsummer Night's Dream* — to replace the old Mendelssohn stuff everybody knows, I guess. They did the whole play. And a comedian I used to see on television a lot named Red Buttons played Puck—even though he was getting pretty old. The orchestra did the music, which was all in unison, with lots of gongs and drums. Then they took the whole stage down. A chorus came out. And Stravinsky conducted the premiere of a piece he'd just written, *Cantium Sanctum*. It was very atonal. The audience wasn't very appreciative; when people left the music tent, there was a lot of snickering. But I liked it more than the Orff." I stood on tip-toe because some of the paying audience just entering—about twelve feet in front of us — hadn't sat yet. "Tonight Craft is going to conduct *The Firebird*. Then Stravinsky's going to do *The Rite of Spring*. It's an awfully conservative performance for him to go out on. But..." I shrugged. I'd read the whole concert program two days ago. I wasn't sure why I hadn't wanted to tell Trevor.

"*Mmm,*" Cosima said.

Trevor said: "You're going to be leaving in a couple of days. I bet, after you've gone, that English fellow, John, would let me stay up at DeLys's—if I went there and asked him. Nicely, I mean. He's supposed to like boys. And, after all, DeLys is my friend, too."

"I don't know," I said. "I'd stay away from him if I were you, Trevor. What are you going to do if he gets after your bum?"

"I'd beat the shit out of him, if he tried anything!" Trevor pulled himself up, to turn from the fence.

"But why would you go up there if you didn't want him to try?" I asked. "Besides, people will *think* you wanted him to try. If you went up there, knowing the sort of fellow he is, if something happened, no one would ever believe you hadn't egged him on to it. I certainly wouldn't believe it."

A couple of times, when we'd hitched to Istanbul together, Jerry's fear of John and anything else queer (except me) had annoyed me—like the afternoon he'd flatly refused to go up to see John for tea in Turkey. But Trevor's "I'll beat you to a pulp if you touch me, but aren't you supposed to like me anyway because I'm cute?" (and often with a "Can you spare a hundred drachma while you're at it?"), and all with perfect Dartington manners when he chose to drag them out, actually made me mad. John had had a tough enough time; I wanted to keep Trevor out of his hair.

I waited for Trevor to say something back. But my own position as a self-confessed queer, married, and with an occasional girlfriend, made Trevor, if not most of my friends, not know what to say to me at all. I liked that.

Cosima said, "Oh! They're starting...!"

Applause swelled as, in his black tails, Craft walked out across the platform in front of the orchestra.

The Firebird, The Rite of Spring — they're pieces you've heard so many times you'd think they couldn't be interesting anymore. But precisely that music, when it's done well, is so embarrassingly moving. The Athenians certainly applauded enough.

Listening, however, I remembered when Trevor had gotten a recording of the Ninth Symphony. (Jerry hadn't yet gone back to Kentucky.) Above the orchestral photograph, the Deutsche Grammophon label was brutal yellow. Cardboard on European albums is thinner than on American albums. And Trevor had held this one in both hands, in front of his jeans. Both the knees were torn. The sun made his hair look like some white plastic fiber pushed back from his soap-white forehead, reddened here and there by a pimple. I stood a step below him on Mnisicleou Street, while he said: "The Swiss Bitch told me all of us could come up to her place tonight and hear it. I hope you and Heidi can make it."

"All of us" turned out to be: my recent roommates, John (who was from London) and Ron (who was from New Jersey); and [English] John (the Cockney electrical engineer); and Heidi (we'd locked Pharaoh in her room, but he barked enough while we were going down the stairs that, in her wire-rimmed glasses and green apron, Kyria Kokinou came out and started arguing that the dog was not healthy for the children in the apartment upstairs—which, finally, we just had to walk away from; with Kyria Kokinou, sometimes you had to do that); and the tall redheaded English woman (who had been first Ron's, then John's, girlfriend); and DeLys (who was from New Orleans and whose gold hair was as striking, in its way, as Trevor's); and Gay (the American woman who played Joan Baez and Leonard Cohen songs at the 'O kai 'E); and

Jane (Gay's tense, unhappy, mid-Western traveling companion); and
Jerry (who, with his slightly stooped shoulders, was about twice as tall as
anyone else, and had huge hands and feet like some German Shepherd
puppy); and sports-jacketed law-student Costas (DeLys's landlord, who
kept laughing and saying, "Well, we'll squeeze… I'm sure we can think
of something…there's always a way, now…"); and me.

"Oh, my God…!" Cosima said, at the head of the stairs. "I don't
think we'll all *fit…?*"

In a kind of attic tower, Cosima's single room had a desk and a bed in
it, with a couple of travel posters on the walls — one from Israel, one
from North Africa. It wasn't any larger, though, than the chicken-coop
arrangement I'd left on the roof of Voltetsiou Street; or, indeed, than
Heidi's at Kyria Kokinou's, which I'd left it for (though Heidi's room
had a shower). I wondered what Trevor had been thinking when he'd
invited us. The phonograph was one someone's ten-year-old sister
might have gotten for her birthday: a square box with a pink cover that
swung up from a yellow base with dirty corners, on which the table
turned.

"I'm going to put it out here in the hall," Cosima said, "so as many
people can hear as possible."

We sat on the steps, most of us. DeLys, [English] John, and Heidi
rested their heads against the gray, unpainted wall-boards. In his black
sneakers and white jeans, all scrunched up on the step above Jane, Jerry
took his pink-framed glasses off to listen, his eyes closed, his head to the
side. (Probably he was taller than the tall sailor.) At the bottom, hands
in his jacket pockets, Costas lounged against the newel. The orange
light from Cosima's open door fell down among us. A window high in
the stairwell wall showed a few raindrops outside on the little panes.

We were very quiet.

Cosima started the record.

The opening intervals of the Ninth dropped through the stairwell—
from the scratchy speaker. Where I sat, the step above digging into my
hip, my back pressed against the wall, I had one hand on Heidi's knee;
she put one hand on mine.

After the second movement, while Cosima turned the record over, DeLys started coughing. Costas pulled out a handkerchief and handed it up to her—but she waved it away.

"Oh, it's clean," Costas said, laughing. "Don't worry."

"I *know* it's clean!" DeLys coughed again, the back of one hand against her mouth, the fingers in a loose fist that grabbed after something with each head-lowering hack. "That's not it at all and you know it...!" She coughed some more.

Then Cosima played the adagio.

When the choral opening of the "Ode to Joy" finished and the baritone solo began, Heidi squeezed my hand and I thought of Beethoven, arthritic, deaf, and thinking his work a failure after he'd finished conducting the Ninth's premiere, because he'd heard nothing behind him. Then the Soprano stepped down to take him by the arm and turn him to see the standing Viennese, clapping madly—

Without any noise, I started to cry, while, there behind the fence, we listened with a silent avidity—to *The Rite of Spring.*

—but by the end of the Ninth, for our several reasons, all of us had been moved:

Jammed together on Cosima's steps, the physical discomfort and social preposterousness of the situation had made us listen with intense attention. A number of us in that stairway had been wet-eyed.

We'd said, "Goodnight," and "Thank you," and "Ciao," to Cosima, quietly. Then, our hands against the narrow stairwell walls, some of us, we'd filed down to the street, now and again glancing back to smile. In the doorway at the stairs' head, holding the album cover, Trevor had stood, raggedy-kneed. Just behind his shoulder, in her long skirt, Cosima had watched us.

Outside, it had rained enough to slick the sidewalk under the corner lamp. Heidi and I had walked back to the bottom of Mnisicleou...

Between the standing Athenians, clapping madly, I could see, down on the platform, someone hand Stravinsky another pink and yellow bouquet. In his black tails, with his white tie, bald head, and glasses, he held two in his arms already. Three more lay on the gray wood beside him.

Craft came out again to take Stravinsky's arm and lead him off. Once he shifted the flowers and waved at the audience.

On the other side of Cosima, the Greek boy closed two buttons on his shirt. With his friends, he turned to leave the fence—the school girls beside me, whispering and worried that they were already late, had hurried off as soon as the applause began.

Applause swelled again. I said, softly, in Cosima's ear: "There. Now his career as a conductor is finished. It's over. Like that."

Her face near the wire, black fur moving in the wind that, with the later hour, had started, Cosima nodded.

V

To construct oneself, to know oneself — are these two distinct acts or not?

— Paul Valéry, *Eupalinos, or the Architect*

A good number of people were on the platform when I got there. I had my guitar case — and a shopping bag. At the bottom of the bag was Heidi's Vian. Then my underwear and my balled-up suit. On the top were my novels. Two had actually been published while I was here — though I'd written them before. My wife had sent me a single copy of each, as they came out. I'd figured to reread the newest one on the train — for more typographical mistakes; or for stylistic changes I might want to make. And maybe reread the typescript of her poems. It was as sunny as it had been on the Piraeus docks when I'd seen Heidi off to Aegina. Shabby-coated lottery vendors ambled about. Ticket streamers tentacled their sticks. A cart rolled by, selling milk-pudding and spinach pie and warm Orangata, big wheels grumbling and squeaking. Sailors and soldiers stood in groups, talking together, among the civilian passengers.

When I saw him—the tall one—with four others in their whites, my heart thudded hard enough to hurt my throat. From the surprise, the back of my neck grew wet. I swallowed a few times—and tried to get my breath back. But—no!—I wasn't going to go up to the other end of the platform. I wasn't going to let the son of a bitch run me all around the train station. I took a deep breath, turned, and looked toward the empty tracks.

But I hoped the train would hurry up.

Not that he could do anything here, with all these people.

The third time I glanced at him, he was looking at me—smiling. He was smiling!

Another surge of fear; but it wasn't as big as the terror at my initial recognition.

Next time I caught him looking, I didn't look away.

So he raised his hand—and waved: that little "go away" gesture that, in Greek, means "come over here."

When I frowned, he broke from his group to lope toward me.

He came up with a burst of Greek: *"Kalimera sas! Ti kanis? Kalla?"* (Hello, you! How you doing? All right?)

"Kalimera," I said, dry as a phrase book.

But with his big (nervous? Probably, but I didn't catch it then) smile, he rattled on. In front of me, the creaseless white of his uniform was as blinding as a tombstone at noon; he towered over me by a head and a half. Now, with a scowl, he explained: *"...Dthen eine philos mou... Dthen eine kalos, to peidi..."* He isn't a friend of mine...he's no good, that fellow... Where're you going? It's beautiful today... Yes? (*"Orea simera... Ne?"*) You all right? He's crazy, that guy. He just gets everybody in trouble. Me, I don't do things like that. I don't like him. I go out with him, I always get in trouble—like with you and your friend, up there, that night. That wasn't any good. You're taking the train today? Where're you going? You're Negro, aren't you? (*"Mavros, esis?"*) You like it here, in Greece? It's a beautiful country, isn't it? You had a good time? How long have you been here?

I didn't want to tell him where I was going; so I mimed ignorance at half his questions, wondering just what part he thought *he'd* played in the night before last.

I was surprised, though, I wasn't scared anymore. At all. Or, really, even that angry. Suddenly, for a demonic joke, I began to ask him lots of questions, fast: What was his name? (*"Petros, ego."* Peter, that's me.) Where was he going? (*"Sto 'Saloniki."* To Thessalonika.) Where was he from? (Some little mountain town I'd never heard of before.) Did he like the Navy? (With wavering hand, *"Etsi-getsi."* So-so.) He answered them all quite seriously, the grin gone and—I guess—a slightly bewildered look, hanging above me, in its place.

Finally, though, he dropped a hand on my shoulder and bent to me. He'd come over to me, he explained, because he had something to show me. *No, no — it's all right. Let me show it to you. Here.* He went digging in his back pocket—for a moment I thought he was going to pull out his wallet to show me pictures. But when his hand came back around, he was holding a knife. *No, don't be afraid. Don't be afraid — I just want to show you something.* I pulled back, but, by the shoulder, he forced me forward—still smiling. *Here,* he said. *Here — go on. You take it. Go ahead. Take it. Hold it.* While he held the knife in his amazingly large hand, I saw the nails on his big fingers were clean, evenly clipped, with ivory scimitars over the crowns—under clear polish.

Like many Greek men, he wore his little nail half an inch or more long.

I hadn't noticed any of that, the night at DeLys's.

I took the closed knife from him and thought: Greek sailors don't usually have manicures. Briefly I wondered if he was queer himself.

He said: *"Orea, eine…?"* (Beautiful, isn't it…?) He didn't make any other gesture to touch it but, with motions of two fingers together and the odd word, told me to open it up. *It isn't very expensive. It's cheap — but it's a pretty knife. Good. Strong. You like it? It's nice, yes? Come on, open it up. A good knife. That button there — you push it up. To open it. Yes. Come on.*

I pushed the button up, and the blade jumped out, a sliver of light, of metal, of sky.

Here! He laughed. *It's a good knife, yes?*

I nodded—that is, moved my head to the side, the Greek gesture for Yes. *"Ne,"* I said. *"Kallos to eine."* (Yes. It's a good one.)

He said in Greek: *You want this knife? You like it? Go on, take it. For you. You keep it. You like it, yes? I give it to you. For a present. Maybe you need it, sometimes. It's a good knife.*

"*Yati...?*" I asked. Why are you giving this to me?

You want to kill me now. He gave a sideways nod, then added a chuckle. *Cut something of mine off, I bet. I wouldn't blame you.*

"No," I said. I shook my head (or rather, raised it in negation). "*Ochi.*" I told him, *You take it.* I pressed the button. But it didn't close.

He took it from me now. There was another pressure point you had to thumb to make the blade slip in. With his big, manicured fingers, he thumbed it. The metal flicked into the silver and tortoise shell handle. Like that. *You sure? You don't want it?*

I said: "*Ochi — efharisto. Ochi.*" (No — thank you. No.)

He put it in his back pocket again, and regarded me a little strangely, blinking his green-gray eyes in the sun. Then he said: "*Philli, akomi — emis?*" (We're friends, now — us?)

"Okay," I said, in English. "Just forget it."

"*Esis. Ego.* O-kay!" he repeated. *You. Me.* "O-kay. You like...I like..." With a flipped finger, he indicated him and me. "O-kay. Friend: me, you." He laughed once more, clapped me on the shoulder, then turned to go back to the others. As he walked away, knife and wallet were outlined on one white buttock.

How, I wondered, were we supposed to be friends?

The other sailors were laughing — I'm sure about something else.

I watched them, wondering if I could see some effeminacy in any of their movements — queer sailors, camping it up on the station platform. Him...maybe. But not the others.

Just once more he caught me looking and grinned again — before the train came.

When we pulled from the station, his group was still talking out on the platform — so he wasn't on my train. I was glad about that.

That night, in my couchette, while we hurtled between Switzerland and Italy, in the dark compartment I thought about the two sailors; and when my body told me what I was about to do, I had some troubled minutes, when it was too easy to imagine the armchair psychiatrists, over their morning yogurt and rolls at the white metal tables in front of American Express, explaining to me (in three languages) how, on some level, I had liked it, that—somehow—I must have wanted it.

While I masturbated, I thought about the thick, rough hands on the squat one, but grown now to the size of the tall one's; and the tall one's hazel eyes and smile — but deprived of the Sen-sen scent; and about sucking the squat one's cock, with all its black hair—except that, for the alcoholic sweat and cologne, I substituted the slight work-salt of a stocky good-humored housepainter I'd had on the first day I'd got to Athens.

Once I tried to use the knife blade, as he'd held it, full of sky: nothing happened with it.

At all.

But I used my waking up with the sailor beside me, his leg against my arm, his hand between his legs. I did it first with fear, then with a committed anger, determined to take something from them, to retrieve some pleasure from what, otherwise, had been just painful, just ugly.

But if I hadn't — I realized, once I'd finished, drifting in the rumbling, rocking train—then, alone with it, unable to talk of it, even with John or Heidi, I simply would have found it too bleak. I'd have been defeated by it—and, more, would have remained defeated. That had been the only way to reseize my imagination, let go of the stinging fear, and use what I could of both to heal.

VI

Unknown and alone, I have returned to wander through my
native country, which lies about me like a vast graveyard...

— Friedrich Hölderlin, *Hyperion*

In London one night beside a neon-striped eating place, I'd stood outside plate glass, a triangle of blue sliding down at my eye, listening to a
record on the jukebox inside, by a group that sang, in the most astonishing antiphony, about "Monday, Monday..."—as rich with pop possibilities as new music could be.

In France, for a day, I'd hitched north toward the Luxembourg air-
port through a stony landscape — sided with crumbling white walls,
shuttered windows and planked-up doors that recalled so many of that
country's warnings, from so many of its writers, about the meanness and
a-sensuality of its strict, strict provinces.

And, in New York, three weeks later, I was sitting at the foot of my
bed, when, after some argument that had to do with neither money nor
sex, my wife walked in and slapped me, about as hard as I'd ever been
hit, across the face—the only time either one of us ever struck the other.
A week later, with her poems and the red clay casserole, she moved into
another apartment, down on Henry Street. Which left me nothing but
to plunge into the ending of the novel I'd been working on last fall and
spring, full of Greece—but with no Heidi or Pharaoh, no Cosima or

DeLys, no Trevor or Costas, no Jerry or [Turkish] John.

Two weeks after that I got a letter from Heidi—which surprised me: I hadn't written her at all. I sat on the bed in the back of my empty Lower East Side flat to read its more-than-dozen pages. The light through the window-gate made lozenges over the rumpled linen.

The return address on Heidi's letter was Munich, which was where her family lived. Its many beige sheets explained how she was with them now, how glad she'd been to see her mother once she'd arrived—and how the problems she'd sometimes cried to me about having with her father seemed, briefly, in abeyance. Had I gotten to the Deutsches Museum? (I had. And it had been quite as wonderful as she'd told me. But she seemed to think I'd probably missed it.) She hoped things were going well between me and my wife.

Then, in its last pages, she wrote:

"Before I left Greece, I killed my poor Pharaoh—whom I loved more than anything else in the world. Even more than, for that little time, I loved you. But there was no one I could give him to. The Greeks don't keep pets. And the quarantine laws are impossible—they would have put him in kennel for six months; and that costs lots of money. Besides, he was just a puppy, and after six months more he wouldn't even have known me. But the day before I did it, I saw a dog—all broken up and bloody, with one leg and one eye entirely gone, and his innards—Oh, I don't want to describe it to you! But he was alive, though barely, in the garbage behind Kyria Kokinou's, because of what some boys had done to him. He was going to die. And I knew if I just let Pharaoh go, with the stones and the glass in the meat, and the Greek boys, he would die too. That's when I cried.

"Since I was leaving Greece in two days, what I did was take my poor, beautiful Pharaoh out in the blue rowboat that David said I could use, with a rope, one end of which I'd already tied around a big rock (about eighteen kilos). I was in my bathing suit—as though we were going for a swim, back on Aegina. And while he looked up at me, with his trusting eyes — which, because you are such a careful writer, you would say was a cliché, but I could really look into those swimming, swirling eyes and see he *did* trust me, because I fed him good food every day from the market and took him for his walks in the morning and at night so he could make his shits and his pee-pees, and I had protected him all winter and spring from those horrid Greeks. I tied the rope around his neck, the knot very tight, so it wouldn't come loose. Then we wrestled together in the boat and I hugged him and he licked me, and I threw him over the side. He swam around the boat, as he used to when I'd take him out in the skiff on Aegina, with most of the rope floating in curves, back and forth, snaking to the gunwale, and back over. Once he climbed in again—and got me all wet, shaking. Then he jumped out, to swim some more.

"He just loved to swim. And while he was swimming, sometimes he glanced at me. Or off at a sea bird.

"When he looked away, I threw the rock over.

"The splash wet me to my waist. Over the time of a breath, in and out, while the boat rocked up and down, all the curves in the rope disappeared.

"And still paddling, Pharaoh jerked to the side—and went under.

"There were ripples, moving in to and out from the boat.

"There were the obligatory gulls—one swooped close enough to startle me, making me sit back on the seat. Then it flew away.

"The paper mill squatted in its smelly haze across the harbor.

"But it was over.

"Like that.

"I waited ten minutes.

"I'd thought to sit there perhaps an hour or so, being alone with myself, with the water, with what I'd done—just thinking. But after ten minutes—because of the gull, I think—I realized I'd done it, and I rowed back to the Pasilimani dock.

"Although I cried when I saw the poor dog out behind the house, I didn't cry with Pharaoh. I'm really surprised about that—about how little I felt. I suppose I didn't feel worse than any other murderer who has to do things like that daily for a living—a highway bandit; a state executioner. I wonder why that is?

"Cosima thought I was just a terrible person, and kept saying that there must have been something else I could have done.

"But there wasn't. And I hope she comes to realize that. I hope you realize it too.

"I used to say the Greeks were barbarians, and you would laugh at me and tell me that people's believing they could deal with the world in such general terms was what made it so awful. And I would laugh at you back. But now I know that I am the barbarian. Not the Greeks who are too hungry to understand why anyone would keep a dog. Not the Germans who managed to kill so many, many Jews with their beautiful languages, Yiddish and Hebrew, and who, still, someday, I hope will let me into their country to study. Not the southern whites like Jerry and DeLys who lynch and burn Negroes like you. Not the Negroes like you who are ignorant and lazy and oversexed and dangerous to white women like me.

"Me—and not the Others, at all: not you, not them.

"Me.

"I loved my Pharaoh so much. He's gone. My memories of him are beautiful, though.

"I hope someday you will write something about him. And about me —even though you have to say terrible things of me for what I did. And because of how little I felt when I did it. But, then, you haven't written me at all. Maybe you'll just forget us both."

That was her only letter.

— *Amherst*
September 1990

Edited, designed, and produced by
Incunabula.
Edited by Ron Drummond.
Book design and composition by John D. Berry.

The type is Adobe Caslon,
designed by Carol Twombly in 1990
as part of the Adobe Originals series of digital typefaces.
Adobe Caslon is based directly on
specimen sheets of William Caslon's text types
from the early 18th century.

Produced with Aldus PageMaker 5.0
on an Apple Macintosh IIvx.
Printed and bound by
Braun-Brumfield of Ann Arbor, Michigan:
printed on 60# Glatfelter Natural Smooth acid-free paper,
sewn & bound in Roxite C linen cloth over boards.

Thanks to the following for their assistance:
Margaret Di Salvi, Doug Faunt,
Rachel Gugler, David G. Hartwell,
Dave Howell, Greg Ketter,
Neil S Kvern, Kate Schaefer,
David Sherrard, Suzanna Tamminen,
& Tom Whitmore.

UNIVERSITY PRESS OF NEW ENGLAND publishes books under its own imprint and is the publisher for Brandeis University Press, Brown University Press, Dartmouth College, Middlebury College Press, University of New Hampshire, University of Rhode Island, Tufts University, University of Vermont, Wesleyan University Press, and Salzburg Seminar.

LIBRARY OF CONGRESS CATALOGING-IN-PUBLICATION DATA

Delany, Samuel R.
Atlantis : three tales / Samuel R. Delany
    p. m.
Contents: Atlantis—Erik, Gwen, and D.H. Lawrence's aesthetic of unrectified feeling—Citre et trans.
ISBN 0-8195-5283-6
1. Title
PS3554.E437A85   1995
813'.54—dc20   94-48726

I don't feel
like talking to
you in this weekend.